THE CRYSTAL BIRD

BY

HELEN DRAYTON

ISBN: 1475225075

ISBN 13: 9781475225075

Library of Congress Control Number: 2012907400
CreateSpace Independent Publishing Platform
North Charleston, South Carolina

Printed by CreateSpace, an Amazon.com Company
Editor: Julie Morton, Morton Publishing, Trinidad and Tobago
Map designed by Orion Holder, Trinidad and Tobago

Available from Amazon.com, https://www.createspace.com/3855167,
www.thecrystal bird.com and other retailers

Until the lions write their history
the tale of the hunt will always
be glorified by the hunter.

–AFRICAN PROVERB

THE CRYSTAL BIRD is a work of historical and contemporary fiction.

All characters are products of the author's imagination. All places and events are either the products of the author's imagination or used in a fictitious context.

Historical, biblical, geographic, and archaeological facts are placed in a fictitious context.

For Selwyn, Michael, and Elizabeth,
who kept me grounded when I landed
in the mythical land of the Crystal Bird.

For Margaret, Robert, Raymond, Betty,
Vincent, Charles, Helena, Richard, Rodney,
Annmarie, Jason, Jade, and Che.

My special thanks to Julie Morton,
Lorraine Rostant, Corinne Baptiste-McKnight
Rosalind Wilson, and Simone Jacelon,
for their generosity and friendship.

CHARACTERS AND PLACES

1450 – 1900

WARRIORS

Mbtani Djedkare: leader of warriors

Abayomi Menelik: shepherd and first Keeper of the Forest

Debele Traore : lion hunter

Akele Selassie : warrior

Jomo Selassie : storyteller and poet

THE KINGDOMS OF ASHAISE AND AMARA

King Tariku : king of Ashaise

King Sahure : king of Ashaise

King Asefa : king of Amara

King Kepi : king of Amara

King Kibwe : king of the United Kingdom of Ashaise—Land of the Crystal Bird

Prince Askia : son of Kibwe

King Mbtani and Queen Eliye I : King and Queen of Ashaise

1900 – 2004

THE KINGDOM OF ASHAISE—LAND OF THE CRYSTAL BIRD

Queen Eliye II

King Meleke and Queen Teye

Prince Nehsi, Princess Jiena, and Prince Meke

Chinua: Keeper of the Forest

Aatum: warrior chief protector

Sahure: warrior protector

Allan Cline : archaeologist

Christopher Ward : archaeologist

Kevin Springer : anthropologist and adventurer

Robert Armstrong : international geographic writer

Joe Dodd, David Cazeau, Timothy McIntosh, and James Mathews: security team

Raymond Johnson : head of the rescue mission

Brother Caftie : missionary

Charmaine Bruce : environmentalist

DEFINITIONS

Enkai: the Maasai's god with a dual nature. He rules over the sun, water, fertility, and love. Enkai Narok (Black God) is benevolent, and Enkai Nanyokie (Red God) is vengeful.

Laibon: prophet, leader of rituals, and healer.

Alkebulan: African name for Africa.

Manyatta: a Maasai community made up of several huts.

Assegai: a Maasai spear.

The Valley of Sade
Kingdom of Ashaise—
Land of The Crystal Bird

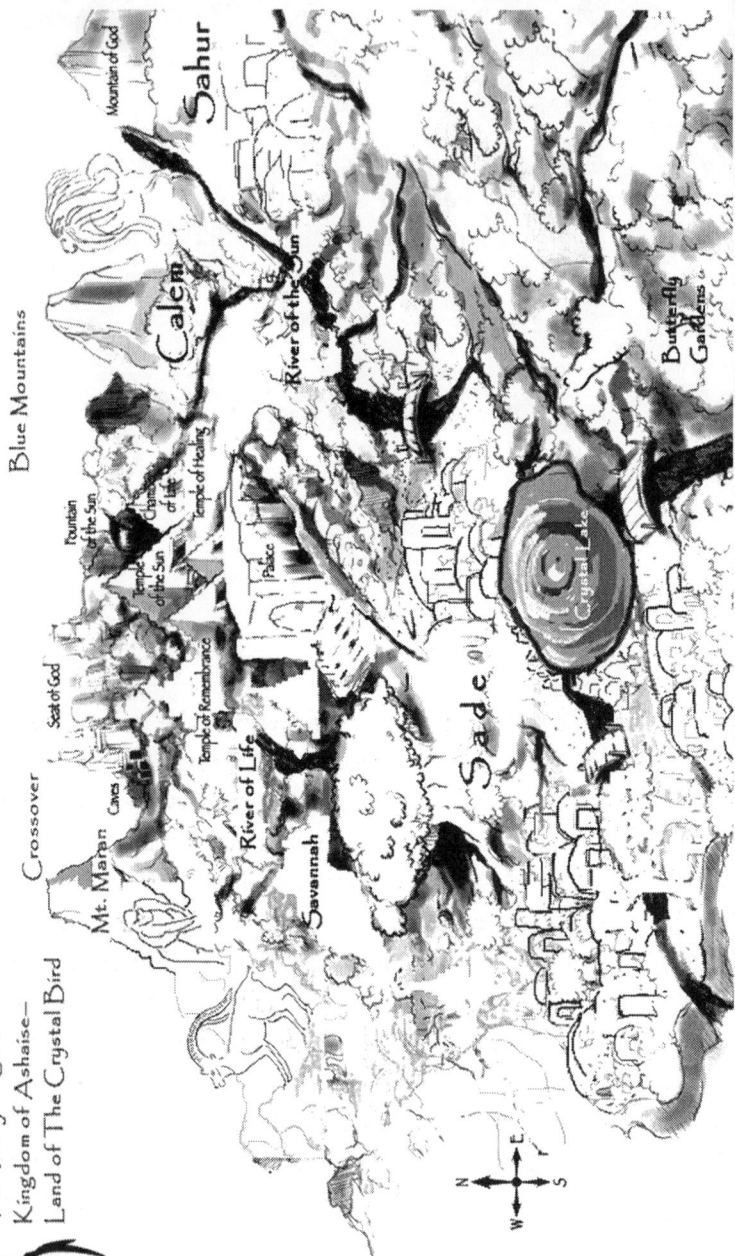

Blue Mountains

Mountain of God

Sahur

Calem

Crossover

Mt. Maran

Caves

Seat of God

Fountain of the Sun

Temple of the Sun

Chamber of Isis

Temple of Healing

Temple of Remembrance

River of the Sun

Palace

River of Life

Savannah

Sade

Crystal Lake

Butterfly Gardens

N
W E
S

CHAPTER 1

THE YEAR 1450

The warrior's searching eyes scanned the tall grasses. He nervously moved a few feet away from the small group and stood in silence. Mbtani turned his pensive face toward the horizon from where the early morning spectacle would emerge. Soon dawn would fade and the bright-orange orb would rise and combust over the open cathedral where man and beast drank together the wine that flowed from the House of God.

The young warriors would usually go to the bank of the Galana Stream and fetch water before the moon turned its back on the Valley of Life. By the time the sun pitched its sequined veil over the savannah plains and woodlands, they would be ready for a day's work. The youth looked forward to the sunrise ritual, as it was the best time to prepare for the day's activities while they sipped tea with honey. Of course one of the most enjoyable activities took place just before dusk. The evening would be breezy and warm, and the girls, after they finished their chores, would get together to chat and play in the shallow water.

On this splendid morning, the warriors were restless. An ominous feeling subdued their chatter. There was an expectant aura, and glances at the surrounding shrubbery disrupted their conversation. They did not hear the usual raucous chirping of hungry chicks or the musical rustling of leaves. Morning was always peaceful, but never quiet.

Mbtani heard a noise—a muffled voice. Heat surged through his body. He turned toward the sound, clenched his teeth, and sprang up an acacia tree. Not seeing anything or hearing the unusual sound again, he swung to the ground, where his feet quietly connected with the dewy grass. He strolled back to his cousins and friends. Mbtani held his assegai horizontally against his sinewy thighs while he stood protectively over the other warriors.

The sun continued its brilliant show, changing from orange to pale yellow to white. The warriors finished their meal and kicked dirt over the low, cindering patch. Akele, Debele, Abayomi, and the other warriors picked up the calabash gourds full of water and, with their shukas thrown over one shoulder, headed back to the manyatta to prepare for taking the cattle to a new grazing ground. Later they would go in the forest to hunt.

On their way back to the living enclosure, Mbtani stopped. He stood still like a lion poised to sprint for fresh meat. His body stiffened. Not a muscle moved.

"Quiet," he whispered. The others felt the vibrations of galloping hooves and heard sounds that became louder as the animals got closer. They thought it was a stampede. Suddenly, the leafy windows of the forest broke open as Jomo Selassie, Akele's father, ran in the direction of their huts, shouting his son's name. Assailants pursued the wounded elder. One threw a net over him. He struggled to free himself.

"Move quickly and get the bastards," said a rider.

The young men observed that one of the attackers was from a rival tribe.

"Father!" shouted Akele as he threw the assegai. The spear reached the target, and the morning splendor of the African plain turned macabre. A loud noise pierced the air.

"Akele, Akele, Akele!" Abayomi called to his cousin. A bullet had entered Akele's chest, and Abayomi saw him fall, his lifeless body draped over a rock.

Before the youths could fully grasp what was happening, the men on horses surrounded them. A pockmarked slaver who stood next to Akele's killer held a scythe. The others pointed weapons at the warriors, and a blotch-faced man with greasy, auburn hair shouted. The young men heard chains dragging and expectancy in the devil's voice.

"These will bring more money if there's no damage." The slaver came up to where Akele's body lay, dismounted, and kicked Abayomi, who fell to the ground.

"Take them with the rest in the village," the slaver yelled to his lackey.

The warriors did not hear another man's voice that rose in the din. It was a muffled, guttural sound like a hyena devouring a carcass. The hyena would be dead before it could finish its meal.

THE CRYSTAL BIRD

Soon after their first steps, the warriors had been trained in the open university of grasslands and jungle. The laibon, a spiritual healer, circumcised boys at twelve years old in an impressive community ceremony. Thereafter the boys would spend five years preparing for warrior protector status. The time for the young men to be initiated fully into the cycle of adulthood had ended, so they knew pain. Life-threatening challenges were everyday tests.

The initiates had survived many harsh, cold nights deep in the rain forest, where darkness was a convenient cover for predators. They learned to swim across infested rivers and streams, run with stampeding buffalo, and balance while running across the backs of cattle from one end of a herd to the other. They dared to hunt large animals and looked forward most of all to the lion hunt. They became adept at throwing spears as straight as the pitch of a star. Courage and tenacity were their strengths—the collective traits of the respected military that protected the tribe and all the cattle their god, Enkai, had put on earth solely for them.

It was their custom to prepare for war by psyching themselves into a frenzied state, jumping higher than gazelles chased by a big cat. Then they attacked the enemy with brutal force. All other tribes knew that. The others knew them to be valiant fighters, adroit at outsmarting, outrunning, and out-killing anyone who threatened their way of life, even the beast others feared. The Maasai warrior, in accordance with the will of Enkai, was king of the earth.

Abayomi had known worse pain. But the beast that kicked him saw intense loathing in his eyes—wide, deep, dark pools narrowed to slits of penetrating light. Abayomi slowly turned his head to catch the eyes of Mbtani. The two warriors exchanged a look that meant it would be a fight to the death.

Mbtani Djedkare, the descendant of generations of chieftains, was usually contemplative. The other warriors respected him for his thoroughness. He planned and executed events with precision and brought order to the daily lives of the warrior team. He inspired and motivated them when challenges became difficult. Now he had to protect them. His mind raced. The beasts had to die.

His cousin, Abayomi Menelik, had been shrewdly preemptive. He marked a target well, and nothing escaped the reach of his spear. He was skilled at outmanoeuvring his challengers, and in the hunt the team relied on him to mark the tracks of prey and guide the warriors along safe paths. Abayomi felt overwhelming grief because of the traumatic separation from Akele. His heart was a drum beating against his chest. His temples throbbed.

The warriors respected the power of the gun; they had heard about it from other tribes that had managed to escape bondage. The slavers raided villages and abducted men, women, and children, shackling them together at necks and ankles. The chained captives walked miles over hills and across treacherous rivers to the seafront, where they would be put up for sale. The walk took more than three days and was the first stage of the journey to hell.

Some escaped and hid in the jungle. Bullets felled others who attempted to run away, or as they retaliated. The captors violated the women and children. The iron chains ripped the prisoners' flesh. The weight of sick or dead bodies dragged other victims to the ground. In the dark of night, moaning saddened the forest, and the spirit of the mountains took souls on its wing.

The avengers focussed their attention on the kill. Now they saw their quarry: predators that had to die.

They heard the faint screams of women muffled by the vulgar words of men on the attack—reasons to act quickly. Time was in flight. Every moment counted. Mbtani and Abayomi quickly gauged the scene. They were a few feet away from each other; farther to the right were Debele and other warriors guarded by another horseman and footmen.

The villain who had kicked Abayomi remounted his horse. Abayomi eyed the animal, hoping its rider would turn it to face him. He did. Abayomi now looked into the eyes of the slaver's horse and lowered his head.

The warriors had extraordinary abilities to communicate with animals. They occupied the same space with their cattle and breathed the same air. So close were they, the creatures understood a silent language. When the warriors looked into their eyes, the animals obeyed an unspoken command.

Of course Akele's pet bull, Zete, was different because he thought he was human. He had long antlers and an unstable temperament. The grand creature also had an unusual horn in the middle of his forehead, so the tribe believed he was a great gift from Enkai.

The tribe killed cattle when necessary and extracted blood from the animals' jugular veins to drink for health and strength—a custom from the time when the moonbeam first shone over the land.

Mbtani and the other warriors saw Abayomi's sign. Suddenly the slaver's horse sprang up on its hind legs, baring its teeth as it neighed. The other horses raged. Man and beast were at war.

Out of nowhere came Zete. He charged a slaver who was on foot. As if the horses were sensitive to the plight of the warriors, the noble creatures threw off their unwanted burdens and their owners descended to hell. The strong hands of justice inflicted agony and death.

The warriors got their spears, which the fiends had thrown in the grass, and caught those who were trying to escape in their backs and legs. Terror filled the air. The green ground turned red. Abayomi caught the slaver who had kicked him. His spear penetrated the man's eye. Abayomi withdrew it before shoving the howling man to the ground. He took the slaver's chain, brutally wrapped it around the man's neck, and tied the other end to the rock where Akele's body lay. The slaver's trials had only just begun. He bawled, writhed, and covered the bloody socket of his left eye with filthy hands.

Abayomi glanced at Jomo, who was still struggling in the net. He released Jomo and gently wiped his face.

The middleman who was a member of the warriors' rival tribe knew all along that he should not have betrayed the children of Enkai. He tried to escape. Abayomi grinned and pursued his prey. It took only a few minutes to catch him, but the warrior was not interested in killing him. Not yet.

The fresh morning air was heavy with the scents of blood and rancid sweat, of riled up animals and death. Monkeys shrieked, birds flew in fright, and the wind blew furiously, as if angered by the invaders who brought their ugly trade to the open temple of man.

The Maasai youths stood together in a circle around Akele Selassie's body, which they had lifted and laid gently under a sprawling tree. Zete knelt and nudged the body. The animal's moaning sounded like distant, rolling thunder. The warriors raised their eyes and hands to the sun god and performed a ceremonial dance, jumping high and chanting. They buried Akele under the tree.

Abayomi and Zete stayed at the burial site for a while. Abayomi thought of the loveable, merry friend with whom he had sparred and shared secrets. Akele was a chubby warrior. They called him "fatty" as a testimony to his appetite, but by no means was he fat. He was just abnormally thicker than the average seventeen-year-old warrior. His face was as smooth as a glossy river stone.

The jovial youth used to break into infectious laughter at the slightest jest or funny semantic. He often told comic tales. His skilfulness in defusing arguments endeared him to his peers. Naturally he was a trickster, and Abayomi often bore the brunt of his ruses. Only a day earlier, Akele had taken Zete near the latrine pit knowing full well his cousin was there. Abayomi had heard a low grunt, a bellow, and movement in the bushes nearby. He'd looked up and seen Zete's ferocious face. Bull and youth had stared at each other for a few heartbeats. Abayomi's deep mahogany face had turned pale yellow, then white. Zete was a bull who felt his horn should be tested on both moving and stationary targets, so he had gracefully moved his plump, buff-white body two steps back—a warning sign well known to all Maasai.

Abayomi respected animals, but the latrine pit was no place for a bull. He had lowered his eyes; Zete was acutely sensitive and easily insulted—an impudence that had to be punished. Abayomi was an agile teenager, and his statuesque, six-foot-tall body, which had been in a squatting position, flew up and bolted from the pit. The crabby bull had grunted and charged a nearby tree, then looked at Abayomi from the corner of his eye for the rest of the day.

Abayomi smiled through tears as he remembered his beloved cousin. "Akele," he said softly.

Before returning to the manyatta, the warriors dealt with the man from across the river. His vulture-like face contorted as they dragged him to the river's edge where a lion had once engaged their attention. Abayomi easily sliced off the man's nose with a scythe. Then he chained the man to a rock so the lion would not have to hunt for its next meal.

They left two other severely wounded men where they had fallen. In such condition the men would not get far, and only predators attracted to the scent of blood would hear their groans. Abayomi's interest was in the slaver who had killed his cousin. He walked to the rock where he had tied up the man. Zete was at Abayomi's side. Bull and warrior stood before the howling, one-eyed man. Zete did not like noise. Abayomi patted the terror of his village and walked away without looking back. He heard Zete's bellow and a guttural, gurgling sound. Akele's spirit was free. The youth went off to find their families.

※

Hundreds of cattle grazed in the areas surrounding the village. The animals moaned and behaved as though they were calling for help because of a gathering storm. The bullocks' curved, ivory-colored antlers stood out against the lush, green vegetation.

The warriors knew some of the men had left the village and would not return to their women and children until evening. Some of the younger women would be with them, which left mothers, children, and a few men in the village. The likelihood of tragedy crowded the warriors' minds.

They heard sobs. A dog whined. A vulture flew off a roof. Huts, village gardens, and the community ground bore signs of fierce struggle. A crying, naked child walked away from a dwelling unit holding a bloody cloth—his mother's wrap—in his hand. This was the brother of Akele.

Each warrior called out the names of his family members and went to the wounded. They lifted the victims one by one and took their broken, bruised bodies under the shade of a baobab tree. The warriors made stretchers from strong branches and hooked them to animal bracers. They carried their people to a neighboring village for care. Sixty members of their immediate families remained from a village of more than four hundred. Of the survivors three died before they reached the next village. Two were children.

Mbtani searched for his younger brother and Eliye Diop, a pretty girl he had played with as a child. Eliye was the daughter of distinguished elders, and at just sixteen years old she was elegant and graceful as a flamingo. She wore a necklace of tiny river stones and shells, and a bracelet of jade with yellow beads. Braids framed her face.

When Eliye smiled, Mbtani saw the sun. He knew one day he would marry her. She liked him too–all the girls did. When they went to the river in the evenings, they talked about him more than any other man. They became shy and giggled when he smiled at them.

Mbtani now felt fear. He was also ready for vengeance. The thought of his sibling and Eliye brought waves of anger and an aura of super strength. His focus was sharp, his eyes as cold as diamonds.

But neither of them was among the dead or wounded. He thought of Eliye's innocence and charm, of her egg-shaped, mahogany face and large, eyes that sparkled like polished, dark brown gems. He had once seen her bending over to reach a yellow stone on the river bed.

"I'll get it," he had said, then gone into the water and picked up the stone. He'd handed it to her. She'd run away as soon as she had taken it from him.

When the warriors reached the nearby village, the entire neighborhood ran toward them shouting, wanting to know what had happened. An elderly member wearing a calfskin shuka attended to the wounded. He beckoned the youth to bring them to a large hut and place them on beds of hay to await the healer. The doctor abated their bleeding with tourniquets made of wide, flat vines, dried their wounds, and dabbed on astringents. He covered ravaged flesh with potions and leaves of the verbena.

After that there was business to be done. Mbtani sent his comrades to gather the tribes of other villages. Afterward he returned to the river bank where they had gathered earlier that morning. There he crossed to a tree and picked up the slavers' guns. The slavers' horses lingered at the place where the warriors had slain evil by the will of Enkai, the sun god who protected them.

Mbtani gathered the guns and took the clothes from the slavers' sacks. He had little time to rehearse his plan.

As word spread of the murders and abductions, a thousand tribesmen migrated to the open savannah. The sea of tall warriors with painted faces, colorful headpieces, and beaded neck jewelry jumped in unison, reaching higher and higher, chanting solemnly. Their voices hummed in the wind like thousands of taut strings. They readied themselves for war.

Their dancing feet stirred a thick dust cloud that flooded the energy-charged landscape with a golden haze. Mbtani made his way through the throng of warriors to a mound where he raised his assegai against the orange sky. The voices hushed. His shuka ballooned in the wind. His long, thick braids lifted around his handsome face. His imposing figure silhouetted against the sun and a purple aura surrounded him. Everyone on the savannah stood silent as he spoke in a steady, authoritative tone.

"The river will run with their blood. Vultures will pick their bones. Let no one live."

One thousand assegais glistened in the sun. One thousand muscular bodies leapt high off the ground in a jumping, war dance. One thousand voices stilled the heavens and the sun god above the clouds travelled with them. They ran over hills, rivers, and rocky terrain. They chased the night to the edge of the forest into open, dewy plains and across swamps, onward to the outskirts of a town—Mombasa, where the slavers came to auction their human goods to merchants from Portugal, Zanzibar, Turkey, Rome, and countries across the Atlantic.

From a distant hill, the warriors saw the dhows rocking under the ebbing tide. Vessels waited to be filled with human cargo packed head to heel, heel to head in chains. No space would separate the naked bodies in the holds of Satan's vessels.

Mbtani sent Abayomi forward to survey what was happening in the town. He wanted information on the locations of family members and the slavers. Abayomi took off his headdress and shuka, wrapped the dirty, white turban of the slain slaver around his head, slipped on a white tunic and foul trousers, and went into the town.

The marketplace hummed with vendors from the east and west plying their trades in ivory, animal skins, gold, silver, and humans. A variety of essences mixed with sweat, rotting animal flesh, vomit, excrement, and the slick, oily greed of merchants filled the air. As Abayomi entered the path to the port, taking care to hide in the shadows, he heard voices shouting and the clanging of chains. He stealthily approached the scene and saw his people. They were naked, wet, and standing under guard at the side of the auctioneer's stall. The slavers had doused them with seawater to make the merchandise presentable to bidders. He saw his little brother but not Mbtani's. Cold sweat ran down Abayomi's face, blurring vision. His body stiffened, and he knew how a spear to his heart would feel.

As soon as the slavers auctioned one person, they placed another on the ramp. The guards scanned the area and kept a keen watch over the human treasure, taking them in groups to a holding bay to be loaded onto the dhows.

Then one of them ushered Eliye to the block. She was pearl; she would fetch a fortune. She would not work

13

in fields but be kept in the master's house. Her statuesque body stood proudly; she lifted her head high and her eyes were afire. The ugly bruise on her right cheek indicated resistance.

Abayomi saw a tall man go to the block and walk slowly around her. He touched her breast, ran his hands over her body, and drooled. Several merchants repeated his actions. Then the bidding started. Abayomi ran faster than lightning back to his fellow warriors and told them what was happening.

"We must hurry," he said. "There is no time to spare."

Dressed as slavers and with guns in their hands, Mbtani and Abayomi mounted the horses. They arranged the rest of the warriors in a coffle and made their way to the town.

The morning was unusually humid and slushy. A pale, gray cloud hung like a teardrop, the sun was reluctant to shine, and a dog howled somewhere in the distance. There was hardly a breeze, but when it blew it carried the stench of the town to surrounding areas. The warriors moved with the silence of a snake, their pretense seeming as real as the fright of the slavers' victims.

As they reached a busy thoroughfare, Mbtani and Abayomi gave some members of their family orders to crack whips on the backs of their brothers. As they made their way through the town, Abayomi shouted obscenities as the local middlemen slavers did. The warriors in their disguise as slaves created a stir as they had made their way through the town. The large number of strapping, youthful goods for sale had merchants running to their bosses. The warriors were careful to hide their spears, bows, and arrows.

Not long thereafter the spectators of the devil's trade heard the low thumps of spears and arrows connecting with flesh. The blood-curdling cries of the warriors reverberated throughout the town, above the din of gunshots. The warriors ran like the River Nile. Their loose clothing blew up around their bodies like the wings of avenging angels. Zete gored, raged, and ripped flesh that would later be a feast for the vultures.

When Mbtani reached Eliye, he looked deep into her eyes, which held his with softness.

"Where is Masigonde?" he said almost in a whisper.

"He is not with us," Eliye replied.

Mbtani lifted her and commanded his warriors, "Take our people and leave."

They chanted as they made their way up and over the hills, and deep into the jungle. Some returned to their homes. Others followed Mbtani, their new chief, on a long journey, first to find the children. They searched the orchard areas where, early in the morning, they knew the young ones would usually go to pick oranges. The warriors went into the forest calling their names. They returned and combed village after village for the missing boys to no avail. Finally they assumed they were among a group the slavers had captured earlier.

After several days the warriors reached the majestic mountain and made their way farther and farther up her slopes. They gave thanks to the sun god for saving them from bondage and for keeping them alive.

As they continued on their journey to the summit, Eliye kept count of all members of the tribe and made sure each child had the care of an adult. She took responsibility for those who had lost their parents.

Zete was a clumsy climber. He showed displeasure at the cold, windy weather but was corporative when Abayomi put tired children on his back. He bellowed his way up the steep slopes.

Not long after they had begun to climb the mountain, Abayomi became aware that there was an addition to the group: a sure-footed shadow that the warriors had seen near the river bank several nights before the slavers had invaded their village. It had been a moonlit night, and they had trekked about a kilometer beyond the boundary of the man-yatta to catch blue crabs. As they'd reached the river, they'd seen a large lion standing a couple of meters from the bank, silhouetted against the brilliant light of the moon. His long mane blew in the breeze. Instinctively, and without missing a step, the warriors had formed a circle, eyes scanning the surroundings. They had picked up the scent of predators and knew the lion's females were likely to attack. The warriors stood still, listening and hardly breathing, feeling vibrations beneath their feet. Their senses were alert. Their spears, bows, and arrows were ready.

A monkey barked. Suddenly a clamor sounded in the night. Debele Traore, a lanky youth and a cousin of Mbtani, saw a hulking shadow. He made a low, deep sound, and arrows pierced the heads and chests of three lionesses whose spirits took flight to the silent kingdom of the forest dead. When the warriors looked again, the beast had left the river bank. In the hunt the warriors were rhythmic in motion; each was the other's responsibility. That night they had slain the lion's pride.

Since then, the warriors had seen the lion on a few occasions and they had ignored it, but only Abayomi was aware that the beast was following them up the mountain. He did not think it was a threat. He felt as though it merely wanted to be with them. A creature was always at Abayomi's side; his fellow tribesmen believed he was the reincarnation of a king bird. His deep-set, dark eyes peered into one's soul. His narrow, high, slightly humped nose flared at the end, and his high cheekbones, which accentuated his wide mouth, gave him an intimidating look that belied his gentle demeanor. He often went to the mountain with his spear, shield, and dog in tow. He would cover his braided head while he sat on a rock and talked to the animals.

The lion was a magnificent creature. He was a shadow at night but by daylight became an unusual beast. His mane was velvet black with silvery-bluish streaks; his prodigious body was a silvery blue-black. He moved like a lurking panther. He was no ordinary cat. He became known as the lion of the sun god.

As night fell the warriors took shelter in a cave full of large boulders. The night was bright and aglow with fireflies. The breeze was mild and comforting as it swished the leaves, making its own music.

Jomo, the serene and gentle elder, sat on a boulder a few meters from the entrance of the cave. From there he could see the night's magnificent stars and the cloudy light of the Milky Way. Abayomi gently touched his arm.

"Why, father?"

"Why?" He looked at Abayomi with both love and sadness.

"Yes. Why do they take us? Why do our people betray us? Why do they curse our god?"

Jomo bowed his head in thought. He looked up at the stars and then at the faces of the warriors, the children, and the others. "Evil leaders of other tribes betray us because they fear us. They fear Enkai. They sell their enemies to the devil's merchants who come from faraway kingdoms, and who pay for slaves in cattle, weapons and trinkets." Jomo reflected for a moment. "We the people of Enkai, do not make good slaves. The captors must look over their shoulders because they know we would kill them. If we cannot take their lives, we will take our own by starvation or other means. We do not bow to the will of other men. We, brave children, do not take enemies alive. The wicked strangers who come here to plunder the land, and capture our brothers want many strong backs and hands to sow seeds in their lands, to reap harvests, work in rivers and caves for gold, to cut trees in forests for their dwellings, and to help build their world. They want women to work in the masters' dwellings, and they take our children to increase their wealth."

The taut skin on Jomo's oval face had a healthy shine, and his soft, teary eyes stared as though he were in a trance. He stood up and pulled his shuka, which covered a calfskin tunic, tightly around his reed-like body. He looked like a willow branch on a windy hill. Jomo held his staff and began to walk slowly among the captivated group. "This is not the first time, my sons. Many moons ago, when our ancestors lived far away on the banks of the Nile god, in the land of Kush, the strangers came. Tales handed down through generations speak of men of war."

"Who were they?" asked Mbtani.

"They were strangers who travelled on the river in wooden vessels and came ashore on ancestral lands. The strangers had the eyes of the fox and brought our ancestors gifts. Our people welcomed the cunning men, who loved the land's rich soil, maize, and fat sheep, goats, and cattle. The ancestors and their allies from Punt understood the ways of Enkai, the sun god and Olapa, the moon god. Their wealth was plentiful. They built beautiful dwellings and temples in the mountains and buried their loved ones in buildings made of stone, shaped like the spear's blade, to reach the heart of the rising sun god."

Jomo continued walking around the group, and after a while he sat near Eliye, who had her arms around two children. He looked at them. He bent and gently touched Eliye's face. He smiled at her.

In almost a whisper, Eliye said, "Tell us more, Father Jomo." He was the elder of their group, so they all called him "father."

"They had traded with peoples of the desert and from across the seas, gold, silver, frankincense, myrrh, wood, and medicines. Our forefathers defended their land but also attacked enemies who lived close to the river god, and others across the ocean.

"What happened to them?" enquired Mbtani.

"After bloody battles some of them followed the mighty river and came to the valleys below. We are their children."

Like a priest with an adoring flock, Jomo looked at the children. His benevolent manner comforted them. "If only I could borrow a day from times past," he said, "so you would understand the passions of the warriors who died for their cause. They followed the river god, scaled mountains, and walked these valleys with eyes cast to the sun god and their backs to the dead."

He was silent for a long while. Everyone was quiet. The cave took on the aura of a sacred temple. Jomo raised his voice slightly.

"My children, many strangers will come from everywhere to plunder, steal, and enslave the people of Alkebulan. I see a vision of them arriving from many places to divide this land among their people. This is the home of men with much wealth, and these others will always return, just like the moon that comes every night. We are children of the sun god, descendants of fearless warriors. Never yield to the sons of other gods. Children, wear your shields, hold your assegais with pride, and follow the sun."

The following morning they continued their ascent. It was a gruelling climb to the top; thirteen members had perished. Ten days after leaving their villages, they reached a place their tribe believed was Ngaje Ngai, or the House of God. They stood on the summit of the mountain, and the clouds engulfed them. They held hands and prayed to the sun god. The sun was an orange ball. They had seen the moon rise. It had moved toward the sun.

That year Jomo and the tribe of 250 Maasai warriors, 165 women, and 75 children heard a strange whistle, and before night blanketed the cradle of humanity, they disappeared in the clouds. Their people in the plains below never saw them again.

CHAPTER 2

They arrived in a strange and hauntingly beautiful land, and their sadness over having lost several members on the way up the mountain receded. They would always remember the courage of those who had perished. Some had been too young to cope with the high altitude and moody weather. Some had died in accidents during raging storms. Others had succumbed to infections and wounds from chains and whips. Their bodies had cringed from cold and pain.

Besides his brother, Mbtani had lost his mother. He saw his brother's face in every leaf, flower and stream. His agony was acute, gnawing at the pit of his bruised body. His inner being screamed.

As the weary group stood on the mount and surveyed their surroundings, Mbtani held Eliye's hand and asked his people to give praise to the sun god for bringing them to a place where they would feed and regain strength. The men held their assegais high, and the people jumped as high as their tired bodies could take them. They hummed and gave praise.

Then they descended the mountain. As the mist cleared, they heard a loud bark—a familiar sound but much louder, deeper, and sharper than what they were used to. It shattered their sense of security. Mbtani saw the source of the intimidating noise: a gorilla of a size they could not have imagined. There were more—several more—in a habitat with their young.

The warriors were ready should the giant animal approach. She did not. She gave them a look that said, "This is my place. Do not venture in." They did not challenge her by staring into her eyes or quickening their pace—reactions that could have resulted in their deaths. They simply watched the gorillas from the corners of their vigilant eyes and continued along the path.

While passing the habitat, Abayomi, the shepherd, placed one hand on Zete, who remained calm. He had struggled to climb ridges and ledges but had eaten up the rocky mountainsides and weathered the blizzards. The beloved Zete and the lion the warriors had named Matai had provided warmth and guarded their masters steadfastly. Abayomi looked around now for the lion and saw it in the far distance, as if it knew the place. Then it disappeared from his sight.

On this day, their day of salvation, the group walked together as they always had done, except that now their families were with them. The warriors dedicated themselves to their loved ones' well-being and to protecting them.

Eliye never left Mbtani's side. She was content and happy to be his woman and knew they would be husband and wife soon. She would be with him forever. She would fight at his side and be ready to give her life for the young warrior who had saved her from the worst death a human could suffer: captivity.

That night Mbtani and Eliye rested on a pile of leaves close to each other. He turned his head and looked into her longing eyes. They studied each other's faces. The emotional and physical pain of the past weeks ebbed. Warmth surged through their bodies. The desire to hold her was overwhelming. He wanted to kiss her. He reached for her hand and brought it to his lips. Her moist lips parted just slightly, revealing pearls. She placed her other hand on his body and caressed him. The silent night engulfed them. The universe opened up, and they explored its firm gentleness. It was a universe only the two of them would traverse. Its sun rose beyond clouds bursting just after the thunder. Rain fell and cooled the intensity of its rays. It subsided temporarily, and the second and third tumultuous heat waves tumbled them to the shores of dawn.

〰️※〰️

On the top of the mountain, on an expansive ledge, canopied by a wide overhang and too far away to be seen, stood a small group of men. They had followed the movements of these people who had just arrived in their land. They had monitored their every move. The leaders of the land already knew strangers had arrived carrying spears, bows, and arrows and wearing ragged garments.

Mbtani, Abayomi, and Debele the lion hunter were watching. Intuitively they knew people were around. They wanted no regrettable surprises. Their eyes searched the tall grasses and forest. Debele's instinct told him to look up into the mountain, toward the east. The mountain was far away and misty, impossible for the human eye to detect any movement. Yet he could not stop gazing. He had an uncontrollable urge to find out what was happening. The same urge had led him to pursue and kill lions that hunted the village cattle. Now he picked up his assegai, threw his shuka over his shoulder, and slowly jogged until he was midway between the mountain and where his fellow warriors were. The people of the land had seen him as he'd progressed along the savannah. The mist-drenched trees still hid them.

Mbtani knew Debele was investigating something, and was ready to move in whatever way or direction was necessary. The inhabitants also knew the one who was approaching the mountain was not simply taking a stroll. While they could not make out much, they had seen enough to know Debele was suspicious that other people were around. They decided it was time to speak with the visitors. They began to descend the mountain.

Debele slowed his pace as he approached the savannah's edge and the jungle beyond. He observed his surroundings with a keen eye and saw the movement of small animals. After a while Debele turned and began to make his way back to his family, aware that many eyes followed his movements. The lion hunter felt no fear although he knew his people were not alone.

The men on the mountain made their way down a familiar path. They were adorned with colourful, intricate necklaces of small, precious stones and amulets of gold. Plaited hair hung to their shoulders. Coarse red and gold threads fashioned braids on their buffalo hide skirts. They held the assegai. Among them was one of regal bearing wearing a gold headband.

Debele returned to his family, but the jungle at the edge of the savannah occupied his mind. He would bide his time and would not sleep. Later that day, as he and the other warriors were about to leave the camp to perform their duties, Debele saw the figures standing at the edge of the savannah looking in his direction. His senses had been right. He had known people were around. Instinctively Debele looked for the lion and only then realized it had wandered off into the jungle. The last place he'd seen it was in the long grass a few yards away from the giant baobab tree under which he and his family camped.

The people in the distance began to walk in the warriors' direction, and Mbtani called his team. When the two groups were in full view of each other, both looked for signs of aggression. Mbtani made the first move. He stepped ahead of his warriors, indicating to them to stay as he went toward the other group of men.

The man with the gold headband stepped away from the other group of people and approached Mbtani. The groups watched every move their leaders made. Eliye moved away from the women and children and went to stand closer to the warriors.

The two men looked into each other's eyes. Mbtani wore a ragged robe. His unkempt, braided hair hung just below his bony shoulders. His body was thin, having been starved of solid food for weeks, but he remained a stoic force of unusual strength—just like the thoroughbred he faced. Still he looked surreal silhouetted against the colourful landscape.

Neither group predicted what happened next. Mbtani held his assegai out and placed the bottom end firmly on the ground. It was about equal distance from both men. The other man did the same with his spear. His eyes twinkled. Mbtani's narrowed slightly as he broke the silence.

"We do not know where we are."

The regal one did not respond, but his eyes were reassuring and friendly. Mbtani interpreted their message as a nonthreatening engagement. The man placed his hand on Mbtani's shoulder, flashing his gleaming teeth. "We welcome you who the sun god has brought to us from the other place. It is from where our forefathers came. My father asked that we bring you to the temple."

"It is not our intention to stay. We must return to rid our home of evil. The sun god has brought us here temporarily for a purpose. My name is Mbtani."

"I am Askia, and these are my soldiers." He called the six men behind him, and they each extended a hand to Mbtani's shoulder. They looked past him as well.

"Come, meet my family," Mbtani offered.

The warm welcome infused the rustic atmosphere with the murmur of greetings in a language that had a distinct Nilotic lilt. The women made sounds of joy.

Askia looked into Eliye's eyes as he greeted her. He no longer grinned. She turned away and went to the girl tugging at her clothes.

As everyone chattered, Mbtani heard a roar and observed activity in the distance. He heard another roar, and another.

Beyond the grassy fringes at the southwestern perimeter of the valley, two huge, black lions viciously struggled in the sienna-colored soil. One disengaged, ran a few yards in the direction of the people, then stood its ground. It lunged at the other lion. Its yawning jaws closed on its rival's head. The frenzied pawing and wrestling to the sounds of their sonorous growls signified a battle to the death for a prized asset: the handsome pride.

As the two moved apart for a fleeting moment, Abayomi recognized the sun god's gift that had followed them up to the House of God over the past several days.

The battle ended as suddenly as it had begun. The much larger and older beast surrendered all possessions of its kingdom to the one the warriors had named Matai. The pitiful image of the beast limping across the wooded valley and out of sight wrenched Abayomi's heart. The victor licked the wounds on his paws and shoulder while flicking his tail up and down and from side to side. He grinned and bounded toward Abayomi as if to reassure his master he would be back soon. Then he took off to take control of his new lionesses.

He had returned home.

Askia and his men had seen the lion and the bull from where they had stood on the shelf called the Seat of God. The lion perplexed them. The new people showed no fear of it, yet the lions in this land were vicious predators that lived in caves and hunted both humans and animals. The beasts had killed many in stealthy attacks. All adults and children were at risk, especially those who ventured into the wrong cave.

The caves held many secrets, and the people believed the bird god lived in them. Whenever the people heard whistles, they came and looked for birds. The magnificent creatures flew above the clouds, but at times swooped to the trees and springs. Their crystal-like bodies gleamed in the sun's rays as they flew from the cave and across the mountain, where mist draped giant trees.

The people of the land watched with admiration as Matai licked Abayomi, then bent his head to receive the master's benediction before proceeding on his business. Matai would kill the cubs of the king he dethroned and sire many of his own seed, ensuring his lineage for generations. Each lion that became the leader of protector lions in the land beyond the House of God would bear the name Matai.

〰

Word spread among the villages like feathers taken by the wind: others had arrived, led by a valiant warrior name Mbtani. Askia's father, King Kibwe, instructed his men to take the strangers to the valley of Sade, where they would stay.

As the warriors and their families travelled there, they wondered whether they were in the place where the sun god lived. Never had they seen such dwellings, built discreetly between the trunks of giant baobab trees of indescribable girth, spread, and height. They knew the tree from its leaves; its exaggerated, pendulous, sweet-smelling flowers; its egg-shaped fruit; and its massive trunk. The women often used the fruit to make refreshing drinks and to reduce fevers. The warriors and their families could not see the crowns of these towering trees, nor could they have imagined the size of the glorious ficus and yellow-wood trees that decorated the slopes of the valley.

On the way Askia stopped to show them a magnificent building called the Temple of the Sun. This was where successive generations had recorded the history of their people, going back to when their first ancestors had come. The drawings were outlines of naked people hunting deer and fighting large beasts. Some danced, and others played. Many walked with the day's catch along a riverbank or sat in front of dome-shaped huts and around fires. The people appeared similar to the warriors in height, complexion, and shape.

Mbtani and his people had heard tales of formidable warriors who had gone into battle on elephants, wearing skins of leopards and lions, and such events were recorded within this building. On one marble stone was a fighter larger than the others, wearing a blue crown with two cobras. He was in combat against others who wielded clubs, long spears, and knives.

Many thousands of years were recorded on these walls, starting back when the current inhabitants' ancestors had made sacrifices. In the images they prayed to the ram-headed god Amun-Ra, father of all gods, creator of all things. He was the sun god. The images also portrayed the flight of warriors to a valley that was familiar to those who had just arrived. Later, Mbtani and his people would hear stories of what the drawings, etchings, and engravings meant. The Ashais, people of the land of Ashaise, would dramatize the tales with the same pride and enthusiasm as Askia's foreparents when they'd passed the tales down to his generation. Mbtani and his warriors heard about the lands of Kush, Punt, and Kemet, and about the kingdoms north of the river god: Asante, Nri, Ife, and Oyo.

The stroll through the temple ended with stelae of black lions, hippopotami, crocodiles, flamingos, and many other creatures. There was an illustration of an unusual bird flying over the Blue Mountains.

The two groups left the Temple of the Sun, and Askia took the others across the forest. They rode through thick, mountain bamboo and into another valley where large ferns, shrubs, and wild coffee grew in profusion. Tree creepers hung like a continuous downpour of rain upon the cradle of wild foliage. Askia took the warriors and their families to where they would stay. They did not know that the place, which was nestled on the southern end of the valley of Sade, would be their home.

The king gave each family the gift of life—a head of cattle. Mbtani and his tribe wandered freely across the land and far away into the neighboring forest to hunt, fish, and play.

After seven days Askia and his compatriots visited the newcomers on handsome ibexes. The animals were practical means of transport in the strange, mountainous land. The time had come for the new arrivals to meet the king. While speaking to Mbtani about the event, Askia kept his eyes on Eliye—an impertinence not missed by her man, who chose to ignore it.

"We take pleasure in knowing that your people are well and comfortable," said Askia. "You have great hunting skills. The shepherd, the one called Abayomi, has a way with cattle and beasts that makes us very enthusiastic about you. He tames lions and speaks to birds. Come with us. We have brought you the carriers." He gestured to the ibexes. Mbtani and his men mounted the handsome beasts.

They journeyed across the valleys and rough terrain. The sure-footed beasts moved with ease on the steepest of hills with sharp, jagged stones and dangerous overhangs. They all but flew across the surface. The group reached the home of King Kibwe, dismounted their animals, and entered a columned palace with few furnishings besides wooden stools and chairs. Images of kings, queens, the falcon, the black lion, and the god Amun-Ra lined the walls. Askia ushered the group to a passage that led to a courtyard where they would meet the king.

As Mbtani and his men entered the courtyard, the king stood next to a lily pond. He wore a leather kilt with blue and gold bands, a large chain of gold links connected by beads, a ring depicting a falcon on his middle finger, a bracelet, and a gold headband with two cobras in the middle of the forehead. His height was striking. His eyes were soft and engaging. He had a thick, plaited beard that hung to his chest.

"Welcome, Mbtani. The sun god has smiled on us." He placed his hand on Mbtani's left shoulder.

"Your generosity humbles me," Mbtani replied. "We are strangers in your land, but your son and people have not made us feel that way. We are comfortable, and we owe your people for the gifts they have given us. The cattle are healthy and feed us well. We must return soon to our homes across the sun and below the great mountain."

"We have witnessed your great powers on the hunt. You are brave warriors who are not strangers. You followed the path of our ancestors—the same ancestors as yours. We came here by the will of Amun-Ra. Do not turn your back on fortune."

"We must protect what the sun god gave to us. When we fled to the House of God, we intended to return and defeat the enemy. We did not know what happened. The sun god hid behind the moon god and plunged the path into darkness."

"The opportunity for a crossover to your home may not return," the king advised.

"Tegene, our scientist, has been studying the ways of Amun-Ra and we have not yet been shown the path. We know there is an alignment with the land from which we came. We are still not sure that we have left there. Do not trouble yourself. If ever the forces open the door, you will know. Teach us the way of the lions. The elder father called Jomo must tell our children about the place from which you came. The shepherd impresses me—the one who goes fearlessly into the forests and tames the lions. He has unique powers."

"We will do as you desire and will be happy to share our customs."

"We will meet your people and welcome them at the Sunrise Festival in the next ten moon days."

Kibwe and his guests enjoyed a tasty meal of fruit, bread, and goat meat. Mbtani and his people left in the evening. It was the time of the midnight sun, so it was safer to travel through the forest than it was during dark nights.

Mbtani was in deep thought as the animal beneath him gobbled up the terrain on the way to Sade. What he had seen and experienced over the past few days drove him to question himself. He was growing attached to Ashaise and its people. To him they were not just other people remote from his own. He felt comfortable with them and could detect no insincerity or latent malice among their ranks, and this made him feel a tinge of guilt. His elders had nurtured him to be a defender of his people and their possessions. He should not have developed affection for these others in the time it took to catch wild boar.

But the king's embrace had perplexed him. There was something mysterious. The Ashais seemed to have a need for something that was elusive to his understanding. He wondered about his hosts' obsession with security. There was an extraordinarily large contingent accompanying Askia, which reinforced Mbtani's belief that the Ashais were wary of an attack from some dangerous force. He had heard much about animal attacks, but the attitude of Askia's protectors suggested they were guarding against a source more cunning than wild beasts. He had seen a fortress-like, interlocking brick building. Its walls were sufficiently high to deter invaders from reaching vulnerable citizens such as elders and children.

Mbtani did not know of the toxic undercurrent in the land where black lions roamed, and where a strange bird flew above the clouds. He and his people did not know there were two kingdoms, but they sensed there were others apart from Askia and his men who watched them.

"Askia, are there others here, apart from your people?"

"Why do you ask?"

"Your warriors constantly look around the trees and mountains. You have many warrior protectors. My people are watched by others who do not have garments like yours."

"Yes there are others—enemies who want our land. There is much to tell you. Let's talk later."

The sky was a sheet of pale orange before the dance of the midnight sun contrasted the bluish-leaf fescue grass. Creamy, feathery panicles decorated the grassland. The wraithlike herders with blanched sheepskins hanging off one shoulder gracefully guided droves of oversized cattle with shining horns to enclosures. In other areas gazelles gambolled along pathways and through patches in the forest.

The children had eagerly awaited Mbtani and the others' return and ran to them as they dismounted the gentle ibexes. A little later Askia sat with Mbtani and his men and related to them the wars with his neighbors—the Amarans.

CHAPTER 3

A skia told them that beyond the mountains there was another land called the Kingdom of Amara, led by a king called Kepi. Askia's father, King Kibwe, ruled over the Kingdom of Ashaise. This division had come about with the arrival of a king named Tariku more than two thousand moon years earlier. He was the great ancestor of Kibwe.

"Tariku had been eighteen years of age when he and other fighters in the army of a great warrior named Taharqa, fled an invasion of their homeland—the Kingdom of Kush. They had travelled along the river god into the Valley of Life where they had settled and commingled with other tribes. Several years later Tariku and his family had gone up the mountain. They had wanted to be closer to the sun god. The chronicles said they took refuge from a storm in a cave. After the storm subsided, they climbed to the summit of the mountain. There on the mountain where the clouds swirled, they stood. They observed the moon god as it moved toward the sun god, which it eventually covered except for a brilliant light, then Tariku and his people heard long, low whistles and thereafter, they vanished."

"That is what happened to us," said Mbtani. "And your people too."

"Yes. When King Tariku and his family arrived on the mountain of this beautiful land, they met others who were similar to them. In those ancient times, there was only the kingdom of Amara ruled by a King named Asefa. Asefa believed Tariku and his tribe had arrived by the will of the sun god, so he welcomed them. He agreed to share the land and decided on boundaries. Asefa created two kingdoms. He ruled the Kingdom of Amara, and Tariku ruled this kingdom called Ashaise.

Tariku was formidable, as was Asefa, but they lived in peace, and both kingdoms prospered. Things changed when the sons of King Asefa and King Tariku got into a conflict. They agreed that after the death of their fathers, the kingdoms should unite, but Prince Asefa felt since he was the eldest he should lead the united kingdom."

"So why didn't their fathers unite Amara and Ashaise again?" asked Mbtani.

"There was no need to do that. Both peoples lived in harmony and no one bothered with the boundaries. Their fathers had discussed succession with the elders and decided that whosoever, in the collective wisdom of the council of elders, could best advance the welfare of the kingdoms would succeed the kings, though this did not necessarily mean their children. Prince Asefa fumed. He thought the decision was unjust because he saw himself as the heir to both kingdoms.

Two moon years later, when King Tariku went hunting he suffered severe blows to his head and body from a fatal fall over a rocky cliff. His animal had suddenly swerved to avoid a deep sink hole. He had not fully recovered, and within six moon months of the fall, Tariku died in the arms of his son—Prince Sahure. The council of elders here agreed that Sahure would succeed his father.

The elevation of Sahure to king of Ashaise created anxiety for his rival—Prince Asefa. Asefa felt that since Sahure had succeeded his father as king here in Ashaise, then the council of elders in Amara had to make him king of Amara after the death of his father. Prince Asefa couldn't wait. He got rid of council elders he did not trust. He created conflict, which resulted in the deaths of two council elders. Prince Asefa's men had assassinated the elders.

It was one of his father's trusted protectors who told the king that his son had killed the elders. King Asefa was no fool. He had been aware that his son was a threat and he had confronted him on more than one occasion. The king grieved over the death of his trusted elders. He had to take action against his son. He'd waited too long. King Asefa left his dwelling place to meet with his son. While the king was on his way, a group of men attacked and killed him and his protector."

"You mean his son killed him."

"Yes," responded Askia. "But, the council of elders refused to make Prince Asefa king. They defied his orders and appointed a laibon named Geteye the king of Amara. Prince Asefa called his warrior protectors and told them, 'Geteye must not live another day.' Hatred burned in his eyes. The heat of rage scorched his soul. Asefa assassinated Geteye and the council of elders. He appointed a new council. He then plotted to kill King Sahure, unite both kingdoms and become king of a united land. He underestimated the young king of Ashaise.

Asefa and his gang attacked our land at midnight. They had forgotten great warrior blood ran through Sahure's veins. The young king was ready. It was a time when the midnight sun shone. The sky was a silver sheet of light, and Sahure fought Asefa from the mountains, the trees, the boulders, the rock protrusions, the temple, the lake, and every other strategic location in Ashaise. The sun god's archers sent arrows into the hearts of Asefa's men. In the end, Sahure lived up to the expectations of his elders. He repelled Asefa's army. As Sahure was close to striking the fatal blow, the coward fled.

Driven mad by his failure, the twisted, self-appointed king of Amara used every tactic to foment division across both kingdoms. Cunning and malice consumed him; he bided time until it was advantageous to initiate war again.

Since then, this kingdom of Ashaise, and the kingdom of Amara have been in a state of mistrust. There is much hostility. The new king of Amara—Kepi, like his predecessors, believes that if he controls our Temple of the Sun, he will conquer Ashaise."

When Askia had finished telling Mbtani about the challenges of the Kingdom of Ashaise, it was clear to Mbtani that the peaceful rhapsody of life in the kingdoms had ceased a long time ago. The children of both kingdoms grew up knowing only war. The energies of the people were no

longer occupied with hunting, fishing and peaceful liveli-
hoods. Successive leaders of Ashaise and Amara spent most
of their time strategizing, plotting, and building weapons in
order to protect their territories, and to make war. They had
launched constant attacks on each other.

Askia said, "We want peace, and my father has approached
King Kepi for a solution. But Kepi is cunning. He greets my
father and shares a meal, then his soldiers kill our shepherds
and protectors."

It was late in the evening when Askia bade farewell to
his guests. He lingered a little longer to watch Eliye as she
ushered a couple of boys to their huts.

※

In between her daily caregiving and other domestic tasks,
Eliye strolled to the lake and sat in a cozy space between boulders. While contemplating the future with her lover, she had
drawn pictures of animals and was now sketching swans. On
previous visits here she'd written songs and crafted necklaces
from precious stones she found at the lakeside.

From the nearby grazing ground, Abayomi watched her.
He considered it his duty to see no harm befell her when
Mbtani was in the forest hunting or preoccupied with other
duties. This day he observed Askia approaching her quiet
spot. Abayomi smiled because he knew the man wanted her.
Askia was love-struck. Still, Abayomi hoped he would not
have to intervene on behalf of his leader.

Askia showed no concern that the woman he would
ask to be his wife belonged to someone else. He would face

39

Mbtani and tell him of his intent if Eliye gave any indication that she would consider his request. She intimidated him, and he felt foolish. It was not a man's way to contemplate how to approach the woman he wanted. He knew his men were amused by his clumsiness.

It was the day before the Sunrise Festival when Askia seized the opportunity to speak with her. His men had kept watch of her movements, so he knew she was alone. Looking regal on his decorated ibex, he approached the woman at the lakeside. She was aware of his presence but chose to keep her eyes focused on her drawing.

Askia stayed on the animal, waiting for Eliye to acknowledge him. When he realized he and the beast would be there to welcome the Sunrise Festival the next morning, he dismounted and moved toward her. Her impudence in ignoring the son of King Kibwe crossed his mind, but he was a wise young man and thought better of using his position.

"May I see the image?" he asked.

She looked up and extended the tablet. He bent down to examine it.

"You are as beautiful as the swans." He extended his arm to draw her eyes to the graceful water fowl. She was neither flattered nor amused, and walked to the water's edge. He followed her and said, "I want you to be my wife."

"I belong to Mbtani and you know that, so why do you ask? It is not our intention to stay in your land. I have many responsibilities to my people."

"You will not be returning home, Eliye. That was our ancestors' wish when they came here. Ashaise will not be aligned again unless the sun god opens up a way. Tengene has made drawings in the great temple about the path. He told us there are many places in the universe. Our place is within the sphere of your land, and the path will only align with your home if Ashaise moves. My people are afraid of that because when the earth opens it shakes everything, trees move, the animals become silent, and then there is much noise. When that happens we lose many cattle and loved ones who go into the earth. I know you will remain here. I have seen you with the little ones and you will be the mother of my children."

Eliye felt sorry for him and did not respond.

"My father is anxious for me to marry and have children," Askia continued. "I've told him you are the woman I want."

"I am committed to another. I have known him since childhood and love him. I cannot love another. You must understand. I am in your house, and my fate and that of my people are in your hands."

Eliye looked without blinking into his eyes. He focused on hers and knew he would never have her. They studied each other's faces for what seemed like ages to Abayomi.

Askia saw Eliye's eyes softened, and he realised that she understood his sincerity. He touched Eliye's face, letting his fingers rest a moment under her chin. He then turned away slowly and mounted the ibex but looked at her for a while. A smile was on his lips. His eyes showed his longing.

Eliye returned to what she had been doing and hummed a tune as she drew the squawking cygnets paddling behind their mother.

CHAPTER 4

D
awn received the people of the strange land as they
unfurled from villages across the country with expectant faces. The Ashais would kill a bull. Their sacrifice
would be grand, and they anticipated the benediction.
The Ashais headed to the temple where the rite of purifi-
cation would be performed. The people sang and waved
palms as they walked in procession. Their voices rose in
concert with the sudden downpour—the cleansing before
the rebirth. The citizens of Ashaise were going to see the
golden orb that at noontide would pour its rays directly over
the temple, drenching it with powerful light. When it crept
over the valleys, they would sing of love and beautiful things.

Time devoured light as the moment drew closer. The
people heard the calling sounds of drums atop the mountain
where the temple stood—sounds that reached their souls,
making their bodies move involuntarily to the rhythm.
Voices hushed; a child led a magnificent bull to the sacri-
ficial table. The laibons, in white cotton shukas trimmed

with gold, came and stood around the animal. A warrior herder held it and placed a reed around its neck. Another warrior stooped about two feet away, aimed his arrow, and, with precision, pierced an artery in the bull just enough for blood to squirt into the temple's golden gourd. The animal did not move. The warrior then gently squeezed the wound and eased the reed.

The laibons drank, and at the last sip the drums rolled. The people focused their eyes on the sky. The sun combusted over the temple and showered the mountains and valleys with golden ribbons of light. It was an act that could only be perpetrated by the sun god, who gave life. The people sacrificed the animal before celebrating the rebirth of all that was in the universe. Crystal birds whistled low as they flew into the clouds.

The drums continued to roll. The people stood still. Their silence was acknowledgement of their insignificance in the grandeur of nature. In unison they raised their hands and voices in a valorous crescendo, giving praise for all they had received. The melding of Meroitic, Maa, other Nilotic, and Niger-Congo languages was musical.

While these wondrous events unfolded, Eliye looked at Mbtani, who seemed anxious. She was uneasy too. She was familiar with his moods—his pensive, searching ways. He knew she looked at him, so he turned his head and looked at her. He gave a reassuring smile. They planned to be married the following day and had confided this to Jomo.

As the elder of the tribe, Jomo had lived an exemplary life, though he was still a young man at sixty years of age. He looked at Mbtani, searched the faces of the warriors for signs of unease, and finally looked for Abayomi. Their eyes met, and that was when Jomo knew something was wrong. It was a sensation he understood well. It was what he had felt when the slavers came.

Mbtani's eyes roamed. He noticed when Abayomi slipped away. It was time for him to let his warriors know evil was at hand. They were already on full alert.

Askia was shrewd. He also felt ill at ease and had observed the eye contact between Mbtani and his men. He looked toward his father, who was conversing with the elders as they drank a beverage of strained, fermented millet grain.

The king's camaraderie with the elders and other members of the royal family masked his disquiet over the dream he'd had the previous night. In it he'd fallen into a deep crevasse. He'd called his beloved wife, who could not hear him.

Askia called Narma, an accomplished archer, and whispered to him.

Abayomi returned and hurried to Mbtani. This indicated something was about to happen. Simultaneously, Mbtani saw Narma racing toward Askia and pointing in the direction of the eastern mountain range. There was a piercing whistle, and into the air six flaming arrows flew. The sound confused the visitors, who did not understand the meaning of the Ashais' codes and symbols. Soldiers gathered the women and children and ushered them to the western valley trail that led to various shelters made of stone. The soldiers sent some of the women and children into caves with heavy stone doors.

Mbtani, Abayomi, and the warriors gathered their kin, and Eliye led the women, children, and elders to where the Ashais had ushered their people. Mbtani looked around quickly for areas where Ashaise was weak. He decided to position some of his men at the northwestern side of the temple, with some close to where the king was. Some went to defend Askia, and other warriors protected the safe houses where their families went.

※

King Kepi of Amara had plotted for several moon months to accomplish the goal which had eluded his predecessors—to conquer Ashaise. Kepi had timed the attack for late evening. By then, he thought, the consumption of fermented drinks would have impaired his enemies' alertness. "This moon day I will conquer Ashaise," he said.

At the height of sunset, he gave his men orders to invade, and they engaged in battle. Amara had more military resources than its rival, and for all of Kepi's scheming he had underestimated the resourcefulness, skill, and tenacity of the Ashais' soldiers and archers. Unfortunately for Kepi, he also was not aware of the superior fighting skills of the warriors from the land across the sun.

Arrows flew from under the leafy shelters of massive branches, from behind boulders by the lake, from boats, and from crevices on the slopes of the valley walls, and men fell. The aggressors made headway among the smaller army of Ashaise. Warriors on horseback from Amara came in droves from various directions over the mountains. As they approached the temple, they were surprised by an army of massive bulls led by Abayomi, who sat atop the finest of them all: Zete. They charged and gored the riders and horses, driving them to the fringes of the village, where black lions savaged some of them and enraged, mammoth gorillas massacred others.

The pyramid temple was difficult for enemies to reach, as three layers of soldiers surrounded its base and Askia had stationed archers randomly in alcoves on the three sides. In the melee below, the tallest and heaviest of the Amarans' best fighters, led by Kepi, breached the wall beyond a moat. Stealthily they moved along the path to where Kibwe and his son were.

Mbtani and his warriors were valiant, fearless fighters who moved like shadows. Their strides were swift, graceful, and quiet, and the surrounding trees hid them. The presence of Debele, the lion hunter, had alerted Kibwe and his son that the warriors were fighting alongside them.

The king, his son, and their guards were now in a full-scale battle for their lives. Mbtani and his warriors took control; though they were slightly shorter and lighter in weight than the Amarans, they were deadly in their nimbleness, discipline, and strategy. They were brutally adept with spears and short blades, and their arrows flew like diving gulls. In short measure they eased the pressure on Kibwe, Askia, and their protectors.

After Eliye had taken the women and children to the safety of the cave, she returned and stayed hidden among shrubbery near the temple. Jomo was aware she was there. She had a good view of the raging battle. No one else saw from where the arrow came, and Eliye made sure that the Amaran warrior, who shot an arrow into Askia's side, never shot another. Her assegai took flight and pierced the Amaran's forehead. Then she ran to the edge of the bloody courtyard and dragged Askia, with the help of Jomo, to safety behind two boulders.

Eliye had to act quickly. She grabbed a handful of grass, which she placed on Askia's wounded flesh and said to Jomo, "Pull it out now." Jomo extracted the arrow. With deft hands, Eliye placed a tourniquet made from long reed stalks and covered the wound. She knew it was only a matter of time unless she could get Askia into the temple, where he would be given an antidote and anti-inflammatory medicine.

Jomo picked up his spear and helped Eliye to carry Askia. Mbtani saw what was happening and wanted her out of the way. She too was a skilled warrior, but even warriors died, he thought.

Blood flowed from a nasty gash over Kibwe's swollen-shut right eye. He was now in Kepi's line of vision. It was an opportune time for the Amaran king to throw his blade, but King Kibwe shifted his position, and the sun was now directly in Kepi's face. Kepi was not sure what he was seeing. There was a shadowy figure. Kepi lifted his arm to throw the blade and felt a force grip his wrist. Kepi was a bigger man than Mbtani. It was a struggle between malice, and courage. The iron grip of Mbtani's hand and the blinding light of the sun god sentenced Kepi.

Except for a handful of fighters, Kepi's disintegrated army fled, leaving the seriously wounded and the dead.

The fighting had by and large ended except for the battle between Kepi and Mbtani. The blood-curdling sounds of the past hours—the roar of lions, the gorillas' thunderous bark, the zip and swoosh of arrows and the thuds of spears—had ceased. The spectators stood in expectation. King Kibwe who could barely see because of his wounds stood still where he was. He knew any movement that distracted Mbtani would cause the young warrior's death.

Kepi could not move the force. He squinted in the glare of the sun and used his other hand to reach out for the shadow. It was a wasted effort. He then lifted his leg, aiming for Mbtani's groin. Mbtani's willowy and nimble body spun like a top, and he thrust his foot into Kepi's stomach. Kepi hit the ground with a thud that sounded through the forest. The last thing King Kepi saw was an assegai aimed at his heart. The villagers looked up as they heard the long, low whistles of crystal birds flying to the Seat of God.

※

In the pyramid Temple of the Sun, Kibwe and Mbtani found Eliye and Jomo attending to Askia. He was in and out of delirium, drifting toward a light, yet he tried to reach out to something. There was something to go to, and he wanted to go to it. The light pulled his body toward it, but at the same time something tugged him back. He did not understand.

Eliye looked up at the king. "The poison is strong."

It was some time before Askia rested less fitfully. Eliye looked at Mbtani, whose eyes were glazed. He smiled at her. She heard a faint voice calling her name and saw Askia's eyes fixed on her. She held his hand. His restlessness subsided, and he calmed under the influence of the drug she'd given him.

Jomo got up from the other side of the bench, and the king sat beside his son. Kibwe reached out and caressed Askia's pale, hot forehead. Askia placed his hand over his father's. He tried to squeeze it but was too weak. Mbtani stood next to Eliye as Askia looked at him.

Askia whispered, "Take care of them."

The people of Ashaise buried their dead. There were many ceremonies to send the spirits on the rays of the sun successfully through the passage of time. The new people from the land across the sun had not suffered losses. Their courage became legendary in the chronicles of Ashaise.

Abayomi was hardly seen thereafter. He wandered the forest with the lions and Zete. He learned the path of many caves. He listened for the long, low whistle of the crystal birds. Often Abayomi went to the Blue Mountains and stayed on the Seat of God. He waited there to see the birds, but they flew above the clouds. He became enlightened about the ways of all creatures, and they came to know him. The birds ate from his hands, and the deer gathered around as he slept under the sky. The animals slept with him.

The king mourned his son and often went to the temple, where he stayed for long periods. He had grown close to Mbtani. He loved the warrior from across the sun who every day demonstrated the wisdom of a man far exceeding his age and filled the king with immense satisfaction. Kibwe loved Mbtani's wife, Princess Eliye. She was the daughter Kibwe and his beloved wife had longed for. Mbtani and Eliye became his children. His joy was his grandchildren.

※

The people of Ashaise made peace with the land and vowed to resolve all differences without bloodshed. Anyone who threatened the peace had to surrender their possessions to the kingdom. The king banished beyond the mist those who committed serious crimes against humans and animals.

The king gradually handed over many of his daily responsibilities to the prince, in whom he had the greatest confidence. During the time of Prince Mbtani, the sacrifice of animals was no more. Abayomi, who lived in the forest with the lions, gorillas, and Zete, influenced the decision. Abayomi said to the people of Ashaise, "The sun god does not need the blood of animals to give you blessings. Caring for creatures is the greatest sacrifice you can make. Without the animals, you will not survive."

People throughout the land loved Jomo. He was an inspiration to them. He became a famous storyteller and was responsible for updating the chronicles of the Kingdom of Ashaise. When he wasn't in the temple, he was with the children of Mbtani and Eliye. On nights when the midnight sun shone over the temple, he would tell the children stories about the land across the sun and the ancient kingdoms of Kush and Punt that were ruled by their ancestors.

It was the first son of Mbtani and Eliye—Askia II, who found the body of Jomo Selassie at the side of the lake early one morning. The sun shone on Jomo's gentle face which reinforced the Ashais's belief that when people died, the rays of the sun god took their chis throughout aeons. The artists recorded the storyteller's life in the Temple of the Sun.

The other young warriors became leaders of the realms. Debele and Abayomi contributed greatly to reforming the kingdom of Ashaise. They learned much from the native people and founded schools of science, astronomy, art, sports, and agriculture and laid the foundation for the modernization of Ashaise. Abayomi made a garden in the name of Akele.

King Kibwe's chi went on the rays of the sun when he was 120 years old. King Mbtani and Queen Eliye ruled with firm, benevolent hands for sixty years. The Land of the Crystal Bird prospered under their leadership. Successive leaders built upon the legacy of their ancestors.

Ashaise progressed from a kingdom of agrarian communities to a kingdom of diversified agricultural, commercial, and light industrial realms. They were guided by an underlying philosophy that each and every citizen had the potential to advance the kingdom.

Many moon years passed. During the reign of a great-granddaughter of the legendary Mbtani Djedkare—Queen Eliye II—the development of the people became a pillar of progress. Like Mbtani she was a transformational leader. She studied his strategies.

Gradually the Ashais abandoned all of their doctrines that stigmatized people based on their personal beliefs, occupations, lifestyles, and handicaps. They eschewed anything that inhibited their freedom to grow in harmony. Queen Eliye II married a distant cousin whose name was Akele Djedkare. Together they layered earlier foundations with institutions of leadership and mind development. They had three children. Their last son was named Meleke Djedkare.

※

Mbtani's brother, Masigonde, and some other boys had disappeared the morning the slavers had killed Akele. Five of them had left the manyatta at sunrise to pick fruit. They were not easy targets, as the slavers had thought, and were able to evade captivity by hiding in the forest. A day later they snuck back to their homes. No one was there. The boys thought the slavers had killed their parents and siblings. Fear overwhelmed them, and they wept. They vowed they would get revenge when they grew up.

They left the village, travelled miles away, and eventually joined a tribe of Samburu nomads who protected and nurtured them. Masigonde and the other young boys grew up to become formidable warrior protectors. At the age of twenty, they returned to their place of birth not far from the Galana River. Masigonde married the daughter of a chief protector. After several years of successful exploits for land and cattle, he ruled the largest tribe in the region.

Masigonde expanded his empire across many villages. He was a menace to foreigners and had brutally dealt with middlemen slavers. People of other kingdoms and tribes called Masigonde Black Lightning because he struck with speed and stealth, leaving no enemy alive.

His people loved and worshipped their king. His enemies feared him. King Masigonde Djedkare died from natural causes at the age of 113 years.

In 1619 slavers captured a twelve-year-old direct descendant of the illustrious warrior king. The boy sailed in the stench of Satan's ship bound for the New World. His parents named him Masigonde after their legendary ancestor. He was tall and wise for his age, with twinkling, smiling eyes and dimpled cheeks. He resembled his great-uncle Mbtani.

CHAPTER 6

THE YEAR 1999

"This, I think, is the spot."

Shoulder-length Afro-locks fell to the sides of Allan-Michael Cline's face. His dark-brown eyes sparkled with enthusiasm. He bent his athletic body over the map of East Africa spread out on the mahogany table and traced the path into the Rift Valley.

"This will be an ideal place to begin the search since it's where archaeologists found drawings and artifacts in caves fifty-five years ago. Remember that?"

Christopher Ward turned around and swept back a patch of unruly, dark-blond hair. At six and a half feet, he was about half a foot shorter than Allan. He rolled up his shirt sleeves and went to the table to examine the map.

"Okay, so we would start off in Tanzania. Let's leave as soon as we finish the manuscript on Ethiopia."

"I'll call Jennifer and the dean and let them know what's happening. This will be our biggest project yet. Some good information already exists, but we still have a lot of work to do before the traces of ancient sites completely vanish." Allan swung around and picked up the telephone.

"I don't understand why some of our colleagues and the Egyptian authorities responded so negatively to our proposition. The evidence is not new," Chris said as he walked across the room, opened the refrigerator, and took out a beer. He took a long swig and held the bottle to the sunlight before guzzling what was left. "Well, at least we have them talking."

"Let them talk all the shit they want."

Jennifer's line was busy, and Allan slammed the handset on the receiver. "If it's more evidence they want, we'll find it. Did you read that silly headline this morning about how we risked our reputations with a controversial theory? They got it all wrong. It's not what we said. It's what the evidence that's been staring the world in its face for millennia shows."

"Anyway," said Chris, "we would leave within the month to search for unexplored caves in Tanzania. If we don't find anything there we would move on to Kenya. The progenitors of the ancient northern kingdoms had to have made their way up through Eastern or Central Africa."

Allan tried calling again and this time heard Jennifer's laughing voice. "Jen," he said, "we've decided to go to Tanzania and Kenya before returning to Ethiopia. Let the dean know we'll meet with him tomorrow."

"How long will you be away?" the sing-song voice asked.

"About nine months." After flirting on the phone for another few minutes, he went back to studying the map.

※

Chris and Allan arrived in Tanzania on March 18, 1999 and lost little time hiring guides and an experienced security team. The rigmarole of bureaucracy caused delays, but they got permission to set up a headquarters between the Kenyan and Tanzanian borders and to explore the territories. Thereafter they journeyed to the Magamba rain forest, where they camped.

The team included a Kenyan anthropologist named Kevin Springer and a British international geographic writer, Robert Armstrong, who had worked with Allan and Chris on previous expeditions. The two Archaeologists hired ex-Marines to provide security; Timothy McIntosh was a land surveyor, James Mathews a construction engineer, Joe Dodd a geographic mapper, and David Cazeau a soil expert. These men had provided similar services for various missions throughout the continent, and their specialized training and knowledge of the region were useful. The archaeologists were well aware the security men were soldiers of fortune.

The camp was in the heart of colobus monkey habitat, and the aristocratic-looking, arboreal creatures kept watch on the interfering trespassers. The monkeys pretended not to see the group but alerted all relatives far and wide in the forest about their human predator cousins who had the audacity to gawk at them.

The days were drizzly and humid but uneventful. The long nights, however, were full of hungry hunters.

A combination of experience, skill, and intuition was necessary to keep a person alive in this beautiful place, so full of the arrogance of sublime superiority that is the natural environment.

There were other essential requirements for survival: passion and inquisitiveness—the burning desire for knowledge of this place called Earth and people's early passages through time.

The group combed the area for unusual tracks that would have been created by generations of animals. Their focus was on paw prints and spoors of lions and other species that were likely to hide or make their homes in tight spaces between boulders and in caves.

Three days after establishing camp, the group came upon the entrance to a cave. They would not have found it if a flask had not fallen, rolled down a small hill, and rested within the swards of thick shrubs that grew between the large tectonic rocks. The men cut their way through thorny bush for closer observation, often stumbling over rocks. One of the guides warned the others of certain caves that were reputed to be explorers' graves.

Allan and Chris had heard many stories. Experience had taught them not to dismiss such reports as mere folklore. They had heard the one about the soldiers who had ventured down a similar opening. The men had never been seen again, but their dog had returned from within a cave many miles away across the border. There was another one about black lions in caves and a large, white bird that flew above the clouds.

Such tales did not discourage them. Their mission was to uncover facts. They made a decision that the guides would return to base camp and await their return within two hours, failing which they would alert headquarters.

It was Allan and Chris' intention to assess the site and get an idea of its topography. Depending on the results of the assessment, preparation would commence immediately for extensive exploration. They made their way with enthusiasm through an opening and down a narrow pathway. Within forty-five minutes they realized it was no shallow cave. The vast local river system extended into the mountain where, at various places, natural light flowed, revealing enormous stones that formed an intricate design in a rain forest ecosystem of evergreens, ferns, and palms. It was a complex labyrinth of limestone caves. They could not get a sense of its size and scope unless they penetrated the rooms full of stalactites and fossilized formations. Pitch blackness morphed to brilliance where pencils of light beamed on white ferns.

Given their limited supplies, they decided to go back to the base camp. Exhilarated by the prospects of the cave's secrets unfolding for their cameras, they resumed exploration the following day and progressed deeper into the network, which was blistered with obsidian and pumice stone. Within the cave's bowels were hot springs that splashed musically, with swirling, babbling steam jets. An immense lake, the depth of which was yet to be determined, was surrounded by remarkable, marble-like, textured stone that contrasted the colourful flora.

Farther into the network, the group of explorers pursued the cave's secrets. They smelled faint musk and felt the warmth of the cave while examining its rugged structure. All eyes stared at the amazing graffiti ancient hands had drawn. It was a naturalistic art record of daily life: hunters carried clubs and spears, a deer was slung over a shoulder, a wild hog roasted on a stake, women waited around the fire, and children ran out of the village to welcome the food bearers. The strangers were trespassing into the past. They walked through the thoughts of man. Ideas budded and crystallized to create a mural upon which successive generations would paint with symbols of their creativity and passion.

The only sound they heard was the echo of silence—a sacred quietness; the voiceless awe for the sanctity of the early human story. It unfurled from fingers that had held stone and chalk to infuse future man with the essence of who he was in his naked innocence.

The expedition was now back in time, watching people perform rituals of sacrifice to a god in the likeness of an animal. They walked to where light filtered in, revealing a profusion of vegetation of every shade of green. With a few strides, they were in a chamber where they watched women harvesting corn, some with babies on their backs. The women put the food in baskets made of fronds. Children played around their unshod feet.

In their passage through time, the group stopped to admire the fisher folk carrying their catches to the village and young people splashing in the forest river. With the next step, the group found themselves in the middle of an invasion of a village by men with spears, clubs, and feathered headpieces. The tribe defended its territory. There were many dead. There was no relief, no respite from the ancient hands that held to the visitors' faces the foundations and pillars of civilization. They needed none.

The men now stood in the center of another room, and everywhere they turned there was life. Each generation and each tribe that had made the cave its home, in the crevices of her skin and the folds of her skirt, had told its story.

"They're talking to us," whispered Allan.

He and the others held their breath as they entered the temple. There, in the belly of the gargantuan cavern, light dispensed its rays over a rock where craftsmen were making blocks. Chris observed something unusual about the illustration.

"Allan, they made the blocks as they built their pyramid of worship. Upon each dried layer, they mixed the substance we know was granite and poured it into molds onsite. The theory that thousands of men hauled twenty-ton blocks from miles away is all wrong."

The expedition members were stunned.

Next images of a procession of priests filled the massive stone wall. They carried large bowls, jars, and animals. Another drawing showed a priest sacrificing an animal, people raising their faces and hands to the ram-headed god Amun-Ra, and performing a ritual dance. The mural ended with images of men with bows and people taking flight.

"Who were they?" Chris said softly. "Look at this. It appears to be a colossal lion. Just look at the sprawl of its mane."

"I suspect they were ancient Nubians, otherwise why the sun god?" Allan pointed to the image of Amun-Ra. "From what I can make out of their physiques and clothing, they must have been among the earliest peoples of the northern region."

"The unusually tall ones were perhaps priest-kings."

The cave was home to different generations of tribes, starting with those who had made crude drawings of animals probably more than fifty thousand years ago. It was surreal. The drawings appeared on walls, stone slabs, boulders, hanging rock formations, and wall indentations and created a superb, prism-like impression.

The most surprising of all were the illustrations of pyramids and a temple estimated to be about eighteen thousand years old.

"If we're correct, it predates the magnificent structures in Egypt by at least twelve thousand years," Chris said as he studied the drawings. "If that's the case, it confirms what other information indicates: the earliest architects of pyramids were Nubians, or desert people from the lost Kingdom of Yam. I wonder from what or whom they fled. Were they nomadic people who travelled along the river with their cattle and by chance made their home here?"

"No, I don't think so, because of their clothes and the background structures," said Allan.

There was a long pause before Chris resumed the conversation. "A piece of the human story has emerged in this cave that could fill a gap in information about ancient civilizations and rewrite history."

※

She lay upon the highest shelf of the cave with three cubs that suckled hungrily. The beast kept her eyes on the intruders while she continued to do what any mother in that situation would have done: rest and feed her young until such a time that she had to feed herself.

On this occasion she was alone. The cubs' father had left with the rest of the pride to hunt and more than likely would not return for another two or three days. The cave had been the den for generations of her family after the last human inhabitants had left about three centuries earlier.

At the moment she was quiet, and her cubs were so new their cries were faint. In any event it would have been difficult to detect her against the dark, volcanic rocks, which were similar in color to her fur. Her interest was in protecting her young, and for the time being she would not concern herself with the intruders.

※

The archaeologists could not believe their luck. No amount of acclamation could compensate for the joy they felt over their discoveries in the massive cave system. Over thirty-six hours they had unearthed spears, arrowheads, iron blades, pottery, religious artifacts, and many other treasures made of precious metals.

"Look at this." Robert gestured to the others. He had walked a few meters along a passage.

Chris worked on the area using a small pick and brush to remove layers of dust. It took a while before they were able to make out some of the signs. "What do you think?"

Allan went closer to where Chris was and examined the tablet. "It's cursive. Some signs seem similar to Meroitic script. A few others look like Nigerian Nsibidi writing. It will take months of work to make sense of all this."

"It may very well confirm what we've suspected: Meroitic script is probably a derivative of ancient Central African script."

They chatted quietly about the discovery. Robert, the British, professorial looking geographic writer with a patch of gray at his temples, joined in. "A significant number of stories about the early kingdoms of Africa was the work of arch rivals and colonists. It's a lie that prior to colonization this continent was nothing more than cannibalistic savagery."

"They should have eaten us," said Springer. Laughter echoed around the cave.

"Be quiet," said Robert, who continued to inspect the script.

"In past times this entire region, stretching through to South Africa, thrived with innovation and enterprise. Egypt has always seemed more Mediterranean than African. The fact is her roots are in the belly of the African continent, and there is abundant evidence to substantiate that Ethiopian and Kushitic civilizations predated that glorious civilization by well over three thousand years. When those kingdoms were already in full flight, the Egyptian civilization of antiquity did not exist. Diodorus chronicled how the Egyptians received the greater part of their laws, religion, funeral rites, and culture from the Ethiopians' ancestors."

Springer, the jovial anthropologist, was quiet most of the time. He was a charming man with deep-set, gray eyes, a little less than six feet tall. He chuckled because the others were discussing issues he had long ago settled in his mind. "Kenya is where I was born, and as we sit in this sacred cave of ancient dwellers, I can say the pioneers and writers distorted stories and twisted the history about the place my family made their home centuries ago. That was how colonists and rivals subjugated and indoctrinated generations." He paused and looked around the cave. "But, in the northern region along the Nile, more than five thousand years BCE, illiterate, wiry-headed, broad-nosed people established a central food production system, and I am hungry."

Chris, while tucking his blue and white striped shirt into his jeans, dismissed him. "You just ate. It's time we get moving." He pulled up his boots and grinned.

"How are we going to protect what we've discovered?" asked Chris.

"That will be a challenge," Springer responded.

"Well, you know the situation here better than any of us, and the security of the site is a priority right now," Chris retorted.

Absorbed in the revelations of the newly discovered cave, they were oblivious of their position. The sunken, ancient living area beside a subterranean waterway came to an abrupt end. All they saw was a tunnel through which the water gently flowed. They turned around to the passage through which they had entered the area, then turned again and again. While engrossed in the work of ancient cave dwellers, they had ventured off the main pathway into a subtle, crisscrossing network.

They had no clue where they were, but estimated they had penetrated the cave about fifty-two kilometers. They mapped the area and began to retrace their steps. Suddenly they heard a deep, bellowing sound. Was it a roar, or was it the rush of water? They did not know exactly.

The lioness was making her way from the roof of the cave across the waterway. The only option for the explorers was the watercourse—to move with the water through the tunnel that had to lead to a basin where it would empty. Without a second thought, they grabbed their equipment and fled like bats from hell.

The team waded through the cold water for many hours before the river narrowed, allowing them to emerge on dry, rocky terrain within another cavern of volcanic rock. They followed a path through another narrow tunnel, first crawling on their hands and knees, then dragging their bodies on the rugged ground before walking and climbing over miles of rocks, sandy soil, clay, and stratified gravel.

The explorers emerged bruised and ragged, without some of their valuable equipment, one gruelling day after they had left the place where the lion tended her cubs. They exited in Kenya, miles from the border with Tanzania. At first the explorers weren't quite sure where they were. They spent a day exploring the area and later crossed back to Tanzania.

⁂

"I suggest we resume tomorrow up the mountain of many myths," said Allan.

"After what we've just come through, I think some of the stories are probably not myths at all but actual events. What happened to us is more than likely what happened to the dog that entered the cave on the Tanzanian side and came out miles away right here in Kenya. I wonder whether lions got the soldier," Chris speculated.

The promise of more discoveries was too tempting to ignore, Allan thought. He had to admit the calling he'd heard was far louder than the call of the archaeologist part of him. It came from a space waiting to be filled, from deep within his tribal self. He wondered whether it was the call migratory animals heard.

When he was a child, he'd wondered about things. He had not seen images of angels and saints that looked like him. There had been no fairy tales with children like him. He had asked his father why.

"Well, the angels and saints are there, but we have to write the books," his father had said.

He would watch an airplane until it disappeared behind a cloud, a ship until it crossed the horizon, and he would wonder. He now raised his seven-foot-tall body, clothed as usual in jeans and a loose, white shirt, and strolled off to lean against a tree. His height, square shoulders, high forehead, and slightly humped nose gave him an imposing presence. His dancing eyes and dimpled cheeks lessened the authoritative look. He pulled back his thick locks, which accentuated his defining facial features. He stayed under the tree for some time, taking in the landscape and contemplating the following day's activities.

During a meeting the following day, the group discussed the security of the cave and agreed Springer would inform the Tanzanian authorities. He would warn them about the lions and other dangers—although lions in the cave were insurance against raiders.

Across the green, grassy plains they looked at her majesty. She was the woman in the same white top that she wore every day—that she had worn before man trampled the valleys below. No red lava or pretty flowers adorned her head; there was just the white bodice covering her volcanic crest and bosom.

They watched as the sun shone over her head. They were captivated by the white cap of snow where a scorched summit should have been. Many had climbed her for pleasure, but they were explorers whose sole objective was to peer behind the folds of her clothes and into her rocky skin. They were on their way to scope out her forests and find out whether early man had left her pregnant. In the distance a herd of giraffe sauntered across the foothills.

Early on the morning of March 28, they left camp for the mountain. The day showed off its sunny, diaphanous dress with style, attracting butterflies, hummingbirds, and grazing animals to the green, scrubby grounds. The lonely call of a hornbill was ignored by blue herons pecking for food in the wetlands. Wildebeest moaned; other bovid chewed juicy grasses or socialized near water holes. Giraffes necked and sparred against the background of a white sky over the cradle of man.

The mountain, as formidable as she was, had been scaled by many experts and amateurs, but such achievements were no indication of her mercy. Her stately charm, viewed from the surrounding plains, was an entrapment. She was moody and nasty. Those who climbed her sweltered in temperatures over one hundred degrees and shivered in her freezer. They were no amateurs but seasoned archaeologists, explorers, war veterans, and adventurers. Up her slopes they went into bushy areas, grasslands, and shady woods, scrutinizing the volcanic rocks and flora that could hide the entrance to a cave. The beauty of the colorful, blooming shrubs and giant groundsel trees was a respite from the difficulties of the search.

On the fifth day of the team's excursion, the weather changed drastically to almost white-out, bitterly cold conditions. It was wise to camp.

Robert held between gloved hands a cup of black tea. He was savoring the hot, sharp brew when he observed a space between the steep, sloping stone wall. His eyes fixed on the area for a few moments before his curiosity got the better of him. He got up to examine it more closely. Chris saw him disappear into the space. He too was about to get up when Robert emerged. Robert called out to the others that it would provide good shelter until the storm ended—or until the following morning, as it was already late in the evening.

At first Robert had thought it was a shallow inset, but it turned out to be a spacious chamber once they advanced through a very short, rocky pathway to level ground. They were inquisitive. They got a spike of adrenaline, and all they wanted was to get her to reveal her full identity. The storm outside was forgotten and stiff limbs became nimble, and there was no need for cups of invigorating tea to awaken their senses. Their lamps lit the way.

The security team was alert as they searched the area, moving through very short passages and sometimes climbing over huge rocks. Time flew, and they lost all sense of direction. From where they'd entered, they knew they were moving in a north-westerly direction within the mountain. According to their watches, they had been walking for just about two hours when Springer spotted a peculiar shape high up on an isolated rock. He climbed up. His voice resonated with childlike excitement.

"Hey, guys, there's something here. It's a sculpture. It's massive—bigger than anything else we have seen."

The peculiar shape was a sculpture several millennia old. Its features were barely visible after years of calcium deposits. Under close examination they saw the shape of feet and the form of an animal. It was a lion at the side of a warrior.

The expedition was now on a second level of the cave, and they estimated it was even larger than the one in the Magamba rain forest. Springer speculated the two caves were in fact part of one system stretching across Kenya and Tanzania. The reliefs, marble sculptures, drawings on rocks and walls, and script on tablets in this cave were similar to what they'd discovered in the last cave.

A distinguishing feature of this new find was the running artistic commentary on an ancient war. There was a cavalry with shielded horses, horsemen in tunics, and an infantry with battle axes, lances, bows, and spears. Across the width of one mural was an army of Nubian archers. It confirmed Chris' theory that whoever the ancient people had been, they'd fled for their lives. Another panel depicted warrior archers in canoes engaged in a naval clash. It was difficult to decipher specifics.

"Who were they fighting?" asked Chris.

"I'd like to know what became of them. Where was their ultimate destination? Was it this mountain?" Allan asked.

Robert looked up at the ceiling and around the cave. "I'm sure they will tell us."

The group continued searching the mammoth cave. Two days later they followed slivers of light that increasingly expanded. The climb out was slippery, the path narrow and treacherous, and it was bitterly cold. When they reached the glacial summit, thick, rolling clouds engulfed them.

They stood just outside the cave's mouth for quite some time. The clouds gradually cleared, revealing an orange sky. They walked a few meters and witnessed the darkening of the sky. Encroaching darkness succumbed to a black night, except for a halo around the sun.

CHAPTER 7

Darkness yielded to mist that was similar to the white-out conditions they had experienced on the mountain before they had entered the cave. As it cleared there was confusion. They wondered whether they were suffering from altitude sickness that left them bewildered. There they were, on the summit of a mountain that was certainly not the one they had just climbed.

As the mist cleared, the men looked around and realized they were in a place of extraordinary topography. Treetops were not visible, but there were mountains covered with colorful foliage. Eden could not have looked more beautiful.

In the hushed moment, Allan pulled out a compass. They walked across the summit of the mountain and came upon a lake. Clear water rippled, flashing silver in the sunlight. Large shoals of colorful fish moved close to the surface, and on the rim flowering weeds attracted dragonflies. They hovered over blossoms in between dips. Hummingbirds with wings that spanned at least eight inches fluttered busily over water lilies and did not shy away from the strangers. The men ran along the lakeside like children. The sound of water led them to a waterfall that poured its mass of silvery tulle from clouds like the beard of an ancient god.

The sun vanished across the western sky, leaving an early moon to light the way. The men settled under a tree they estimated to be at least five hundred feet tall and more than one hundred feet in diameter. Its branches seemed to span the universe.

"I don't think we're alone." Springer looked around. He had a hunter's instinct. The others were too engrossed in the wonders of the flora and animal life to pay attention. In the light of the white, full moon, they found comfortable beds in the deep insets of the massive tree. After a lengthy discussion about the strange set of events, they tried to settle in.

The watchers surveyed them with some consternation but decided not to make themselves known to the strangers until they understood their intent.

※

Dawn broke, and soon after sunrise long, low whistles awoke the strangers. They got up feeling invigorated but wondered about the peculiar sound. They looked up, and all they saw were twinkling specks of sunlight between the leaves of the trees.

They needed water, not only to satisfy their thirst but to feel its coolness on their skin. They shed their winter clothing for jerseys and windbreakers.

In the shallows they splashed and admired the variety of fish. To their surprise the creatures they saw were the same as those in the other lakes and rivers of Africa. The one difference was their very large size, which made them definitely out of the norm.

"Now, guys, don't pollute the water," said Springer

"Shut up and speak for yourself," responded Robert. Everyone else laughed.

Their stomachs grumbled. Fresh food was abundant, but they were too hungry to cook, so they ate the tinned stuff. Afterward it was time to try to find out where they were. With their limited weapons it was best to stay together.

At midmorning they heard the sound of hooves approaching from where they had camped for the night. Was it a vision of the horsemen of the apocalypse? Were they hallucinating? Had they fallen to sleep on their feet and were they now dreaming?

No, it could not have been those fabled horsemen. These men were not on horses. As the vision drew closer, the group saw the strikingly handsome beasts. The group's eyes were attracted not so much to the ibexes but to the people who rode them. They were like cave murals come alive. The riders had an air of authority; they wore white shukas, simple leather sandals, and gold bands around their arms. They stopped, slowly dismounted, and stood at the sides of the splendid beasts, which had the biggest and longest curved horns the strangers had ever seen. If the men were armed, the weapons were not visible.

"Keep your weapons hidden," Springer cautioned his team. "No sense in doing anything that could be interpreted as a hostile act."

There was silence as the two groups summed each other up. The strangers were cautious and more astonished than anything else. The riders were young men. One of them—the only one with a gold band around his head, clearly the leader—stepped forward. He placed one hand slowly over his chest. It was a neutral indicator that the group of men should not be afraid. Their training had conditioned them not to mistake local courtesy for a welcoming gesture.

The young men eyed Allan and glanced at the others one by one. The leader's eyes became playful as he looked again at Allan, who did not know what to make of the behavior. Was the leader condescending? Allan held his gaze and moved forward, extending his hand. They clasped hands and searched each other's eyes. They were about the same height.

"My name is Allan Cline."

The young man said nothing. Allan repeated what he had said in his twisted version of the Maa language. The man grinned and looked over Allan's head at Springer, who repeated the sentence in perfect dialect.

"My name is Nehsi. We saw when you came on the rays of the sun." The leader spoke a language that was Maa amalgamated with other African dialects.

"On the rays of the sun!" Springer translated for the benefit of the group, each of whom had a familiarity with at least one African dialect. They and the other men understood each other, although with some effort.

"Where are we? What is this place?" Allan asked.

"You are not far away from home," Nehsi replied. "Now is not the time to explain. I can well ask you what you are doing here."

His dark eyes still twinkled mischievously, but he no longer smiled. In Allan's mind he was no ordinary native. He had a commanding presence, with his head held high, distinct cheekbones, a Nubian nose that flared slightly at the nostrils, and broad shoulders on his otherwise slender body. His hair was medium brown. The sparkle in his eyes and the touch of sarcasm in his voice gave an impression of haughtiness.

"Who are you, and what is your business here?" He directed the question at Allan.

"This is Christopher Ward, my friend and fellow archaeologist. We're exploring ancient cultures of Africa. We climbed up a mountain, and because of a snowstorm we went to find shelter in a cave. When we got out on top of the mountain, it was very misty, and then it became very dark. Eventually the sun came out, and we found ourselves here. Now, this is Joe Dodd, Timothy McIntosh, David Cazeau, and James Mathews."

Nehsi acknowledged the four men.

"This is Robert Armstrong, who is a writer and photographer, and this is Kevin Springer, who is an anthropologist and an adventurer."

"So what have you found?"

Allan hesitated. He felt naked even speaking of it. "We found many things in the caves, and now we have found *you*. Where are we?"

"This is Ashaise, which is in your world."

"I do not understand," said Allan, looking puzzled.

"You will in time. Come, meet my brothers."

Nehsi introduced the five men who were with him. They were all tall and exuded more than self-confidence—it was sheer strength and power.

"We will take you where you will be given all you need," Nehsi told Allan. Then he made a signal, and immediately more men with horses appeared as if from nowhere. Nehsi gently commanded Allan's team to mount, then led them in the direction from which they had come. Not too far from that spot, the party turned on a pathway and journeyed through thick mist. They arrived at another side of the mountain through a habitat of gorillas that were much larger than the giant silverback species of Central Africa.

The visitors could not take their eyes off the awesome creatures, which glanced at the men furtively—all except one that stared openly until the humans disappeared once again in the thick mist.

They travelled for at least an hour before arriving in a village where people went about their daily business. The Ashais seemed uninterested in the visitors, which aroused the group's curiosity. The explorers were men who specialized in cultures and behaviors, albeit of the past, and it seemed to them that the Ashais' behavior was unusual.

The gait and beauty of the people were striking. The women braided their hair and wore white wraps around their slender bodies, with gold clasps on the shoulders. Their accessories were gold, which more than perked the interest of Timothy, James, and Joe. Even the everyday utensils appeared to be made of gold and silver with insets of precious stones.

At first sight it was evident to the visitors that they were not seeing typical village life as it existed in every part of the developing world and the rural areas of some developed countries. It was a much higher level of order. The homes were all built in a manner complementary to the natural environment, in between the massive trees and in the mountains. There were gardens everywhere. The strangest of all things was that they saw no one who looked over fifty years old.

As they journeyed, Nehsi and his men kept an eye on the curious visitors, who stopped to view the impressive pyramid and other architectural designs within the mountainside. Finally they reached their destination in the lush valley of Sade, and Nehsi showed the guests to their dwellings. There was a garden not too far from a lake. The men were happy for Nehsi's invitation to have a meal.

Chris could not contain his curiosity any longer. "Nehsi, tell us, who are you? From where did you come? You say we're within our home, but we know of no place like this. You call it Ashaise, and you speak a language that's somewhat similar to languages spoken where we live, but some of your words are strange."

"I am the son of King Meleke. My father wishes you to be at peace. He will meet with you in due time."

"What is the population of Ashaise? I mean, how many of you are here?"

The twinkle returned to Nehsi's eyes. At best Chris' local dialect was as distorted as Allan's, but he knew Nehsi understood him.

"We are many. We have twelve realms."

Long, low whistles rang out above the trees. Allan, Chris, and the others looked up just in time to see a spectacle of the largest birds they had ever seen. The men made 360-degree turns, hoping to see the birds come from behind the clouds.

"I will leave Aatum with you," said Nehsi. "Ask him for anything you want. Aatum is a special assistant to my father, the king."

The visitors did not hear what he said. They were still unsure about what they had just seen in the sky. Robert and Springer moved a little away from where the other members and their hosts stood but did not stop looking skyward, hoping to see the birds return.

Chris turned to Nehsi and looked up again. "What was that we just saw?"

"They are birds sent to us by the sun god."

"The sun god?"

"Yes. They are Kriziantu."

At this time another man, who wore a red shuka, joined them. His eyes were engaging, and he had a soft, angelic look. He leaned his head slightly to the side and acknowledged each member of the expedition with a smile.

"This is Chinua. He is Keeper of the Forest." The laughter returned to Nehsi's eyes. "We know you want to explore, since your wish is to know about people. You were distracted by the birds from the sun god when I said you can ask Aatum for anything you need. Chinua will accompany you when you want to go into the forest."

Nehsi mounted his ibex and took off with his party.

※

That evening the visitors gathered in the garden surrounding their impressive dwellings. The pyramid-shaped dwellings made of green marble, blended with the environment of enormous trees and flowering shrubbery. From a distance it would have been difficult to know that buildings existed there; flowering vines had latched on to large areas of the surfaces. The bay-type windows opened to mountain and savannah views. Sunlight poured in from the ceilings, which were made of a transparent material that was not glass. Walking into a dwelling was like walking into a garden. A wooden door led to a spacious living area with knotted, wooden beams and furniture. A winding stairway, also made of wood, led to upper rooms and a balcony with a view of the lake.

The team recapped all that had happened since the day they had discovered the cave in the Magamba forest. They were enthralled, perplexed, and anxious to know exactly where they were. There was no hostility from the people here, who resembled Ethiopians and the Maasai. They had a civilized and modern disposition. Yet there was something very ancient about them.

And what had the team seen flying into the clouds? They did not know of any bird that had such a low, penetrating whistle or crystal-like color.

Most of all they wanted to understand what phenomenon had occurred that had caused them to arrive in this mystical land.

"Let's talk with Aatum," suggested Robert. "He'll probably give us some clues."

Springer, who was taking a keen interest in their surroundings, often looking up in the hope of seeing the extraordinary birds again, was a bit skeptical. "I wish us luck. They know more about us than we think. Why weren't the people in the village curious about us? Back home there would have been traffic jams and a media circus if strange people who looked like aliens walked into town. Take my word for it—they saw us when we came here. They know how we came, and they're watching us. But let's talk to Aatum anyway."

Aatum was not far away when Springer approached him, and without a question he joined the men. Aatum was a handsome man with an extraordinary body. His appearance exuded authority. His muscles rippled with energy. His dark-brown eyes, pyramid nose, and full lips were attractive, and he carried himself with impressive assertiveness. He had a constant amused look on his face that the security members found unsettling.

"Aatum, everything about Ashaise amazes us," Springer began. "It's beautiful. And it has such large animals. Aren't the children afraid of them?"

"You speak as though you are afraid. We have always lived among our cattle and other creatures. Yes, they can hurt us, but we have learned to live with them. Our children will not go into the habitat of Apti or the lions."

"Apti?"

82

"You saw him on your way to these dwellings. He lives beyond the mist," said Aatum.

"Ah, the gorillas. Yes, we saw them. However we didn't see any old people or children as we passed through the village."

"Old?" Aatum asked, unsure of the word.

"I mean people like—people who have lived full lives… those who are much older than you. Like him." Springer teasingly pointed at Robert.

Without missing a beat, Robert retorted, "Why do you think everyone else looks like you?"

Aatum smiled and shook his head. "Yes, I am an old man."

"You are? You don't look old." Springer smiled too. "You look very young. How old are you?"

Aatum laughed. "I am ninety moons." The disbelief on the visitors' faces made him laugh again.

"Moons." Allan tilted his head sideways and looked at Aatum. "You mean you're ninety years old?"

"You say it your way. My father is one hundred and twenty moons, and his father lived to one hundred and fifty one moons."

"What do you mean by moons?" asked Allan.

Aatum pondered the question. "From the first full moon of spring to the last moon of winter is one complete moon cycle. In Ashaise there are twenty nine moon days every moon month. The sun moon is the midnight sun which appears twelve times a cycle—sometimes more frequently. We usually celebrate about 348 moon days every moon cycle."

"OK," Allan interrupted very gently, taking care not to appear doubtful. "Now, tell us about the bird given to you by the sun god."

"She is Kriziantu, the crystal bird or the healing bird."

"A healing bird. You mean the birds actually heal?" Allan asked.

"Yes. Many moons ago, when our children's bodies became ill with poison from creatures that bit them, or their flesh festered, we discovered Kriziantu's egg healed their ailments."

Aatum described the symptoms of cancer, malaria, yellow fever, degeneration of the liver, tumors, and other fatal illnesses. As he continued to speak, there was absolute silence except for the sound of water and a light rustling of leaves. The group's emotions were revealed by small gasps, wrinkled brows, and leaning their bodies closer to the speaker so they would not miss a word.

"The bird god lives not only in the caves and trees but in the daily lives of all Ashaise. She heals and gives us life. She feeds other life in the caves and streams. Without her the forests and caves would not be the same, and many of us would perish."

As he spoke, Aatum showed the group where his leg had been lacerated in a fall on the rocks—but there was no scar. A bit of the puzzle took shape. He had said enough for them to begin to believe they were in a land with a people who had come to terms with themselves and their environment. Ashaise had to be in Earth's atmosphere, hidden by some strange phenomenon.

※

The evening was still bright when Aatum left the team to their thoughts. Allan strolled to the lakeside. Just a short distance away, he saw a woman walking toward the garden on the far eastern side. He stopped and looked in her direction, and as if she knew someone was watching her, she turned, paused for a moment, then continued slowly toward the banyan tree at the entrance to the garden.

Allan was intrigued and decided to follow her. By the time he got within a few feet, she was already sitting on a rock close to the pond, in which yellow lilies grew.

"Hello," he said. She turned and looked at him, slightly tilting her head to one side. He went closer and looked into the largest eyes he had ever seen. In them he saw mountains, a full moon, a pitching star, and many bright lights strung across the ages of time, and his insides became cotton. He did not know how long he stared into the pools of her eyes. He caught himself when she turned her head to the water.

"What is your name?" he asked.

"Jiena." She did not turn to look at him.

At that moment, Chinua, Keeper of the Forest, appeared as if from nowhere. He smiled at Allan before telling the young lady it was time to go.

The visitors went to sleep knowing that prospects were favorable for seeing the healing birds the following day. They felt like impatient children on Christmas Eve—all except Allan, who had forgotten about the birds.

CHAPTER 8

She rested atop the trees that canopied the wondrous Blue Mountains. Human eyes did not have the lenses to see her beauty from the forest floor, which was a far distance beneath her throne. Allan squinted as he looked up and put his hands across his forehead to block the glare of the sun. A large, brown dove flew to the ground and daintily walked by while pecking the rich detritus on the dark earth. She poked her beak into the castle of an earthworm, secured the food, and flew off to a nearby thick, gold-leaf shrub.

The visitors could hear the sounds of new life within. The crackling of dry leaves meant they were not the only early morning guests of the keeper. A few meters away a fox halted, watched the strangers, then continued on its business. A groove-toothed rat scurried to the right of a mountain bamboo patch. A troupe of gelada baboons casually passed by, one with a shy baby on its back. The sounds of the mountain and the scent of a blend of vegetation and animal perfumes were intoxicating.

"Man is so vulnerable in the scheme of things," observed Chris. The keeper's eyes smiled. He said nothing. They kept walking up the mountain. Allan was silent. Whenever he came across any place or thing that looked and felt sacred, which the aura of the Blue Mountains was, he was silent. At such times he never seemed to be the confident, strong person he was. The mountains were humbling.

Timothy, Joe, James, Cazeau, Robert, and Springer walked about fifteen meters behind Chris and Allan. They strained their necks for signs of the bird. The men were a good way from the immediate goal, which was to reach the Seat of God. They would see from there, at fairly close range, the crystal birds as they left their habitat and flew westward across and over the mountain, to return in the late evening.

The group of men camped on the shelf until just before sunset, admiring the scenery and the wide variety of animal and plant life. During the wait Allan walked a short distance to where the keeper sat. At first he thought the quiet man was meditating because of the way he sat on the rock in Buddha style, but the keeper was aware of Allan's approach. The keeper turned and smiled at the archaeologist, who looked a little unsure of himself.

"What do you want to know?" the keeper asked.

"More about you and how and when we will get out of here."

"There's only one way, which is the way you came. The time depends on the next sun moon, and we have to decide whether allowing you to leave would be in our interest. There are dangers to us."

"I don't understand. What are those dangers? We're only interested in our work, and I can assure you none of us would do harm."

"Let us not dwell on that at this time. Come with me."

The keeper took Allan down a path to his home, which was a dome-shaped building surrounded by flowering trees and shrubs. Together they drank tea and chatted while sitting on rugs at a marble table. The spacious interior was simply decorated with artwork of animals and diverse landscapes.

Allan smiled and admired the pleasant living room. He felt no inhibitions in sharing with the keeper knowledge of his work, his aspirations, his world, and what he knew of his ancestry.

The keeper spoke about his people and their endeavors to explore the universe. What he said helped Allan to understand the level of sophistication of the society in which he found himself. The keeper studied Allan. He liked the man sharing tea with him and wanted to learn more about his work. He thought it was regrettable that his life was at risk.

Allan also studied the keeper. There was something about him that was intriguing. It was not only his look of wisdom and gentility. He had large, light-brown eyes and unusually long eyelashes for a man, and his hands were soft to the touch. He had the body of a woman who had kept up a vigorous exercise routine.

The keeper knew Allan looked at him with interest. He smiled and got up, indicating it was time to return to the others.

They went back to join the rest of the team. Not long afterward, the expedition members ran along the ledge with excitement as the birds flew by to enter the cave.

⚒

"You can speak to them. I think they like you and trust you. We need a chick, or an egg, or DNA samples. I don't have to tell you what this would mean to millions of people with life-threatening diseases. I have no intention of betraying their kindness, so we would have to negotiate our way. Not only that, but think of what our work will mean, especially the discovery of a habitable place hitherto unknown in our sphere."

Chris spoke with sincerity and humility. He and Allan exchanged glances, and Allan saw the genuine expression of wonder in his friend's brown eyes. Chris was an affable person who cared deeply for the disadvantaged. He had a strong sense of social justice and often used archaeological conferences to promote the plight of refugees.

"And the money to be made," Allan said. The statement was hurtful and uncharacteristic. As soon as the words came out of his mouth he regretted them. They were indicative of the underlying emotional conflict he was beginning to experience.

"Yes, that too," Chris replied. "But that's not on my mind, and you bloody well know it. That was nasty."

"I'm sorry. I take it back." Allan went closer to Chris and rested his hands gently on his shoulder. "The keeper hinted to me that we are a threat." He bowed his head and took up a stick, which he used to draw a small circle in the rich, dark soil. He drew larger and larger circles around the small one.

The diamond eyes of the lady by the lake danced in the earth. She stretched her hands to reach a water lily, and her feet glided over the ground as she went with the keeper.

Allan looked up and around, sensing another presence, but did not see anything. He looked at his partner—a man he knew well. They had gone through university together and fought in the same company in the Army. They protected each other, explored ancient sites, and shared the open ground under trees in remote places. They considered themselves brothers with a bond that many blood brothers never shared.

Chris was a dreamer and a visionary. He enjoyed sports and had played on his school's football team. In the tradition of his parents, who were of British ancestry, he had attended Stanford University. Chris had studied archaeology and graduated in 1984.

Allan's family had a long history in Arkansas, and like many Americans their ancestors had come to the new world in abysmal slave ships. From an early age, Allan had a passion for history; his desire was to become an archaeologist, explore the continent of Africa, and write about its early civilizations. He was an avid reader of ancient history, mythology, and theology and delved into books on astronomy. Both men pursued their doctorates in archaeology after leaving the military.

"I understand the part about the cures," Allan said. "These people make me think of the African continent, the cradle of mankind, more than I have ever thought about it before. Its natural wealth is vast, and the potential of its strong and diverse people is enormous." He flicked a few stones away with the stick and looked around again before he resumed the conversation. "It also makes me think of my people back home and in all the countries in which they live. Many of us have not yet broken through the barriers to self-discovery. So many children all over the world are living in poverty. How many can we save from the doors of death? How much pain can be alleviated with the cure that is available here? Will it bring peace? Will it stop hatred, wars, strife? Or will these people be pawns in the next round of destructive greed that's messed up our world?"

Chris listened intently. He wondered whether Allan was becoming too involved with the Ashais and was losing focus on the archaeological mission.

Allan thought about what Aatum had said about the healing powers of the birds. From what the archaeologists had gathered, it was the source of medicine for many illnesses, although they had not yet understood how this was so. From Aatum's description of the illnesses, it was evident the Ashais had found a cure for cancer and other fatal diseases. And, the bird god, which was protected by lions, was symbolic of something far more precious to the Ashais than its ability to cure sickness. Aatum had spoken about life. Their lives revolved around Kriziantu, the bird god. The birds flew beyond the clouds, close to the sun god, which was where the Ashais had to reach. The crystal birds motivated the Ashais to strive for a higher level of existence.

"What do you think would happen if governments and commercial opportunists heard about this place, its wealth, and the birds?" Allan asked, then he answered his own question. "They'll send researchers, scientists, and military people to take what they can get. We do not know whether the birds can exist in a polluted environment." He had started to doodle in the soil again, and at the same time he raised questions to which he responded as if he talked to himself. "Can *this* environment be replicated? I don't know. We don't even know what the difference is between here and home. Are we in fact home, or in another place? We have to explore, if these seemingly peaceful people will allow us to do so."

Aatum had told them that usually there was only one queen bird at any given time. The lives of the people would be changed without the birds—it would be a devastating situation. She produced a few eggs every cycle, which was every moon year.

"Chris, the bird is more than a source of healing. It represents life. I cannot ask these people to compromise their lives."

The night sang its songs of rolling waters in a laughing landscape. The music of whistling trees and the low-pitched call of the crystal birds soared across the Blue Mountains, which were splashed with the light of the midnight sun.

"I said nothing about peace," said Chris. "I'm talking about helping sick people. These people will not die if they share the birds with us. We have the technology to clone animals. Once we can clone the queen there will be no need for further help from them. So all we need of the Ashais is to be able to extract blood samples from the queen."

"It's not that easy. We have no guarantee that a clone of the queen will have the same ability to fertilise her eggs, nor have we any way of knowing beforehand that the samples we take will survive once we go through whatever barrier there is to returning home. In fact we don't even know how the bird heals people."

"What the hell is wrong with you?" Chris stood up and began to pace. "Since when are you so negative about the slightest chance of saving lives or making sick children well? It's a risk worth taking."

Aatum had further told them there was a magnetic field, or something similar—a force that protected Ashaise.

"Just look at the trees," Allan said as he stood up and looked around. "We've never seen trees this tall, and the doves are as large as African fish eagles. What is it about this place that makes it so different from ours? I feel stronger and healthier, and even though I haven't slept for nights I'm not feeling tired. Perhaps if we understand this environment better we will be able to ensure the survival of a bird. We could then negotiate with the people for an egg or chick."

Allan walked a few steps toward a giant, flamboyant tree with branches spread as far as the stone fence. He spoke softly. "Let's leave it for tonight. I need to think. In the morning we can explore and research soil samples, and try to find out how to get out when we're ready."

He stopped and kept his eyes focused on a large patch of tall grass growing alongside the fence. He thought he had seen something move.

Allan and Chris strolled to their spacious, warm dwelling—a place with firm beds made of cured grass covered with cotton cloths. The feathered headrests were comfortable. The glow of large, blue stones strategically placed in the rooms provided light. Since the ancient days, the Ashais had learned to harness solar energy. They had embedded silver wires with light-dispersing properties in the blue-crystal stones. All buildings had skylights, and the stones captured and converted the sun's energy. In the dark the stones lit up, and they automatically switched off in daylight or when covered. Refreshing water came up through pipes of cultured bamboo in a stall where waste was treated and flushed out.

The expedition's members were comfortable, but that night sleep did not come easy for Allan. The lady with the moon-sized eyes was on his mind, and he could not understand why the keeper thought the group was a threat to the Ashais.

※

Chris, Allan, and the other members of the expedition gathered in the center of their living area for a morning meal of fish, porridge sweetened with honey, and bread washed down with freshly brewed tea. They observed the children of the village enjoying fruit and nuts. The children's smooth, chubby faces glowed with health, and they smiled shyly but never came too close to the strangers—except for one boy who seemed to like Allan.

The previous evening Allan had seen him running along the path to the lake, and Allan had followed. The boy had become aware of Allan and ran behind a tree. Allan had dashed behind a tree as well, and they'd both peeped at each other from different sides of the trees. Allan had come from behind the tree and held out his hand. The child had inched toward him, but when he was about a meter away he stopped. Allan reached out, and the child's fingers curled around his own. Allan hoisted him on to his shoulder. Their chuckles were heard by the keeper.

They spent time by the lake throwing pebbles in the water. After a little while, the boy, whose name was Meke, took Allan's hand and guided him to his special hiding place. They turned onto a dirt strip that led to a small area with a few dwelling units among huge trees. Meke took Allan to a butterfly garden. The child pointed up into a silk cotton tree, and just overhead was a swarm of monarch butterflies flying from within the leafy branches.

He then pulled Allan to a nearby poinciana tree and urged him to stoop. Beneath a leaf, a caterpillar rested. The worm vibrated and throbbed to the beat of its pressured heart. She was in transition, evolving from slave to monarch of fluttering grace. The deft weaver was at work, spinning a white, silk covering. It hung like a cotton clump soon to emerge from the mysterious, misty chrysalis stage of its cycle. The caterpillar held on to its lifeline. It then began to tear the silky fabric from which a wing shot out and spindly, wiry sticks unravelled. Two moist, gold fans, with black stripes and veins trimmed with fuzzy white dots, spread from both sides of her body. It was obvious she was aware of her radiant beauty as her wet wings fluttered and flapped. Tiny, confident eyes scanned a strangely familiar world. She lifted her feelers, searching and sensing, then released her hold and flew through the ages of time.

Allan looked into Meke's face and drew the boy into his arms, then lifted him once again onto his shoulder. Allan retraced the dirt track along which they had just passed. During the short walk back to the dwelling area, Meke said he had to go. After Allan put him down they smiled at each other, then Meke turned and ran back along the path. Allan watched him until he disappeared. The hollow space he felt within was inexplicable.

CHAPTER 9

THE CRYSTAL BIRD

llan and Chris left the group to continue their exploration, assisted by the keeper. He was patient, though with a strange manner of serene silence and a wizardly demeanor. He was with them always, yet at times, when he was with animals, he seemed far away. He was like a river. There were long periods when the keeper stood still near a tree. He wore his shuka carelessly over his shoulder, and the end of his staff was firmly on the ground. He was one with the landscape as his elegant, slim body merged with the colorful scenery.

They headed east across the summit of the Blue Mountains on their way to the caves beyond the Seat of God. The keeper told Allan and Chris the queen bird would go there to incubate her eggs. The bird laid up to six eggs at a time, four of which would hatch into healthy birds. The keeper would take the other two eggs to mix with a natural preservative—the oil from the holic palm seed. The holic trees grew along the ridges of the high mountains and bore oval-shaped nuts that turned red when fully ripened. The mixture would age in an earthen jar for three moon months, during which time enzymes would develop and mature to a curative liquid. Chris and Allan knew then that the source of healing was the bird's egg, and that it had to be mixed with another property in order to become a potent medicine.

"Keeper, tell us how it is that the lions and birds live in the same cave, and when did you first discover the healing powers of the egg?" Allan asked.

"It's a long story about the birds, as told by the chronicles. This is what it says: Many moon years ago, the king who had united the land, King Kibwe, asked a protector named Mbtani and his fearless warriors to help protect his people from the lions. The lions had faced intruders before. They had killed many men and all manner of beasts that ventured or strayed into their cave. The beasts were the real rulers of the land until the coming of the warriors by the will of the sun god. The lions' allies were the birds, though they were once nemeses because the lions ventured into their habitat." As the keeper spoke, he pulled his long locks away from his face. He looked past the two men sitting in front of him. His strong and beautiful face fascinated Chris.

"One day the lions went into the cave," the keeper went on. "The birds, which blended with the crystal rocks, swooped down and plucked out the lions' eyes. The lions became sightless and had painful deaths. This occurred many times until the birds were under attack by gorillas and the lions defended and protected them. Thereafter the crystal birds never plucked out the eyes of the black lions. They needed the beasts for their survival, as the Ashais needed the warriors from across the sun to defeat their enemy and unite the land."

The keeper's use of the word *survival* had caught Allan and Chris's attention. The emphasis reminded them of their own conversation the night before about the potential of the bird. That night Allan had been preoccupied by the movement in the nearby shrubbery. Now he wondered if the keeper had heard his conversation with Chris and whether the keeper considered them a threat.

The keeper looked directly at the archaeologists and continued to speak. "When Mbtani and the warriors entered the cave, the queen bird fluttered her wings and made a piercing cry. An imposing beast occupied the highest rock. Its head was in the lunge position. The warriors were alert, and they had seen it. They did not wait. Debele, the lion hunter, took aim and killed the lion. The cry of the bird did not distract the warriors, and they shot their arrows into the bodies of other lions. A bird attacked and a spear pierced her chest. The situation was momentous. The warriors' lion named Matai kept the alpha male at bay. That was his battle. Two birds rose to the height of the cave. They were crying. One descended on a warrior like an arrow, attacking with ferocity. She plucked out his eyes. The bloody wrestling of men and birds continued for what seemed to the warriors a lifetime. A bird killed a warrior. All but one lion was alive. It was in battle with Matai somewhere beyond the boulders. The warriors heard what sounded like wind rushing through a tunnel."

The keeper paused. He looked at the enthusiastic men and smiled. Chris blushed as Chinua looked at him. Chris could not understand why. There was something about this elegant, tender person that moved Chris. They were sitting under a flamboyant tree, and not far away deer grazed. A lone deer wandered by them.

"What happened next?" Chris asked.

"The bird with the spear in her chest fluttered deliriously. Her whistle became coarse before she died. Victory was only temporary. Her cry was heard throughout the mist, echoing across the mountaintop, and others flew to her defense. The crystal birds came like arrows upon the warriors, whose assegais were in the bodies of the lions, so their weapons were few. They fought against seven marauding birds that stabbed their bodies with sharp, pink beaks and deafened their ears with frightening cries. Two more men were killed. Mbtani was wounded on his thigh. He shouted to his men. The blood-curdling scream of the warriors terrified the birds. Momentarily they withdrew from their attack position and hovered overhead with wings beating at an immeasurable speed."

"How many men did the birds kill?" Allan asked.

"By that time three men were killed and two had lost their eyes. But the birds were ready for a second offensive. Those angelic creatures turned into devils. They were querulous, talking among themselves. One of the men threw an assegai into the breast of the queen. She fell, and the other birds dove to her side. They opened their wings over her still body. Then flew to the top of the cave, where they perched in mourning.

"The warriors knelt beside the body of the bird. Her eyes were covered with the veil of death. The other birds flew away, leaving the chicks, which squeaked and cried in the motherless nest. Abayomi pulled the assegai from the queen's breast. Matai went to the side of his master. The other lion stopped fighting and ran to the top of the rocks as the birds flew out of the cave. The warriors looked up and saw the lion standing on the uppermost rock. Men and beast looked at each other for a long while. The beast turned and went away."

"Let us continue on our journey," said the keeper. He and the two men got up and walked slowly while he continued to relate the story of the crystal bird. "The warriors sent the corpses of the birds and lions into the lake to be taken by the currents to a destination they knew not. Mbtani went to the nest and held up a chick. In their pain the warriors grieved for their fallen brothers. Tears streamed down Mbtani's face as he held the chick. He handed it to Abayomi. The warrior shepherd took up an egg and told the other warriors to leave.

"Abayomi stayed in the crystal cave, and there he tended the young chicks, feeding them on plankton and other small creatures of the lake. He picked up the feathers that had fallen from the fighters and placed them tightly over the one remaining egg. A day later a chick pecked her way out, and he swaddled her in his clothes. The lion had watched them from upon the highest rock, and that night the beast descended and stayed near the shepherd who held the orphaned chick in the cradle of his arms. Only the running water was heard above Abayomi's breathing. The crystal bird, Abayomi, and the black lion slept together in the cave. Matai kept watch."

As Allan, Chris, and the keeper neared a winding path where geodes scattered the sides, they stopped. The rocks temporarily distracted the archaeologists' attention. They examined them while the keeper waited. The keeper heard their brief chatter. They soon returned to his side, and he concluded the story of the crystal birds' fight with the warriors from across the sun.

"The warriors returned and told Kibwe what had happened. The people heard about the journey of the warriors into the crystal cave of the bird god and black lions. Mbtani showed them the egg, and later he broke it into a gourd and mixed the yolk with the oil from the holic palm, then shared it with his warriors. The following day their invigoration was evident. Their wounds had dried as if days old, and the pains from the stabs of the birds were no more. They had discovered the healing powers of Kriziantu."

"What happened after that?" Chris asked.

"The kingdom thrived like the young crystal birds that grew to be adults. One was a queen. Her whistle attracted the birds that had fled the habitat after the death of her mother. They went back to the cave."

Chris and Allan were under the spell of the keeper as he related the story. "This is one I will tell my children," Allan said.

They continued on their way to the caves. They passed many villages and observed the theater of the Ashais' lives. The people impressed Allan and Chris. There were mothers and caregivers with babies, and toddlers and children at play. There were schools for adolescents to enrich their minds and strengthen their bodies through the paces of rigorous physical exercise. The girls and boys were in separate schools. Allan and Chris heard the merry voices of a choir within the walls of a college, and boys dressed in white salwar pants were undergoing training. With spears in their hands, they jogged around the perimeter of the grounds. Others jumped over wide logs placed sequentially on the grassy ground; some climbed tall poles, the aim of which was to reach the top and return to ground in the fastest possible time.

As Allan, Chris, and the keeper progressed through the villages, they came to a marketplace with stalls of mahogany under the shade of large trees. The branches and leaves formed an umbrella over an array of tempting fruits, vegetables, and nuts as well as other goods. Chris and Allan admired the exquisite necklaces, amulets, bracelets, beads, and jewelry of sapphire, diamond, topaz, and other precious stones. The baskets, pottery, and scores of uniquely designed utensils were superb works of art.

The people smiled at them but continued with their routines as if they saw visitors fairly often.

From time to time, the trio stopped to admire the natural mural of daily life against the backdrop of the Blue Mountains of Ashaise, a place somewhere in the universe. Chinua the keeper was patient with his childlike charges. Once, when they stopped, he observed their excitement from where he stood under a tree. They'd become distracted from the purpose of the journey.

In the realm of Calem, they saw factories for weaving and manufacturing jewelry, furniture, utensils, metalware, and other items. The people in realms throughout the kingdom crafted merchandise to trade with each other. Jams and jellies were stored in jars of clay and marble, and there were medicines made of dried leaves, bark, and seeds. The merchants sold unguents, liniments, and lotions for minor ailments.

There appeared to be nothing in their lifestyle to jar the pristine environment. The mode of transport was quite charming. It was a combination of animal strength—the primary method—and, to a lesser extent, automated vehicles. The choice of animal depended on where a person was going, since some animals were more suited than others to the treacherous, mountainous terrain. It also depended on family circumstances. The elders more frequently used automated transport.

Life revolved around the family unit and extended family members. The family progressed through five cycles, so status had to do with a person's stage in life and not cattle or other material wealth.

In Calem the group met the chieftain and chatted with the residents to learn more about their lifestyle. During a meal Allan asked the keeper about Meke. The keeper's eyes danced, and he smiled.

"The child has a way with animals," the keeper said, "so he spends time with me in the forest."

"What about his parents?"

The keeper did not respond directly to this question but carried on talking in a contemplative manner. "Meke is a gifted child who one day may be a leader. When I was growing up, I spent many days with the animals, dreaming just like he does, and I went to the college you saw in Sade. It is where Meke goes."

"So would he be the next keeper?"

"I do not know. Maybe, or perhaps he will find a woman and leave his father's place."

It was the first time Allan and Chris heard the keeper chuckle.

"But if he becomes the keeper, would he have a family?" Allan asked.

The keeper sighed and looked into the trees. "Ah, I see you want to know about me. I belong to my home in the forest. When young people leave their childhood dwellings, they enter the first cycle. They may start families and would receive gifts of cattle and land on which they would build their homes."

He told them the second cycle was when they were minding children and adding to their possessions through earnings from the land or through other talents. "It is a very difficult stage, and they must rely on their mental strength to resolve problems."

Chris was amused. "Yes, it could be difficult. It sounds familiar. So what if the marriage doesn't work out? My own didn't."

The keeper's eyes looked a little sad, and he hesitated. "Sometimes that happens, but not often. If there are children, the separation is recorded by the realm's council, which is responsible for all children's well-being. If there are no children, the couple goes their separate ways."

He told them the marriage ceremony was an important, traditional ritual that set the boundary of the relationship.

"No contract between two people can bind them for life if they do not want to stay together," the keeper continued.

"They are free to make binding contracts regarding material possessions. All wealth the couple acquires during the union belongs to any children of that union until they reached young elder status."

"What age is that?" Chris asked.

"Age has little to do with adult status. It is when they are ready to build their realms. Once they leave the nest, the parents can do as they wish with the possessions." The keeper was as patient with them as he would have been with children. "Individual aspirations and generosity in relationships are equally important. We value each person the same."

Chris and Allan learned that when a couple reached the third and fourth cycles, the family unit was usually strong and independent. By the fifth cycle, they would have achieved elder status in their respective realms and sat on councils of wisdom to advance the kingdom.

There was something mysterious and magical about the keeper. His charming smile and serene disposition were engaging. All citizens treasured him. They consulted with him on everything, and he was the source of knowledge for young people who needed counsel. The people called him the Keeper of Kriziantu, the Crystal Bird of Life. His compassionate eyes shone like the bird's, his nose was slightly aquiline, and his tall and dignified frame gave him a noble mien. Often children gathered around in the garden of giant lobelia trees, and wildflowers to listen to his stories about the animals and people who lived beyond the mountain in the sky. He led the children in melodious songs, showed them fish in the lake, and played with them in the butterfly garden.

His discretion earned him the confidence of all citizens. His knowledge of their secrets was never breached, not even to the king. Young couples loved their keeper. He would make up proverbs and anecdotes relevant to their unique situations. They took their babies to him, and he carried them to the Seat of God where mountain nyala, klipspringers, and hyrax skipped and jumped. He held the babies out to the universe and cradled them, observed by lions sitting between rocks nearby.

Later, when Chris and Allan were discussing what they had learned about community life, Chris speculated about the gender of the beguiling keeper.

⊛

As they rested in the shade of an acacia tree, Chris observed Allan's distant gaze. Allan felt the pull of an uncontrollable force tugging at his inner self. His profession had taken him across the globe. Often he thought deeply about the status of undeveloped nation states.

He pondered the rest of the world, which often spoke of the African continent as though it were one large country. What, he asked himself, would be Ashaise's relevance to the billion people living in poverty? What was the relevance of education unless it lifted leaders and populations to a higher level of humanity? What was the reality of his world, where progress was detrimental to the survival of all creatures through the existence of nuclear weapons and savaging to the environment? Would the crystal bird mean healing sick people or would it represent a stock price?

He bowed his head and, as he had a tendency to do when in deep contemplation, picked up a twig and doodled in the soil. He drew a circle. In it were nations struggling to provide citizens with life-sustaining needs although there was an abundance of natural wealth. The actions of modern man that were increasingly in conflict with the healthy environment, but that he needed to survive, appeared in the circle. What would happen if Ashaise became known to the world? Would it survive?

Allan did not hear Chris call his name, so deep into his well had he gone. The keeper as well was aware of the stranger's struggle. He decided to keep his noble profile toward the higher mountain ridge where they were heading. He would give Allan time to deal with his emotions.

"Share your thoughts." Chris touched Allan's head.

Allan lifted his face and looked in the direction of the village they had just left. It was now barely visible because of the irrepressible, creeping clouds. Impressed in Allan's memory was the simplicity of the Ashais' way of life, their innovation and progress in isolation. The value they placed on aspiring to a higher stage of intelligence—to tap into the full power of being human—was inspiring.

"I'm thinking about the things we take for granted," Allan replied. "In many nations poverty never sleeps, disease is resilient, civil strife is under the skin, war is a leaking tap, drugs run like the Nile, corruption strangles economies like a boa, and slavery is alive. Too many of our sons are killing each other in gangs and through strife. We know what the problems are, so why? Why?"

Chris studied his friend's face. He wrinkled his brow, looked at the keeper, put his hands in his pockets, took a step or two away, and went back to face Allan. He had realized, over the past few days, that Allan was unusually withdrawn, reflective, and wrestling with internal conflict. They always bared their souls to each other. There was hardly ever a time when one of them had a problem and did not seek the opinion of the other. Chris knew the demons that plagued his friend. He observed the introspective look in Allan's eyes whenever they interacted with the people here or came upon another magnificent structure.

Their profession was engaged in investigating artifacts to learn about cultures of antiquity, and as a natural consequence they interrogated human evolution. Chris knew Allan was intellectualizing antecedents and contemporary explanations for the status of the continent and the descendants of millions of people who had sailed the middle passage on Satan's ships. Chris was sitting next to Allan and looked directly at his friend.

"Is this the same person I've known for all these years?" Chris asked. "You ask why? Maybe it's because there's a group of people programmed to see themselves in a negative light. Why? Because exactly how you feel is a major part of the cause. It's part of the vicious, psychological cycle of self-abuse."

"What the hell are you talking about?" Allan snapped.

"You are personalizing and stereotyping a significant social issue."

"What I've said are facts, and yes, I am soul searching."

"While soul searching, consider these facts: only thirty-five years ago, millions of Americans got protection to vote under the Civil Rights Act. Just a couple of years before that time, countries throughout four continents got independence from colonialism. Apartheid ended just five years ago. Allan, it took the developed world two thousand years to reach where it is today."

"And who gives a shit about that when there are thousands of angry, marginalized youth in inner cities shooting each other up?" Allan retorted.

Chris said calmly, "The progress we've made within a few decades is unparalleled in world history. That should be the focus. It flies in the face of the slavery that severed millions of people from their civilization—their mooring—by denying them their names, education, religion, cultures, families, and language. Just imagine—you triumphed over that."

"And it is for that reason there should be no repression and slavery," Allan replied. "Yes, slavery was brutally traumatic, and is still in the psyche of many people. More than five hundred years of mental and physical violence have not been fully exorcised. The resilience, courage, and mental strength that triumphed over such adversity are traits that have accelerated the pace of our progress, not victimhood. Chris, victimhood is also slavery. It makes us slaves to handouts called social welfare."

"Stop being such an asshole and a victim of negativism. How many other people are on social welfare? You do not appreciate your strengths as a people and how much you help each other."

"I do. I see the beauty and courage of our women who, in places ravaged by strife and disease, are sole parents to thousands of homeless and fatherless children. They have always been a mighty forest, nurturing, teaching, loving, and reaching with strong arms across bridges. I admit such commonplace heroism is not appreciated."

Chris stood up and leaned against the tree. He looked around at the scenery. "People everywhere have their aspirations, but the bitter cycle of mental abuse, like the cycle of poverty, has never been some abstract reality."

"I reflect when I see the confidence and enterprise of these people. For many centuries children internalized symbols and behaviors that patently portrayed the color of their skin as an affliction. That's why bleaching cream is one of the biggest-selling products today." The emotion in Allan's voice was moving.

Chris spoke softly. "There's a problem of esteem, perhaps a legacy stemming from thousands of generations of indoctrination through colonialism, slavery, self-abuse, and the invisibility of inspiring history. Many cultures systematically use images and symbols of success in children's books, movies, toys, and throughout the religious and educational system. Well, think about this: The human in society is like a three-legged stool. There's history, or the foundation, there are the pillars of development, and there is the individual. What happens if the first or second leg or any part thereof is chopped off?"

Allan turned his head sideways, looked up at his partner, and said, "Well, villages don't raise children anymore, and no one can deny the importance of history, tradition, and a sense of community when it comes to identity and self-esteem. As children we learned that our history was a history of slavery, as if we had no other history. It's the way we were and still are portrayed, yet Africa had a past of innovation and enterprise for thousands of years. Now, we are peoples of America, Canada, Europe, Britain, Caribbean, and other regions. Many of us are multiracial." Allan's pause was reflective. He looked across at the keeper, who was patting a deer, then continued. "Chris, all these places are where our struggles were and where we have built our communities and history. After nearly six centuries, the history of these places is our history, and so too is the history of Africa."

There was a long silence. Chris walked slowly, following the pattern of the long roots of the magnificent tree. He turned and said, "My friend, it's precisely for that reason social problems are to be viewed in a human-development context and no other. If you examine the other issues, every group fought bloody wars against their own and engaged in the most unspeakable forms of brutality. They're still doing so. Whatever advancement we've made, we continue to be enslaved by our thoughts and actions. Poverty, gang warfare, and drug abuse are not unique to any one group."

Chris continued passionately, and the keeper listened. "Stereotyping is like the chicken pox virus. The symptoms go away, but the disease lies dormant in the tissues, flares up under stress years later, and morphs into shingles, which cause a hell of a lot of pain and scarring. It never goes away. What's worse, every generation gets the virus, and the first to be infected are children. Corruption is not unique to the developing world. It's a worldwide curse that's also prevalent in the financial capitals of the developed world."

"That may be so," Allan interjected, "but the citizens in those capitals have clean water and health care. The point is, in the distant past there were strong communities and enterprise. Medicines that exist today were used by ancient people with painted faces and feathered headpieces. They built pyramids and temples, and taught their children to hunt, fish, herd, produce food, and revere the natural environment. Their ancestors sharpened stones to fine surgical instruments to perform surgeries. They understood the powers of the sun, wind, and water to create energy. It is why they divinized the natural environment. I see these people and wonder how they built pyramids here. Who taught them to build manufacturing machines? Who taught them about science, astronomy, and democratic governance? Who taught them to write, to capture the heat of the sun to warm their homes, to draw planets in relation to the earth with such accuracy?"

"The seeds of invention are in the genetic memory of all men," Chris said. He moved closer to Allan, and the keeper felt the deep love between the two of them. The keeper did not turn his head. He listened not to their words; he did not understand all of them. He listened to their passion. He turned and walked past them.

Chris touched Allan on the shoulder, and they followed the keeper.

※

As Chris, Allan and the keeper ascended the mountain, soothing sounds filled their senses. There was no room for thoughts of the world left behind. When they started the ascent the temperature was about thirty degrees, and not too long thereafter it plunged to ten, forcing them to stop and put on warmer clothing than the shirts they were wearing.

They continued their rapid pace waist-deep in rolling clouds that sheathed green vegetation and rocks and looked like a cluster of white chiffon balls.

The tousled clouds swaddled mountains, fingers of blue-green light flashed across valleys, and the aurora borealis showed off her splendor to the mesmerized mortals. The Ashais believed its beams represented the sun god's cosmic messengers sent to remind them of the sun god's power over all things. Lenticular clouds became darker, merging with the sun god's breath, and pirouetted across the mountains.

Were they in heaven? The earthlings watched a picturesque cloud formation as light sliced through it, reflecting tinges of blue with a silvery fringe, blending now and then with a hint of pale gray. They stayed respectfully silent. The clouds spoke softly. A glow appeared around a cumulonimbus. The dramatic spectacle of massive, floating balls separated. Suddenly the sky cracked into veins of light before the sonic boom of thunder's roar ushered in tinselled drops that drenched everything. The peeping sun illuminated the raindrops. A rainbow stretched and curved a radiant arm across the sky to the audience of the three who watched the performance with awe.

The keeper spoke softly. "Come."

Allan and Chris followed him, and within a few yards the clouds thinned and looked like white organza. The two men and the keeper reached the large opening of a cave.

After entering, the keeper signalled to the others to wait. As their eyes adjusted to the darkness, Chris and Allan saw him disappear behind a white boulder. They heard no noises except for the sound of water, the source of which they could not see. It came from north of where they stood.

They respected the keeper's advice and did not move except to turn 360 degrees in their eagerness to understand what would unfold and from where. Now and then they saw shadowy movement, and they assumed it was a reflection of something, although they knew not what.

It was not long before the keeper returned and handed each of them a garment made from very soft material of a dusty-white color. He told them to put on their garments. They obeyed, and then there was no sign of Chris and Allan in the cave. Their faces were covered except for narrow slits through which they could see the way. The material was not lost on the visitors. The Ashais had manufactured camouflage fabric. Once they covered themselves with it, they were invisible. The keeper advised them to wear the material because they were strangers to the lions and the birds.

The three walked along a short, wide path before emerging among large, crystal rocks. The area was dangerous—slippery, with shards of crystal as sharp as knives. The expansive habitat reflected subtle rainbow-colored shades with sparkling tips suggesting glints of sunlight.

It was not long before they came to a river. The keeper cautioned them to tread quietly as they descended the rocky terrain to a grassy bank, where they could better appreciate the size of the crystal cave.

Allan and Chris did not speak because there was nothing to say. There were no words to describe its beauty. A nearby waterfall depicted in their minds images of millions of colorful diamonds cascading to the river, where shoals of silvery-blue fish swam just below the surface.

The keeper guided Allan and Chris to where the bird was nestling her eggs. She had heard and sensed the visitors from the time they'd entered the cave. The guardians of the cave—massive, black beasts—sat majestically on crystal rocks. They did not move, so accustomed were they to their master, although the creatures had picked up other human scents.

The visitors had not seen the beasts. But they saw the magnificent bird raise her gorgeous wings and tuck her eggs beneath her huge body. The keeper saw a look of wonder in the visitors' eyes. He had visions of the archaeologists and his heart was heavy because he had to protect Ashaise. He knew these two men were sincere. He looked up at the lions.

The bird rose and again flapped its wings, which extended across the lake. She lifted her body and tipped her graceful legs as her claws curled inward. She lifted off, and her long neck stretched out as she flew toward the cave's ceiling. Allan and Chris looked in that direction long after she had gone. Their eyes went back to where she had just sat. In the nest there were five eggs, each about twice the size of a man's fist—small for a bird her size.

The men turned their sights to the rocks they had to climb. The lions had gone. Ushered by the keeper, Allan and Chris retraced their path to return to their dwellings.

Chris turned to the keeper and asked, "Keeper, will you bring us back to see the hatching?"

The keeper kept his pace and after a brief while said, "Yes."

"Is that a long time from now?"

"Time stands still. It does not rush by. It does not pass. It is us who move on. The bird will return in time."

CHAPTER 10

Later that evening the expedition members sat by the lake, comparing notes as they listened to Cazeau gently strumming his guitar. Aatum joined them and answered many questions on the history of Ashaise.

"Aatum, tell us more about your history?" Robert asked.

"Our ancestors are among many peoples," Aatum replied. "Our forefathers came from the place below the House of God. It is the place from which you came here."

"You mean in the valleys below Mt. Kilimanjaro?"

"I do not know what you call it, but it is in Alkebulan."

"He means Africa," explained Allan. "Africa is the name given by the Romans to a place in northern Africa. The name Libya also referred to Africa in days of antiquity. Alkebulan, or 'mother of man,' is an indigenous name for what we call Africa. Because of the many African languages, I assume the indigenous people called it by other names."

Aatum told them the Ashais's ancestors had come from the source of the god Hep, or the River Nile. They had tilled the land the sun god had given to them, tamed beasts, and herded cattle. They had multiplied and become independent tribes and kingdoms. Some of them had travelled to Asia, and others had gone south of the Nile, which ended in the large delta that poured into the Mediterranean Sea.

Many thousands of moons later, after the great freeze, various different tribes returned from across the seas and intermingled with his people throughout the motherland. Distinct cultures, derivative languages, and customs emerged throughout Alkebulan. Some of the Ashais' ancestors fled back east, west, and to central Alkebulan when foreigners invaded the kingdoms of Ethiopia, Punt, and Nubia, or Kush.

Aatum told stories from the chronicles about Ashais's ancestors' constant wars with Kemet and the Assyrians, and the escape of their great ancestor, Tariku, after the Assyrian invasion of Nubia and Ethiopia. Kemet—Egypt, their neighbor in the Nile Valley had occupied Nubia for about three centuries. Nineteen of the Ashais' ancestors were pharaohs of Kemet.

The archaeologists also shared stories with Aatum about many kingdoms across the continent of Africa and the people who had entered Alkebulan from Rome, Greece, Spain, France, Turkey, Syria, Arabia, and Asia.

Aatum, who was normally well-composed, became excited. He called elders and others in the realm to hear what the visitors were saying about their ancestors.

The keeper and others came over during Allan's vivid narration of the history of the North African region. A few moments later the group heard galloping. A party drew close. To everyone's surprise it was King Meleke accompanied by three men and two women. They dismounted. Everyone stood.

"No, sit," said the king. "I heard about your storytelling and wanted to listen. Do not stop for us."

The members of the expedition looked at the king standing amidst the gathering. Nehsi had told the men they would be visiting the king soon. Instead he humbled them here with his grace and disarming, understated sophistication. It was a spontaneous situation that lifted the mood of the magical moment of storytelling.

King Meleke was about the height of Aatum—close to eight feet—and striking in his deportment. His frizzy hair framed a smooth, comely face. His eyes teased, and creases at the sides of his mouth gave the impression of a permanent smile. He greeted each guest, and in return they extended their hands to his shoulder. Then they returned to their seats on the grass, marble benches, and rocks. Some leaned against trees.

The woman, who had arrived with King Meleke stunned Robert. He was a happily married man, but his tanned face turned almost red as Kiserian, extended her hand to his shoulder. Her black complexion accentuated her gray eyes. Her shaven head revealed her status as a widow. It was Kiserian's smile that haunted him thereafter. Robert thought it was a smile that told the world to come into her arms.

Kiserian, who was the chieftain of Sure sat next to Robert, and Springer sat in the middle of two young women. Later the others had to give Springer a verbal lashing and warn him sternly. Robert called him a womanizer.

Meleke's eyes lingered on Allan for a while. He observed that Meke, who would normally be at the keeper's side, sat close to Allan, who had his arm around the boy's shoulder. Not long thereafter Meke was asleep with his head on Allan's lap.

Chris saw the way the king continued to look at Allan and the boy. It was a pleasant look, but one that suggested the king was thinking. Chris whispered to Robert about the resemblance between the child and Allan.

The group looked at Allan expectantly as he shared stories. He told them that in his homeland, the records showed that Nubia, or Ta Seti—Land of the Bow—had been a mighty kingdom under the dynastic leadership of Pharaoh Piye, followed by his brother, Shabaka, then Piye's sons, Shebiku and Taharqa. They had conquered and united Egypt. During six decades of governance, the dynastic leaders had changed the landscape with grand architecture and revived Egypt's literature and arts.

"'Harness the best steeds in your stable,' said Piye as he marched into Thebes like a raging panther and seized Egypt like a cloudburst," related Allan. "Pharaoh Tefnakhte and the powerful leaders of the Nile Delta surrendered. Piye died, and his brother, Shabaka, who fought the Assyrian king Sennacherib's army at Eltekeh, built upon his predecessors' legacy. The Assyrians thrashed Shabaka's army. Shebiku succeeded Shabaka, but it was Pharaoh Taharqa who defeated the Assyrians. He was a constant threat to their security. The Syrian king said he was accursed by all the great gods."

The mildly cool breeze, Cazeau's soft strumming of Nat King Cole's "Rambling Rose," and the backdrop of the lake and cattle grazing in the distance were arresting. The aura of the moment was captivating. The group felt a strange peace. The people of this land were growing on the visitors.

Chris was in the company of the keeper. The women charmed Springer. James, Joe, and Timothy were absorbed in dialogue.

Robert took out his pocket Bible and infused the tales with an account of Taharqa's war against the Assyrians as told in the Old Testament, in the book of Isaias. The Assyrian army had marched against Judah. At the same time, Taracha, king of the Ethiopians, had been on his way to battle Sennacherib. The Assyrian king had sent a message to Ezechias, the king of Judah: "Do not let the God in who thou puttest such confidence deceive thee with false hopes, telling thee that Jerusalem will never be allowed to fall into the hands of the Assyrian king." Ezechias had prayed God would not allow Sennacherib to invade Judah. God had heard Ezechias' prayer and told him, "Sennacherib shall never enter the city or shoot an arrow into it." After that an angel had smote down 185,000 men in the Assyrian camp. The Assyrian army had retreated.

Prince Nehsi who was listening attentively said, "Our chronicles say it was Taharqa."

Robert said wryly, "The great prophet Isaias said it was an angel, but the testament also says Taracha led an army against the enemy of Judah at the same time." Robert closed the Bible and continued, "Pharaoh Taharqa and Taracha had been one and the same person. He had defended the borders of Egypt and Nubia. He had fought bloody battles against the Assyrians who were under the new leadership of Esarhaddon. He'd had victories as well as defeats and was wounded. He had fled Memphis only to rearm and return with a vengeance, much to the annoyance of Esarhaddon. The Assyrian king had died while marching against Taharqa, who had valiantly retaken Memphis. Finally he had fled back to Nubia with the emergence of a new thrust by a bigger Assyrian army, and established his seat in Meroe.

The Nubian dynasty, the roots of which had sprung from the belly of stout African civilizations of much earlier antiquity, had left a deep footprint throughout the kingdoms of the Nile. Taharqa had been a prolific builder of images of himself. The dynasty's architecture stretched from the city of Napata and the holy mountain Jebel Barkal—the place where the god Amun-Ra was said to have been born—to the cities of El Kurru, Nuri, and Meroë, and across borders to Egypt."

During this time of storytelling, the explorers learned a lot more about the Ashais. Aatum, the keeper, and others had spoken about their gods of the ancient days. The explorers realized that these people had known about the wars, and they knew about Jesus Christ. Long before Piye's dynasty, there had been Akhenaton, called the Heretic King. He had preached the philosophy of one god thirteen hundred years before the coming of Christ and two thousand years before the Prophet Muhammad. He had believed all living things were connected; so too did the Maasai.

In the days of antiquity, there had been many stories and myths about the people from the kingdoms of Nubia or Kush, Ethiopia, and Punt, including the one that some of them had lived until 120 years of age.

The musings and storytelling with Aatum and the other Ashais members stimulated the expedition team's motivation to explore further—not only to investigate Ashaise but to unearth more evidence in the central and east African regions.

The Ashais' philosophy on how mankind first had arrived caused some consternation. The group wanted to hear more of the Ashais' views on evolution and creation. There was a strange mural in the Temple of the Sun that suggested groups of anatomically similar human species had appeared in various parts of the world and evolved along parallel courses everywhere. It was an exciting topic, especially for the archaeologists and anthropologist. They explored the footsteps of mankind out of the continent and the phenomenal impact the glacial period would have had on lifestyle and the evolution of man.

The king and his party got up to leave. He said to the visitors, "I hope to hear other stories."

"It would be our pleasure," responded Allan. The king put his hand on Allan's shoulder, then looked at Aatum, and asked, "Will the visitors join Sade's team in the hunters' game?"

"I will tell them about it," said Aatum. The king turned and went on his way. Meke ran alongside King Meleke.

The cheerful group had spent some time discussing the hunters' game. Aatum invited them to participate in the day's events. The explorers were willing to join the team, but admitted they were a bit intimidated by the prospects of competing with the Ashais.

"Tell us more about the race," said Robert.

"The hunters' game takes place the day after tomorrow. Runners compete for the Spear of Debele," said Aatum. "Debele was the brave lion hunter in the days of my forefathers. The runners would start on foot in the stadium, and mount horses at the entrance to the savannah, then swim, across the River of Life, and afterwards they would continue on ibexes for about five miles. After that, they would run around the perimeter of the Temple of the Sun. This is a difficult part of the track as there are many boulders, streams, and thicket fences. For the next part of the race, runners need speed, and they must hunt animals, but cannot use their spears on the creatures."

"So how would the hunters catch the animals?" Allan inquired.

"Oh, they would hunt for baby animals like goats, chickens, water fowl and creatures like that, then they would let them go. They must use strategy because in the forest there are rocks, winding roots above the ground, and many hills. They have to swing from vines and branches to avoid rough patches of land and swampy places while holding their spears. Then the runners must navigate waves in the River of the Sun. On completion of the river crossing, they would enter the stadium and throw their spears in the middle of the arena, around the Spear of Debele, before running around the track. You must not drop the spear."

The event excited the explorers. They knew it would be a difficult run as they were not familiar with the race course. Aatum assured them that many competitors would not finish for one reason or another. Many would drop the spear, so the team should not feel disadvantaged. He said it was a day of fun. In keeping with the spirit of the event, the explorers decided to participate. They stood a fair chance of completing the race for the realm of Sade.

The moon was magical over Ashaise's lake, casting light on the water that made it a sheet of shimmering, silver foil. A washing calm poured over the men—a sense of deep relaxation and a feeling of brotherhood. They were in an open cathedral where they stayed for a few hours, well into the morning, before returning to their dwellings.

⚒

The following day, the expedition members rested until mid-morning. Over a late breakfast, they reflected on their conversations with the Ashais on Ashaise's history. They were eager to get definite information about when they would be allowed to return to their homeland. The team decided that after the hunters' game would be an opportune time to broach the subject of their departure from Ashaise.

Later in the morning, the archaeologists explored the river bank. It was a glorious day, and just after midday, Aatum came to take them to survey the race course. They were happy to run with Sade's team, and were meticulous in probing Aatum about every aspect of the race course.

The explorers had visited the River of the Sun. The rapids captivated their competitive spirit. They felt the most challenging part of the race would be the forest track. It was a tortuous path. Aatum took them back to the dwellings early in the evening as he knew they had at least six hours of racing the following day.

⚹

The next day, they joined the Ashais sports men and women from all twelve realms to the cheering of thousands of people in the stadium. Half naked in salwar pants, the team from across the sun started off hilariously. While Aatum had given them a thorough briefing, and he'd familiarized them with the course, he'd forgotten to tell them that at the start of the race in the stadium, the runners jogged to conserve energy for the difficult events.

As a drum rolled signaling the start of the event, the explorers bolted like race horses, leaving the jogging Ashais behind to the amusement of the crowd. Some of the explorers realized their mistake and slowed their pace except for Springer and James who were out of the stadium as though chased by Apti.

The team had kept up well throughout the first four events. By the end of the swim across the River of Life, the other members had caught up with Springer and James both of whom felt the effects of their mad sprints. Robert, the eldest of the explorers lagged behind and after the swim he had abandoned the race. He met Kiserian who was watching the race. She took him to feast with her family and friends.

Citizens had gathered at every strategic point of the race course to cheer their teams. Most of the people had put their bets on a warrior protector named Sahure who'd won the trophy at the last hunters' game.

After about three hours into the race, the runners entered the grounds of the Temple of the Sun. The explorers had scaled over the first set of rocks and boulders fairly easily, but as the hurdles became increasingly difficult, they fell behind. James and Joe dropped their spears as they scaled fences. The Ashais leapt over the obstacles with ease, and literally flew into the air as they crossed the high hedges.

The remaining explorers—Chris, Allan, Springer, Cazeau, and Timothy—recovered some ground, but fell back again as they entered the forested area to hunt for small animals. Springer, the hunter, enjoyed this event. He quickly cornered a squealing baby boar, and managed to avoid the rage of its mother.

In the hunt, Allan lost precious time. He chased oversized squirrels, frogs, and lizards. With each dive to grab a small beast, he came up with a hand full of dried leaves, twigs or a lump of dung. After about twelve minutes of hopelessness, he saw the beautiful creature a few feet away. *Ah,* he said to himself, *A turtle. Thank you sun god.* The dignified creature came out from the bushes. He poked its back with his spear, and the turtle pulled its long neck into the massive shell for protection. Allan picked it up, then he dropped the poor thing on its back, and took off to catch up with the others.

Chris was luckier. He had found a cute baby sloth within five minutes of his hunt.

They were now in the area where the Ashais swung from vines and moved at a remarkable pace. As Cazeau grabbed a vine to cross a swampy area, he miscalculated the distance he had to travel. To save himself from falling, he dropped his spear and grabbed the vine with both hands. He was now out of the race. The creatures in the swamp heard a string of swear words.

Springer suffered a similar fate, except he fell in the swamp, and mud covered him which provided another amusing episode for the fun-loving Ashais. He soon found the company of charming women and disappeared. Most of the competitors had to leave the race because they had dropped their spears.

It was now Allan, Chris, and Timothy to catch up with the rest. They had reached the River of the Sun and had to navigate the rapids. They were skilled oarsmen and manoeuvered their boats well. The challenge was to hold their spears while they paddled. Aatum had shown them how to do this. He had taken his spear and held it together with an oar in his right hand as if both instruments were one paddle.

Sahure—the warrior protector from Sahur, had outpaced the other runners in most of the events, and was already riding the rapids. He was halfway to the other side of the river when the boat got stuck between rocks. He struggled to free the boat. The guys from across the sun, and other competitors had gone ahead of Sahure. He kept glancing at Allan who was close to the other side of the river. It took Sahure approximately ten minutes to get the boat back on course.

Allan, Chris, and Timothy arrived at the other side of the river in excellent form, and ahead of most of their competitors. The three explorers headed for the stadium. In the stadium, Timothy and three runners were out front, and about to throw their spears. Timothy's spear landed just outside of the circle. He was out of the race.

Prince Nehsi and other people from the realm of Sade who stood at the sides of the race track rallied Alan and

Chris. They shouted their names. Other onlookers enthusiastically cheered the men from across the sun. They were with a bunch of ten runners.

Chris and Allan reached the spot where they had to stand and throw their spears. Their spears landed just within the edge of the circle, and they began to sprint to the finish line. The spectators in the stadium, including the king, the queen and their daughter were now on their feet.

Two runners were closing in behind Chris and Allan's group. One was Sahure. They moved through the bunch. While they were overtaking others, one tripped at the same time Allan pulled slightly aside. The tripped up runner sent Chris sprawling.

Allan heard the thud. He looked behind and saw Chris on the ground. Chris put his hands over his head and curled up as the runners jumped over him. Allan could not have known that Chris wasn't hurt. He moved to the wings and waited for the runners to pass.

The crowd in the stadium became silent as the accident occurred. The princess gasped, and held on to the arm of her father. Aatum, who had followed his charges, had seen the accident and went over the track to help Allan take Chris to a place where attendants looked after the fallen and injured runners. The blow had stunned Chris more than it had hurt him, and he was soon on his feet. He had hit his forehead on the ground, and sported a rosy bump.

That night the team had replayed to each other the exciting events of the day and had laughed at their mistakes. Chris and Allan had not figured out exactly what had happened in the stadium. It was a fun-filled day. There was great camaraderie, and at no time had the runners blocked or shoved each other.

Aatum who was sitting with the explorers as they told their stories of the day, with amusement and laughter, knew what had occurred. If Allan hadn't pulled away, the runner would have bumped into him and not Chris. A competitor from the realm of Calem had won the race.

CHAPTER 11

The archaeologists knew that, notwithstanding centuries of peace, the gentle, pastoral people were of warrior blood. That their ancestors had conquered the most-feared predators of the African continent and fended off invaders for fifteen hundred years was instructive. The team knew the quaint calm of the Ashais hid some truth that as yet they had not fathomed.

The previous night, after they'd reflected on the thrills of the hunters' race, Allan had asked Aatum whether the time was near for the team to return home. Aatum told Allan he did not know, and he changed the subject. He said, "I will see you tomorrow. I am sure you are interested in seeing a marriage ceremony at the Temple of the Sun."

In the early afternoon of this new day, Aatum had arrived at their dwellings, and he took the explorers to the garden of the Temple. Timothy and James had left the group, and they walked around the grounds. The two men pondered the events they'd experienced since they'd arrived in the Land of the Crystal Bird. The team was watched and followed all the time. The explorers saw shadows but no forms. The security men were gripped with uneasiness whenever they looked into the eyes of the keeper.

"We'll take off in full view of everybody. That should not appear as anything unusual," James said. "They'll believe we're going to survey the area for security reasons. We'll hide the guns and go through the same path we passed a few days ago, keeping our eyes open for followers and watchers. We should not believe we are safe because we had participated in the games."

"I worry about our safety," said Timothy. "There's something beyond our comprehension out there. What we feel about watchers is real, and it's clear the people do not trust us. Aatum has said as much. Remember, the Ashais people have one enemy—we are the enemy, and they have equipped themselves to handle us although we do not see any weapons other than their spears. The Ashais have not claimed or displayed any magical powers, yet they seem to know what is unknown to us. I listened to the storytelling, and Aatum's conversations. These are people the rest of the world knows nothing about, yet they speak of our wars, failures, and discoveries and the injustices of a modern world. The Ashais cannot know about these things unless, of course, they have found a way to get out of here and keep abreast of things. Perhaps they send seekers, but how do they get out? How?" Timothy wondered. The lean, blue-eyed sharpshooter scratched his head. He obscured and twisted facts to suit his purposes, was quick-witted, and, as his friends would say, he could outrun a cheetah.

"The same way we came. OK. Here's the plan," said James—a brawny, cunning forty-year-old with an air of superiority. "We retrace our steps to the spot where we arrived. I recall it was to the west of a cluster of giant, yellow poui trees that faced a high, snow-capped mountain. We go up the mountain until we reach the spot in the thick of the forest where we saw the giant gorillas. There must be a shield that opens to our world."

"So when does it open?"

"That's what we'll have to figure out."

They were silent, observing the landscape, trying to figure out the puzzle.

"You know, it has something to do with the eclipse," said James.

"So what? We wait for the next eclipse?" The sarcasm in Timothy's voice was not lost on James.

"Yes, I think eclipses—or whatever they are—happen here frequently."

"Why do you say that?" Timothy asked.

"It explains the midnight sun. Remember when we were sitting near the river a few nights ago and the sun was low?" James was reflective.

"So you think there's a protective shield around the land," Timothy queried.

"Yes, a shield that deflects space. It's why they have not been detected. I also feel we're not the first outsiders to have arrived here," speculated James.

"What are you saying, you think there were others before us?"

"Perhaps."

"So what do you think happened to them?"

James was silent again. He chewed on the end of a guava stick, pulled his hat down, raised his head, and looked to the sky and said, "Ask the Ashais."

"Assuming we return to the spot, then what?"

James turned around and looked in the direction where the other members of the team were sitting. He realised it was time to go back to the group. "We wait and choose the exact time. When that is, I'm not sure. Let's go back to our charges and carry on as usual. I'm sure we will get a hint. Our hosts are very sociable. They'll be telling other stories of long ago. With the right discreet questions, we might get clues or direct answers."

"These are neither garrulous nor ignorant people. I detect an ability to read minds or have an idea of what we are thinking and are about to say," Timothy said.

"I know—in fact I am fairly sure they have a keener sense of human frailties than we do and intellects that are higher than average. Call it intuition, instinct, super insight, whatever. We are not dealing with ordinary people."

※

Timothy and James joined the other members of the team who were sitting in the garden of the Temple of the Sun enjoying fruit and refreshments.

The explorers watched in awe the activity that was unfolding. It was a ceremony to mark the beginning of a young couple's new life. They had just arrived to be joined symbolically together in the garden, under a canopy of floral vines. The procession stretched across the mountaintop as friends, relatives, and spectators came to wish them well. The people were dressed in flowing versions of the shuka made of a variety of silks and wore silver and gold sandals. Their dark, smooth faces radiated sunny health, and their nutmeg-shaped eyes beamed with the joy of people in love with life. The male guests, resplendent in their robes of various colours, carried gifts of sculptures, jewels, myrrh, and other perfumes.

"They must be royalty," said Chris.

Allan had spent much time with Aatum and the keeper to learn more about the principles by which the Ashais lived. He was still puzzled by many things. Their tendency was to give only so much information and no more. Every time he made progress, the conversation changed or ended quite politely. He nevertheless had a good relationship with both men—especially the keeper, with whom he felt a connection.

"He is the son of a teacher who heads the college for young men, and she is the daughter of a chieftain," answered Allan. "Her name is Lelite, and his is Omeke. They courted for twelve sun moons, which is equivalent to about a year. I think tonight the sun moon is expected to emerge from the east of Mt. Maran. That means it will shine until early in the morning, so festivities are likely to continue well into tomorrow."

Timothy's brow wrinkled, and he looked at James. He repeated softly, "Twelve sun moons." He smiled at the significance. The sun moon, or midnight sun, came on average, about twelve times a year, and each time just before an eclipse. He calculated that the time was nearly upon them when they would have to go to the spot on the mountain where they had arrived.

He took his mind back to the procession. Children held each other's hands in a circle and skipped and danced to the music of the kibangala. Graceful bodies flexed in motion to the beat of haunting drums and the melodious voices of a male choir. The stupendous majesty of the mountains, in a fusion of ceremonial color, echoed the pulsating sounds. The cattle, never too far from their masters, grazed lazily in the shade of the trees.

Prior to the wedding, Allan, Chris, and Aatum had discussed the columned homes carved in the mountains, decorated with intricate designs, and the architecture of the Temple of Remembrance, where a perpetual light shone. The victorious battle of the Maasai warriors against the invading slavers, and their subsequent flight up the mountain of Kilimanjaro, was in the reliefs. A bull goring a man against a tree was depicted in vivid detail. This scene was followed by warriors carrying the body of a comrade. Expertly painted was the history of the warrior leader who ruled the Kingdom of Ashaise for more than sixty years. Jomo the storyteller was by the lake with a lion at his side. Other reliefs were similar to those seen in the caves on the mountain and in the Magamba forest.

They strolled to the next chamber and viewed a detailed drawing of the solar system, which left Allan and Chris even more anxious than before to find out more about where they were.

As the procession reached the temple, a mass of bejewelled, white-robed Ashais encircled the gardens. In the center of the grassy summit there was a large, flamboyant tree. Branches and flowered vines formed a canopy. A layer of petals more than two inches deep carpeted the floor.

Aatum kept the visitors informed about the ceremony.

"This is where the couple will stand as the laibon sprinkles water from the lake over their heads, and where they will perform the ritual of sipping the blood of a bull."

The strangers felt light and happy. Returning home was far from their minds. The purity of the time, the sincerity of the ritual of marriage, and the exquisite seriousness of the elders in blessing the union were events they would remember when their minds needed soothing.

They had not seen it before that moment. It had a garland around its neck and was behind the procession. The huge, light-cream body was rippled with muscle. It had a horn on its forehead, and the proud beast walked purposefully at the side of a child, like a giant next to an ant.

The strangers had seen many unusual-sized beasts in the animal kingdom, but nothing had prepared them for the magnificence of this animal. The procession parted for it. Everyone smiled and welcomed Zete, the pride of the sun god's people, a descendant of another beast owned by a jovial warrior youth five centuries earlier.

The beautiful child Meke steered Zete to the river's edge, where herdsmen in white shukas waited. Something caused the bull to stop and raise its proud head. It looked at the place where the strangers sat. It stared at Timothy, who felt cold. Zete put its right hoof forward, lowered its head, lifted it again, and bellowed—a sound that disturbed the peaceful revelry of the occasion.

The laibon looked at the strangers. The keeper stood quietly with his animals, enjoying, in his own way, the coming together of the people of the land. A chilly wind blew and crackled the leafy garlands around the canopy. The children shivered.

The laibon led the bull to the lakeside and bled it. Afterward it walked away and sat facing the mountains. It sensed evil. Allan felt a chill.

Across the garden, four people approached the gathering. There was no mistaking the striking king in a flowing, wide-sleeved, blue robe. The elegant queen, dressed in a light-blue, silk shuka gown, walked at his side, and next to her was Prince Nehsi. At the other side of King Meleke was a young woman wearing a cream-satin shuka draped over her slender body. She moved gracefully across the grass.

Allan and Chris inched their way forward to get a better view of the arrival. Allan was interested in one person. She had the hint of a smile.

The four members of the royal family approached the ceremonial dais. The large gathering parted to allow them to enter the flowered canopy. The people chanted followed by children singing while the laibon asked the sun god to shower the couple with light. A young shepherd brought the gourd with the blood and handed it to the laibon, who took it and offered the first sip to Lelite. He placed Omeke's hands on hers as she sipped once; similarly Omeke sipped. Thereafter the laibon gave the gourd to the members of the couple's family. When they had all sipped, the shepherd took it to the temple.

The royal family held hands as the chieftain escorted them out of the canopy. They walked ahead of the procession for the final stage of the simple ceremony. Against the backdrop of the Fountain of the Sun, they crossed over a rivulet, which was symbolical of the crossover to their new lives.

The people danced and celebrated the couple. Allan watched the princess swing her body to the rhythm of drums and flutes. Jiena saw Allan looking at her and went to him: "Let me show you how." She placed Allan's hands on her hips, then hers on his and they danced. She released her hold and turned her back to Allan. He turned her around and put his hands around her waist, and they moved their bodies together.

The other visitors found themselves in the center of the celebration. Springer was in heaven. He danced like a Kenyan, to the delight of the Ashais.

Robert and Kiserian strolled along the summit of the mountain. They chatted about her realm. He told her about his world.

Chris, who was in the company of the keeper, described to him wedding traditions at home. While he was talking with the keeper, Chris watched Allan and Jiena as they danced and flirted with each other. Chris also noticed the keeper, as well as the princess's parents, looked frequently in the direction of Allan and Jiena. He worried about his partner.

The splendid day spread its wings, and time took flight as the sun baptised the celebrators with curative liquid light that fell on their foreheads, releasing their fatigue from yesterday's toil. The sun's warm, penetrating fingers shaped mischievous shadows, contrasting the landscape's colored spreads of brilliance, creating a mystical batik. The silent rhythm of magical creatures celebrated the day.

Pencils of fire lit the land, and youthful Ashais sneaked away to love, laugh, and play in the shade of the golden poui trees. They stole time in conspiracy with the wily conjuror that shone above, surrendering to the wistful, playful day. Amidst the foliage, in vespers' light, they wandered freely, revelling in the contagious moment, hurrying to play before the verge of day blended into the sublime moods of night.

The midnight sun quietly crept across the sky, and the wedding party erupted in chant. They sang songs to the sun god. Warriors gathered together with Omeke in the center and performed the celebratory jumping dance of their forefathers. The king watched Allan. King Meleke was puzzled. The midnight sun waned, and the newly wedded couple said farewell, then the guests began to disperse to their homes. A few who were drunk on the variety of fruit wines lingered to savor the happiness of the day that had just gone.

The visitors had enjoyed the ceremony and shared a sumptuous meal. They had whispered their observations and chatted about the similarities of the Ashais to others in the East African end of the vast geographic trough in that continent.

The more the two archaeologists saw of the Ashais, the more intrigued they became. Although gracious, they kept an intellectual and emotional distance. It was vexing that as soon as they engaged their hosts, the conversation came to an abrupt end.

They appreciated the opportunity to participate in all that had happened during the day. Aatum escorted them back to their dwellings. It should have been a gentle night.

※

"It is the night of the midnight sun, and we should take the opportunity now," Timothy said to James. "They are all high, and it's the best time for us to leave quietly, taking only the ammunition we need, some of the precious things we have gathered, and some fruit. Once we get through the shield, we will be back on Kilimanjaro."

James agreed. "There's sufficient light for us to get up to the ridge on the mountainside. When we get to the place near the Seat of God where they store the eggs, we'll take one. We'll make our way to the mount on which we arrived before the midnight sun sets and the shield temporarily breaks. We must keep an eye out for the keeper. He is everywhere."

"What about the archaeologists? We have a responsibility to protect them," said Timothy.

"I thought a great deal about that. If I believed for one moment we would be allowed to leave, I would not do this. I spoke with Chris and Allan last week and told them I had a problem just waiting around for permission. If there's an opportunity for me to get out and get help, I would like to do so. Do you realize we've been in this place for over a month now?"

"What did they say?"

"They don't think we could get out without the consent of the Ashais. In any event they felt any rescue mission would be doomed, but I told them I would have to try."

"And what did they say to that?"

"As expected," James replied. "That we have a job to do and should not underestimate these people. They feel, sooner or later, we'll know exactly where we stand. I know where these people stand. Any soldier would know that and smell a threat to life. The scent is there. They watch us all the time and want to deal with us without the prospect of our people getting here to look for us. Listen, all I want to do is exactly what Chris and Allan pay me to do: protect them. And that means I must get help."

"Did you tell Chris and Allan about taking an egg?" Timothy asked.

"No."

"Did they release you from the contract?"

"We did not discuss that. The contract is to protect them in the Rift Valley for two months. Do you remember?"

"Wait," Timothy said. "Let's think through what we have planned to a logical conclusion. If we get out, a rescue mission cannot reach here under a month because the midnight sun appears every month. If the mission is successful, then for the same reason, the rescue team will not be able to leave immediately. It does not make sense."

"I'm not an idiot. I've thought about that. At home we do not see eclipses every month. I have no doubt that a phenomenon occurs, and whatever it is, it has to do with light—the speed of light, and the pull is from Ashaise's side." James paused. He looked at the sky and then to the mountains. He turned to Timothy, "There has to be a significant time lapse between Earth and Ashaise, so I don't think it's a case of waiting for a month for the rescue mission to get here. The tricky part will be to get out after we have rescued the team. That's where the risk is."

"No, that's not the risk. They may kill the rest of the team as soon as they've realized we've left Ashaise."

"These people have no intention of sending us back home. We have to do something. The Ashais aren't afraid of us. Look, if you're changing your mind and don't want to try, that's okay. I'll go alone."

"How many years have we worked together? I'll go with you," said Timothy. "I wouldn't want them harmed because of our actions. If we get out, that's one thing. If we took an egg the Ashais would know, and that could mean disaster for the others."

"Okay, I agree. We will not take one, but we need a blood or tissue sample, so let's take the necessary gear and the freezer can."

They clothed themselves in khaki mufti with warm clothing underneath, packed their gear, and took off for the mountain.

CHAPTER 12

The following morning Allan awoke early. He had not slept well. His mind had wandered aimlessly, travelling across vast mountains to his world, where he was stuck in traffic, smelling the toxic fumes of motor vehicles. There were fingers on a keyboard. A television was somewhere in the background, blaring headlines about disaster wreaked by the most recent suicide bomber, and the plight of refugees—children with glazed, gazing eyes. They were fleeing, running away from tyranny promoted by malefactors in lands where nature showed off her ingenuity. He twisted, tossed, and saw in his fitful dream people filing in droves to promised lands in the hope of finding succor from yesterday's migrants who had travelled the same path. The refugees longed for shelter and a mouse's morsel.

He turned on his back and saw, in the space between the bed and ceiling, their stained, gaunt faces. They were skeletons on the move. There was no respite from pain. Their stomachs were mounds of gas. Where were their meals? They were staring with hands outstretched.

In the fitful dream, he saw others in boats which had capsized, and the sea that could not digest starved flesh spat their remains on manicured beaches. The scene changed again, and he saw the mothers' anemic eyes looking at him with smiles because their children's pain had ended. The mothers continued to walk with purpose. Their pride was not shattered. They had the courage to survive another tormenting day, to tread on the shame of the corrupt regimes they fled. In his restless, disconnected dream, he saw white mist creeping over him. The mist passed by and hung low over a city dying from toxic waste. When it cleared, he heard bombs. People were screaming.

He had gone to bed that night feeling cold and uncomfortable. He had shared his feeling with Chris, who had been anxious.

Allan awoke to the long, low whistles of crystal birds just as the sun broke over the eastern sky. He stepped out of his unit near the gargantuan balboa trees and wandered over to the rhododendron garden. He followed a path that led to the lake. Its source was the Fountain of the Sun.

He heard whistles again, and saw the birds flying toward the mountain. Their iridescent feathers reflected the morning sunlight. The animals of the forest answered their whistles. The crystal birds flew low overhead to draw attention to their majesty.

Allan felt a deep urge. He knew it was a desire to belong to Ashaise. He stood transfixed, subdued, and humbled. Another voice joined the animal choir. The melody seemed familiar, yet it was not. His mind raced back to his childhood days in church. On a Sunday morning, people had given thanks in the small Baptist church. He had loved to hear the worshipers sing "Amazing Grace." No, that was not what he heard—it could not be that tune. He followed the rich voice as it sang in a language he barely understood. He wondered about the words. The voice ceased as he approached, and Jiena was there, draped in a white shuka leaning against a boulder. He walked toward her, and as he approached she turned her head to the lake. Standing at her side, he looked out to the lake, where he saw ripples—evidence of abundant life beneath the surface.

"I thought I'd heard that tune before," he said.

Jiena was quiet but looked amused by something. He hoped it was not him. There was a long silence.

"It is the tune of my ancestors. After the hunt, my fore-parents gathered around the fire, sang, and told stories to their children."

They were silent again. Jiena walked away, to a rock upon which she sat with her feet pulled up and her long arms around her knees. She looked up to the rising sun and sang. Allan watched the early morning folk in their boats with tall, billowy sails, and others in canoes. She continued to sing:

I reached the sun, which burnt my heart
So I ran away with the moon.
The sun god called, "Come where I shine
To warm your heart, to warm your heart."
I reached the sun, which warmed my heart
So I stayed under its rays.
The moon god called, "Come where I shine
To warm your heart, to warm your heart."

She stopped singing and looked at him. Their eyes met and explored each other's faces. He saw the innocence and curiosity in her eyes. In his she saw wonder, pain, and confusion. Their spirits reach out to each other beyond the blushing moment and the reverence of the morning. She studied his face. Something was happening.

The invisible cord that held them snapped when Allan saw from the corner of his eye the approaching beast. He panicked. The magical moment was shattered. Fear gripped him as the beast jumped upon the rock behind Jiena. It began to descend. Instinctively Allan reached for his weapon, which was not with him. Jiena saw his panic and lifted her head to see what alarmed him. She saw Matai. Allan moved quickly to protect them both against the animal. There was nowhere to go.

"What's wrong?" Jiena asked.

Allan pointed to the animal.

Jiena looked up and then threw her head back with laughter. "That is Matai."

"Matai," he repeated in a throaty voice.

"Yes, he is the lion of the Ashais. Matai was given to me by my brother, Nehsi. No harm will come to you. He is my protector and pet."

Allan stood in horror. He heard the beat of his heart. The beast strode like an oversized black panther toward them and fixed his amber eyes on Allan. Matai came alongside them and sat looking out at the lake.

Allan could not have imagined any animal like Matai. He was jet black with a thick, blue-black mane. He had a distinctive blue streak of fur in the center of his forehead just above the eyes. Stories of the black lions had been told for centuries among the Ashais. The people said the lions were spirits of the sun god that searched throughout the land and mauled evildoers to death.

"Many moons ago, when the evil ones came to take away our ancestors to faraway lands," Jiena said, "the shadow of Matai's ancestors stalked them and gave our foreparents the strength of the sun god to spear their captors to death. Matai and all the lions know that evil is here."

"What do you mean?" Allan asked. "Are there others here? Who else is here? Do you think I'm evil?"

"No."

"Then what do you mean?"

"I have said too much." She rose, and he held her hands. "Jiena."

She looked at his hands over hers, placed hers over his, and raised her head. "I must go."

Matai stood up and continued to look out at the lake. Allan did not miss its movement and let go of Jiena's hands. He did not stand a chance against the beast, and smiled at his folly.

Jiena stepped away. Allan looked after her until her slender figure disappeared with Matai in the morning mist. The lump in the pit of his stomach was not due to fear of Matai.

The warrior stood on a small hill, hidden among the thick shrubbery. For several days he had followed the movements of Chris and Allan as they'd studied rock formations. The other explorers did not interest Sahure—the warrior protector from the realm of Sahur. His concern was the man who looked like an Ashais, the man who people spoke about after the hunters' race, and again after the wedding. The stranger had danced with the princess, and had spent a long time speaking with the woman who was to be his wife. He now looked at Allan and Jiena and thought he was too close to her.

He saw when Jiena retreated, leaving the stranger staring after her. The warrior bowed his head, clenched his teeth, and took a deep breath. He then looked at Allan again. Sahure's eyes had a distant look as he thought about Jiena's behavior when they had met in the garden of her home. That had been the night after the wedding ceremony. He had thought her eyes looked sad, and felt a distance. She had not been like that before the stranger arrived in their land. She had laughed with him and been happy. Sahure was anxious to marry her but knew she could not be rushed.

He turned toward the mountain and said to himself, "The stranger must sail the skies." He left the hill.

※

Allan turned to face the lake. The crinkly, silvery-blue surface motioned with the life beneath in pursuit of a delectable early morning meal. Fish jumped and swam and splashed a slippery, slobbery, merry dash across the rippling sheet. Predators in the air, with long necks and Jurassic jaws, pierced the translucent shield and yielded a feast the sun god would have blessed.

HELEN DRAYTON

Allan sat upon a rock. He was in turmoil. Boats with billowy, golden sails moved silently across the water. He scanned the surface, and his eyes rested on the fishermen lowering jute baskets into the water, which they pulled up filled with the morning's catch.

He bowed his head in deep thought and wondered about the events of the last couple of weeks, and about himself. He saw his world of scientific discovery and technological achievement, the luxuries of wealth and tremendous medical progress that brought immense relief to people everywhere—people who had thought they would never walk or see or hear again. He reflected on the potential of space exploration and saw the faces of healthy children in comfortable classrooms. The charm of the diverse cultures of his world flashed through his mind, so too the generosity of ordinary people, the elegance and style of fashionable women, and the rewards of labor manifested in the freedom to be and to do.

His world had advanced exponentially, yet it searched for its soul. He too was searching. He reckoned one thing: he did not want to go back to his civilized world. He felt uncomfortable and frightened. He did not understand what Jiena had meant when she said the lions knew that evil was present. He did not understand the hollowness he felt. He turned and stared in the direction she had gone.

CHAPTER 13

The team met in the garden in front of their dwellings and considered options for getting out of Ashaise. The Ashais did not interrogate them, and treated all members generously and with respect, but they refused to discuss if, and when the explorers could leave.

The explorers worried their prospects for returning home were grim. At least they did not think it would be soon. They were never-the-less still hopeful, and considered how they would handle the findings they'd made here, whenever they returned home.

The mystical land was a sensitive matter for the two archaeologists. Unquestionably, Ashaise was the biggest discovery in history. They could not think of an event that would rival their encounter with an advanced civilization living in a land that was not within the physical boundaries of Earth. The team still did not know exactly where they were, but they felt certain Ashaise could not have been on Mt. Kilimanjaro or anywhere else on Earth. How the explorers got to Ashaise was another significant event, and even more difficult to explain than the existence of the land.

This was an archaeological expedition, but each man had his aspirations and knew what he wanted from the project. Timothy and James were mates who had experienced many adventures together since leaving the Army. As soldiers of fortune, they had embraced any project that had potential to add to their treasure trove. Cazeau and Joe had joined Timothy and James in Ghana after leaving the Army.

At times Chris and Allan wondered about the security members, who showed interest in the exquisite handsomeness of the place but paid more attention to the visible treasures than the archaeological discoveries. Ashaise captivated Allan and Chris. They felt safe and took little notice when Timothy and James wandered off, which they often did, though they were never too far away and returned after short periods.

Springer, the anthropologist, either lagged behind the archaeologists or stayed with Robert, the geographic magazine writer, close to their dwelling units—the base to compare notes at the end of the day. Springer was always hungry or thirsty, and gawked at the attractive women. His distraction by women was a nuisance to Robert. On several occasions they had seen naked women swimming in the river. Often Robert had had to restrain Springer, who'd been twice divorced.

Robert too, had observed the frequent disappearances of members of the security team, especially Timothy and James. They were the only members of the group with whom he had some unease. Timothy and James tended to keep their own company. They were secretive. Apart from the slyness of these men, it was a competent expedition team. Members were able to share experiences and ideas on various situations, including the current predicament. They were all interested in the crystal bird and wondered about the prospect of having such a creature back home.

Robert spent evenings writing about the daily lives of the people of Ashaise, describing in detail their routines and special events. Their schools of mind development fascinated him. Students spent the early hours of the day meditating, followed by physical exercises before sitting in groups to learn about their environment, history, and subjects that prepared them for adult life.

Robert observed the Ashais' strange ability to communicate with each other from long distances. They spoke softly, with a musical accent. He took photographs of the landscape, ensuring he captured the sizes of trees, vegetation, and animals in relation to the people. He wondered why they did not seem interested in his equipment and what he was doing.

Robert was certain that these people knew what he was doing, although he didn't think they had pried into his business. He thought their discreetness was characteristic of a diplomatic and sensible people who amused themselves at the expense of less-intuitive persons.

He noted that the Ashais conferred and solved problems in realm groups, and that meditation was an individual as well as a group activity. Often Robert saw people of all ages in deep contemplation for at least a couple of hours. They were by the lake or river, under trees, close to animals, or on the grassy, open plains. Their reverie was never interrupted.

He speculated that meditation was the primary source of their serene character and wisdom.

Robert saw too the strange shadow and was never quite sure whether it was a person or an animal, or whether it had to do with the sun, passing clouds, or the movement of trees and plants. With an eye for every detail, he'd witnessed many thought-provoking events and inspiring innovations in Ashaise.

Robert grew up in southeast England, in a family of modest means. He studied geography and the environment and had worked as a consultant for the South African government before joining the international geographic magazine. He authored several books relating to social and economic development. His friends, family, and readers respected him for his forthright, down-to-earth attitude and fair-mindedness. The other explorers thought Robert to be a gentleman, a learned traveller whose writings had inspired thousands of readers.

The writer invited people into the worlds of his subjects, where they experienced the cultures and quintessence of their daily lives. This was what endeared him to his clients. He captured every nuance of people—a skill that came from the deep empathy he felt for whomever he wrote about. Robert had learned how to anticipate people's needs without being presumptuous. Experience warned him that the Ashais were contemplating what should be done with him and the others. He looked up toward the mountain and knew the keeper was there.

※

Timothy and James waited for the moment when leaving their units would not arouse suspicion. Sneaking away was not a smart idea; rather it was better they leave in the usual manner, as if they were going to explore the landscape. They calculated it was time for the next eclipse and planned to climb to the Seat of God. From there they would follow the trail to the cave where the birds nested.

Their world was one of conflict and war. They had experienced living in conditions only men hardened by the harshest situations could survive for prolonged periods. Their arrival in this peaceful, unspoiled land was an unusual contrast. They passed villages while strolling casually, admiring the Ashais as they went about their daily routines.

The Ashais' attitude toward them puzzled Timothy more than it did James. He felt apprehensive because they seemed attuned to something, as if collectively they surreptitiously watched the group. It was a feeling he'd had since their arrival. James and Timothy had discussed the people in hushed tones at night-time.

They moved at a fairly rapid pace, not resting until they reached the Seat of God many hours after leaving their dwellings. There they paused for a few minutes before using their binoculars to scour the landscape. They did not see anyone as they ascended the mountain.

James and Timothy saw the habitat of the gorillas. They observed the quiet, fatherly glances of the beasts, which were presumably tending to their young and husbanding their patches of territory. The animals had picked up the scent of the men when they were still miles away, and heard the creak of every dry twig and the slight shift of grass beneath stealthy feet. One perceptive primate stood to his full height, slightly ghosted by the mist, and appeared to be staring straight ahead.

The temperature dropped rapidly, and it was not long before Timothy and James looked down on dense clouds.

"How do we find the cave?" James asked.

"Keep moving on the path," said Timothy. "Let's move quickly."

They walked until they reached the spot where they saw the mountain and the yawning mouth of the cave. They intended to enter the habitat, extract fluid from the queen bird or an egg, and put the substance in a freezer canister. Afterward they would return to the place just past the gorillas' habitat where they'd found themselves the first day. There it would be a matter of waiting until the eclipse broke the shield around Ashaise.

As they approached the cave, they turned to see the breathtaking landscape Allan and Chris had described to them. Tentatively they entered, looking up and around in the silence and darkness. The temperature in the cave bit through their clothes to their skin. The salty air stung their eyes, and their feet skidded on the mossy ground. This was not the safe path within the cave on which Chris and Allan had recently walked.

Timothy and James stepped into a chamber that mesmerized them with its staggering beauty. The sun poured its rays through the roof. All they could see as they looked up was blinding-white crystal. It seemed they were in a place with mirrors that reflected the rugged, crystalline walls of the enormous scenery. They heard the sound of water and went through a passageway. As they reached the end and turned, they froze, for there the bird sat proudly.

The shadow moved, and then another. Timothy and James both saw them and instinctively backed against each other as they turned around to scan the crystal rocks and cliffs. Whichever way they turned, a black lion watched them. Timothy drew his gun. A force struck it from his hand. Stunned, they both looked around and did not see any human—only the lions.

They continued to protect each other while searching for a possible means of escape. The lions stood up and moved toward them. As the beasts approached, they broke their circle, leaving room for the two men to turn and run from whence they'd come. As they did James turned and attempted to kill a beast. Someone struck the weapon from his hand, and it went into the air. Then someone slammed him to the ground.

Timothy stopped, looked back, and called out to James. Stunned, James struggled up and ran in the direction of his friend's voice. They heard heavy breathing as they ran. It was their own. They turned to see if the lions were following them. There wasn't anything to be seen except the scenery. They hastened down a path that was not the one on which they had entered the large domain.

Quickly they moved along the avenue of majestic stalagmites and stalactites, which were a unique profusion of colors. They wondered whether they were moving in the right direction. They had no choice but to continue apace. As the wondrous avenue ended, the men found themselves in another domain and heard the sound of running water again. They followed it.

Not long afterward they saw a pathway perpendicular to where they were. They stood still to consider the next move and decided to take the path. They came upon what could only be described as a topaz-colored lake of nature's calm. It conjured memories of a clear night when the moon glowed at its best, splashing lightning-white across mountains silhouetted against the night sky. Glow worms speckled the still mass of crystal-clear water, and above the surface fireflies danced throughout the cave-sphere like millions of stars. The enormous domain resembled a city with silhouetted stalagmites that looked like skyscrapers.

A shadow moved. The two men, lost in the subterranean world, felt a rush of adrenaline. They hurried on the shoulder, passing the entrance to many cave rooms. They turned a blind corner and found themselves on a long, narrow pathway that led to the exit.

On reaching the exit, they saw to right of the mouth a myrrh tree they recognised, and they knew they were not far from the gorillas' habitat. They heard low whistles. A shadow sauntered in the mist. It moved parallel to them. They ran in the haze of the mesosphere, and the shadow went between them. James found himself on the mountain-side where they had arrived from across the sun. The sky grew dark, a velvety black; daylight vanished. A blistering wind blew, and James disappeared.

Shadows encircled Timothy, who entered the habitat where Apti the gorilla fed. The sensitive animal picked him up, and all creatures that dwelled within the Blue Mountains of Ashaise heard Timothy's cry.

The keeper stood on the mountainside caressing Matai's mane. The crystal birds whistled as they flew toward the entrance of the cave.

The following morning the others observed the absence.

"Where are Timothy and James?" Allan asked.

"As usual they wandered off. I thought they had returned," Robert said.

"The king expects all of us," Chris responded. "They know who arrived here. Their disappearing act should have been stopped. Should we ask Aatum to advise the king that we are awaiting the return of two members who went to explore?"

"If the king receives such a message, he might not be pleased. Let us proceed as a matter of respect. They already know there are six of us here and not eight," Allan said.

King Meleke Djedkare was a pragmatic leader who was aware of everything of significance that happened or was about to happen in his kingdom. He was a practical father and husband who knew what went on in his household, but he controlled his kingdom better than he managed his wife and daughter. Both of them manipulated him. He humored them, though; when it came to matters of security and governance of his kingdom, he drew the line.

Like Meleke's illustrious ancestors, his goal was the continued development of his people and the progress of the kingdom. He ensured impartiality whenever he dealt with disputes that could have divided the realms. Usually disagreements were over the allotment of lands for dwellings and agriculture, and the relative worth of property, goods, and services.

In Ashaise currency was tangible goods and services; there was no coinage or paper money, but there was a system of credits. So, accurate records and reliable information on prevailing marketplace conditions were necessary for fair assessment of the relative worth of tradable things. Realm leaders had constantly bickered and bartered on the worth of items. The king had dealt severely with leaders who broke the law. He had confiscated their property and ordered them to compensate the society.

The benevolent king allowed citizens the freedom to question and criticize decisions, but no one dared mobilize other citizens to challenge his authority. He had four sons and one daughter. Prince Meke was his youngest son. Prince Nehsi was his third child and part of his inner circle of leaders. Jiena was his fourth child. Two elder sons were among Ashaise's specialists in medicine and agriculture, and lived in other realms.

The group now walked through the gardens, led by Aatum, who had stayed with them since they had come down the misty mountain four weeks earlier. They approached the king's impressive home with marble columns and walked through a corridor. Aatum ushered them to a large room furnished with scattered carpets, several cushioned chairs, and tables. They heard the sound of falling water in the distant background.

Nehsi entered the room, but Allan did not see him. Allan's eyes were on Jiena.

"Welcome." She extended both arms.

"You are a remarkable people," Chris said. "How is it that we have not discovered you before?"

"Discovered? What do you mean?"

Chris pondered the question. "Well, the world does not know you exist, and you are different. Ashaise is different. You have trees that are much larger than any we have seen before. You have comfortable homes carved from stone, you have built pyramids, and it appears to us that you're familiar with our world. You understand much of what we say."

"Why do you believe we are not in the same place you are?" Nehsi's eyes twinkled.

"We are archaeologists, and—"

Before Chris could finish the sentence, Nehsi interjected, smiling. "Not all of you."

"Ashaise remains unspoilt, untouched, yet you have lived here for thousands of years. You are taller than most of us, you live many more years than we do, and you have found cures for life-threatening ailments and diseases. We are very curious about your science and colleges of mental development."

Allan said, "Our interest is where Ashaise is, if it is on Earth."

An attendant hurried into the room and called Nehsi aside. The others saw the prince's expression change. He looked sad. He dismissed the attendant and returned to his guests.

"My father and mother will see you now."

A cool breeze blew into the chamber, and the team's mood changed inexplicably during the short time they were in the palatial room. The door opened and two attendants entered, followed by the king and queen. Queen Teye was an attractive woman. Her daughter had inherited her charming disposition.

The king and queen smiled warmly and welcomed the group to his home. The unsmiling faces of Nehsi and Jiena heightened the guests' tense feeling.

"We know how you arrived," said King Meleke. "Fate brought you with no bad intention."

Queen Teye looked at Allan. "Malice and greed are with you."

There were no noises in the spacious chamber except for the falling water in the distance. Brows creased, feet shuffled, and eyes queried. Meleke studied the guests' faces; his eyes twinkled, revealing no anger or pretensions, although his aloofness unsettled the others.

"What do you mean your majesties?" Allan asked.

The king turned to the attendant and gave a command with his eyes. The attendant came forward and handed the king a gun. Once again there was silence in the chamber for a long time.

"So you came with the sun god, and we welcomed you." Nehsi extended his arms to show how they had greeted these strangers. "You admire the beauty of our land, its riches and the harmony of all who live here. You've learned about our treasures and Kriziantu, the crystal bird. Certainly, as other traitors wanted from our forefathers their land and wealth, you want more than you already have. You want Kriziantu."

The visitors did not say anything. They waited for information. They had discussed, on more than one occasion among themselves, the curative powers of the bird's egg and considered its benefits to the world. More than that, they had decided to approach the Ashais for that very thing. Denial was not an option. On the other hand, they had made no attempt to betray the trust of the people.

But the gun, whose was it? Where did the Ashais get it? At that moment, team members thought about Timothy and James.

"Betrayal is your destiny and your legacy," the king said. "We expected you. We expected the same from you. We watched for many moons. We will always be prepared."

He put his arm around the queen. He looked into the eyes of Allan, then Chris, and glanced at the others. The king and queen turned and left the room.

CHAPTER 14

Jennifer Stephens checked her e-mail, which was a regular early morning routine before the rush of day began. Every day for the past two weeks she had looked for a message from Allan and Chris, who usually either phoned or sent an e-mail if only to say things were going well. The last message on her voicemail, two weeks ago from Allan, had been very cheerful and to the point: "Hey, Jen, things are great here. The landscape is absolutely breathtaking, and we discovered the most beautiful reliefs in a cave. We'll send pictures soon. Tell Hackshaw the project is going better than expected."

Since then there had been no other communication, so she'd called their camp manager, who'd said his last contact with them had been two weeks earlier, but he didn't think there was need to worry. Jennifer went to talk to Conrad Hackshaw, dean of Ancient Studies at the university.

"Conrad, it's been over two weeks and nobody has heard from Allan and Chris. I find it strange, because we usually receive regular reports."

167

"Do you think something is wrong?"

"Well, I don't know. They've been away for long periods without sending messages, but they said we would hear from them at least every two weeks if there were developments."

"Maybe there were none."

"I suppose we can wait another week or so, and in the meantime I'll call the embassy in case there were any unusual events in the region."

The petite, thirty-six-year-old assistant to Dean Hackshaw was indispensable to him and the two archae-ologists. She kept their work lives in order and, on more than one occasion, rebuked the dean for his cluttered office. Exercising control over that area of her sixty-year-old boss was simply impossible.

He knew where every paperclip and highlighter was and told her that moving things messed up his desk. He was very fond of the conscientious woman and accepted he would be miserable without her.

As each day passed, Jennifer hoped the next day would bring good news. A week later she called the undersecretary for government affairs at the American embassy in Kenya. She explained the situation, and the undersecretary prom-ised her the embassy would investigate immediately.

Four weeks passed and she'd had enough of waiting. She told Hackshaw intervention was necessary. The family of the two archaeologists called her office more than twice daily. If even Allan and Chris did not communicate with their office often, usually they called their parents at least every fort-night. The last message said they were in a cave, and sub-sequent checks with the camp headquarters said they had gone up Kilimanjaro. The perils of working in the rain forest could not be overestimated. There could have been animal attacks, reptile and insect bites, and—most menacing—roaming armed rebels who were serious threats to life.

Jennifer and the dean planned a meeting with the foreign affairs office in Washington. The foreign office agreed to send a search mission, headed by one of their soldiers in Nairobi, to search the area where the expedition had last been seen.

※

Tapping his pen impatiently on the desk, the secretary of foreign affairs at the American embassy waited for what seemed to be a rather long thirty seconds before the person in Kenya spoke again. The urgency in the man's voice meant there was news. He mentioned that one of the members of the expedition—James Mathews, an ex-Marine—had returned to camp. James had related a tall tale about a land that did not exist, yet it was where the archaeologists and the others were. It was a place where everything was giant-sized and the people had little difficulty speaking with them. The assistant in the Kenyan office said James had escaped black lions when he and a colleague had gone to take a sample of blood from a crystal bird.

With the exasperated voice of a person who had heard enough of a fairy tale, the secretary asked for the location of the land, and about James's mental state. The officer told him the place was somewhere beyond where eclipses occurred. He rolled his eyes, sighed, and politely said he had arranged a search and rescue mission.

In the car, returning to the university, Jennifer and the dean mulled over what they had heard. When they got to the office, they laid out a map of the area in Tanzania near the Kenyan side.

The dean said, "They went up on this side. Usually it takes at least six days to get to the top, but since they were exploring, it probably took much longer."

"But why would they go up there anyway?" asked Jennifer.

"Perhaps their intention was not to go to the summit. Having spent many days in caves and burial sites within the area, they probably felt there was potential for further discoveries and decided to look for unexplored caves on the mountain. Maybe there *is* something more. The tale about a mysterious land and strange people is not a new one. Across the continent of Africa, there is a strong culture of storytelling. The elders hand down to each generation stories about challenges of daily life in the villages and kingdoms. There is a story as old as ages about people going up into that mountain, which the Maasai called the House of God, in the hope of seeing the sun god or the bird god, and never returning. According to one story, there is a kingdom beyond the clouds where the sun god goes to sleep at night. In this kingdom are great beasts tamed by tall people who live as much as one hundred and fifty years."

Jennifer was skeptical. "But that's only a story—similar to what we hear about the Bermuda Triangle, where people have disappeared without a trace."

Hackshaw responded in his thin voice, "Would they go chasing after a mythical land? Yes, it's possible. Archaeologists take the stories, tales, and myths very seriously—that's why we are still chasing stories of antiquity. I think they were seeking to explore caves in terrain not yet touched by foreigners."

"A meeting with James would be interesting. What do you think? Should we send an investigator?"

"I'll call the foreign office about the most practical means of having an urgent talk with him. It will be useful if one of us is the investigator. We want geological and ecological information to decide on the possible location of the rest of the expedition."

He dialed the foreign affairs office in Kenya. The person who answered said James Mathews was on the news. Hackshaw turned on the television immediately. He and Jennifer watched James's interview. He told a similar story to the one related by the secretary in the foreign affairs office. What struck them was James's apparent sincerity. The graphic details of the land could have been a description of the geological and ecological topography of remote mountain ranges adjacent to the rift valley, which were difficult to access. The interviewer emphasized the bird; James said was as beautiful as polished crystal. He stressed the point that its egg had healing properties, which was the source of the health and longevity of the people who lived there.

In this interview the world heard about the superior mental powers of a people somewhere in Kenya or Tanzania whose lifestyle was pastoral. James, with a haughty expression, told the news media that the unusual people seemed peaceful and harnessed an element similar to electrical power. They call themselves Ashais and communicated sometimes by means akin to mental telepathy. He had seen only one weapon on Ashaise—a spear. He said ferocious, black lions as large as elephants had chased him and his friend, Timothy, through the cave of the crystal bird. To protect themselves they had tried to kill the lions, but an invisible force had knocked the guns out of their hands. He expressed fear for his friend's life.

The interviewer quizzed James on the mental and physical condition of the others in his party. Were they held captive? Were they free to move around? And how did they talk with the Ashais? James described the warmth of the Ashais, who spoke with a lilt. He and his colleagues had moved around freely, but were under surveillance constantly.

"Have you ever seen lions like that before your adventure on Ashaise?" the interviewer asked James.

"When we were in the cave in the Magamba rain forest, we saw a lion. It was difficult to make out its color, but I'm certain it was not the typical lion you see in Africa."

James's extraordinary adventure was the main headline everywhere. Most people dismissed him as a lunatic still suffering from post-traumatic stress disorder from Desert Storm.

⚒

However not everyone saw a madman. Curiosity among the members of the pharmaceutical industry and governments propelled them into action. They had to investigate any opportunity, regardless of how slight, to find a cure for endemic diseases.

This was something more than just a tall tale; it was James's description of the topography of a subterranean cave and the crustaceans it harbored, and of the rain forest. It was similar to what the region had been like in the Neolithic period. The uncanny likeness of the people to the Maasai and Ethiopians, their Nilotic dialect, and the assegai were significant. Geologists and anthropologists were interested. The discovery of graffiti and a range of items made of precious metals in caves in the Magamba rain forest and on Kilimanjaro perked up other interest groups.

Brother Caftie from the Church of New Life Missionaries in Nairobi went to bed that night deep in thought. He had heard many tales about a mystical bird and people of the sky. He had listened to the radio, not missing a word of what James had to say. He had tried to dismiss the report as an exaggeration of what had happened on the mountain, but descriptions of the people and the bird were similar to the stories told by Maasai elders. These stories were about young men who, centuries earlier, had run away from slavers, and warriors who, thousands of years earlier, had fled ancient lands from the kingdoms of Kush and Punt after a bloody invasion. They had gone up into the mountain and were never seen again.

Caftie had arrived in Kenya twenty-five years earlier and established a network of missions across the country and in Tanzania. He was the principal of a prominent missionary school in the sprawling city of Nairobi. He considered the other story about a group of youth who, around the fifteenth century, had fled into the mountain with their animals. The event had occurred in the early days of slavery. He thought, *Could these people be their descendants, by the grace of God?*

The prospect of being the first person to bring God's message to people who had never heard anything from Him was overwhelming. He could not sleep, and he prayed he would be showed a way to reach the poor people.

Jennifer and Hackshaw had heard enough. It was time for action. A meeting with James was now critical. They made arrangements to go to Kenya. Before leaving they visited the distressed parents of the archaeologists, and Jennifer called Allan's girlfriend, Germaine.

CHAPTER 15

Soon after the meeting with the visitors, Meleke called a meeting with the chieftains of the twelve realms. Communication was swift, and they met the following day.

The male and female chieftains from the realms of Sure, Sahur, Sade, Mban, Calem, Naha, Tangani, Masur, Jih, Meble, Ned, and Aman, together with the royal leaders, gathered in the pyramid temple for a council meeting. They exchanged greetings. The king told the gathering the time had come to decide on the visitors' fate.

"We dealt with those who trespassed before without compromising the vow of our great ancestors. The Ashais will not draw blood from fellow men. We must find solutions without killing unless it's necessary to defend ourselves. There is a threat that is very serious because one of the visitors returned to his place. The lions chased the other into the arms of Apti. The one who escaped will bring others to rescue their people. They will have other motives. Ashaise is a land that brothers across the sun will want. They will come again bearing gifts, will tell us stories about their civilizations, and will want us to pray to their god."

"The two who entered the cave of Kriziantu with the keeper have weapons," said Nehsi. "We must be prepared to handle this grave situation. We know what they want. We know the value of Kriziantu to them, and while we want to help the brothers it is not wise to do so now."

Kiserian, the chieftain of Sure said, "The ones who seek knowledge of ancient lands are sincere. It will be regrettable if harm comes to them."

Jiena listened intently. She knew of whom Kiserian spoke.

"We cannot allow them to leave," said the chieftain from Calem. "I agree the situation is grave. We must not risk all in our land but show compassion to those who are sincere."

"We have two matters before us," said Sade's chieftain. "To decide what to do with those who are here and what to do in the event others come."

"Oh, my friend, it is not in the event. They will come as certain as the moon and sun," said Sahur's chieftain.

Another chieftain asked the king, "What if we let them leave? Then we only have to deal with those who will try to come."

The king considered the question and said, "We will solve this problem for all times. No one will ever come again."

The temple was silent. The king continued, "We have ways to stop them. They will fight with weapons. We will use our powers."

They decided on a plan, and when the meeting ended Meleke met with the keeper. Like his famous ancestor, Abayomi the shepherd, the keeper's smooth, earthy face and wise eyes calmed those who engaged him.

Meleke talked with the keeper in the garden of weeping myrrh trees that flourished close to the palace. The keeper's delicate profile was silhouetted against the scenery as he listened to the options for dealing with the trespassers.

Chinua the keeper was also chief protector of the kingdom, and the people had learned not to underestimate his gentle ways. He had punished several citizens for crimes against the land, and the families of some of those citizens never saw them again.

The keeper was a stabilizing force and had delicately balanced the wishes of the chieftains of the various realms with those of the chieftains in the central office of King Meleke. He was a skilful diplomat.

On this misty day, the keeper listened to the king in silence.

"No blood must be shed in Ashaise," said Meleke. "No one must be allowed to enter, and no more visitors must be allowed to leave. They cannot live amongst us, and Ashaise must not be a sanctuary, for we know they are of many schemes. Any words of friendship or loyalty will be like air that surrounds carrion. They will bide the many dawns and watch for the moment we sleep after the sun sets, then strike like zande at the rabbit's burrow. Their minds think of the source of our strength. If we yield then we will feel the coldness of their weapons as the great forefathers felt fire from steel. Stop them on the other side."

The keeper looked to the mountains. He knew the king had something else on his mind, but there was no need for other words. He looked into Meleke's eyes and said, "Their spirits speak to each other, and the cords of their beings run beyond the periphery of our reality."

The king looked at the mountain and again at the keeper. "We must reach Jiena's chi with our collective might and try to break the cord before it tightens around the man from across the sun."

The keeper smiled and rested his right hand on the king's shoulder. Meleke looked into his eyes, then put his hand over the keeper's. He embraced him briefly. The keeper went on his way.

※

The expedition group returned to their dwelling area and contemplated the situation. They wondered what had happened to Timothy and James. Neither of them had come back, and although the king had a gun belonging to one of them, he gave no information on their whereabouts.

Chris and Allan walked a distance beyond the gardens to the lake, where they sat and talked about the dilemma.

"What do you think our prospects are for leaving here soon?" Chris asked. "Do you think they'll allow us to leave?"

"Let us speak to the chieftain of this realm and tell him again we want to leave, although I'm not sure about the prospects. I imagine they've already decided what to do with us. Meleke was not pleased about whatever happened. They used the word 'betray,' so we must assume James and Timothy did something stupid. The manner in which the king showed us the gun suggests the Ashais' protectors captured them."

Chris and Allan had to find out, and decided they should first talk to Aatum, who, like all other Ashais, was friendly and willing to explain his people's way of life. He had taken the visitors to various celebrations, introduced them to his family and friends, and arranged concerts for their enjoyment. One of the most memorable occasions for the explorers was the hunters' game.

As usual Aatum was never far away, and in a matter of minutes he stood with Chris and Allan by the lake. They wasted no time and asked him about the whereabouts of Timothy and James, to which he responded in a serious tone, "One rests in the arms of Apti, and the other went on the sun's rays."

"Apti," Allan repeated. He was more depressed than when the two mercenaries had disappeared because it was clear now the gorilla had taken one of them.

"Who went in Apti's habitat and what will become of him?" Chris asked.

Aatum looked across the lake as if he had lost himself in the water. "Apti and his family do not share their quarry. There was a time when they took the lions, but no more, and they do not interfere with humans unless threatened. The one called Timothy went with Apti."

They all looked out at the lake and saw fishers bringing in the day's catch; families and lovers in small rowboats enjoyed the evening, laughing and chattering among the cackle of wild fowl and the chirping of birds. Pink flamingos colored the sky as they flew to swampy plains over the mountain.

Chris and Allan were somber. They felt a cold wind and heard the sounds of leaves, which made them nervous. They felt Aatum's eyes penetrate their minds, their souls, and they knew he was aware of their thoughts.

The calm Chris and Allan felt in the presence of the people morphed into the realization that the Ashais had evolved to a higher level of consciousness—a level where these people were in connection with another dimension of existence. In isolation, the Ashais pursued a pastoral life and had learned to survive. They understood the natural world and lived in a loving relationship with her, sensing, feeling, and hearing the vibrations of the universe. They took from her only that which was necessary for their consumption and replaced what they took. The Ashais regulated the population by teaching the rhythm of the body. Mind had conquered heart, so they had exceptional control of their emotions, passions, and desires.

There were no animals held in captivity for personal pleasure. The laws of the natural world governed the land's populations. Animals were sacred to the Ashais, and to kill one was a serious offense unless it was necessary to protect humans.

Allan was tall by normal standards, but he looked up to Aatum, who stood nearly eight feet.

"How soon can we leave, and how can we do it?" Allan asked.

"We know your people will come because the one called James is with them. The realms decided you cannot leave with knowledge of us, but you cannot stay."

"James has knowledge of Ashaise, and images."

"We have his things," Aatum replied. "He will try but will not be able to hurt us."

CHAPTER 16

On returning to inform the others of the latest developments, Allan stopped as he saw Jiena approaching the butterfly garden. Chris chided him and told him their situation was too serious to be distracted by the woman.

"Don't worry, Chris, I'll be back shortly," Allan replied, then followed Jiena's path through the archway leading to the garden. A short distance beyond the poinsettia trees, he saw Jiena walking slowly, in the manner of a person deep in thought. He saw Matai not far away from her, and while Allan continued in Jiena's direction with some unease he knew no harm would befall him if it were not her wish.

Since seeing her on that fateful day when he had arrived on Ashaise, Allan had thought of her. His mind often strayed to the reality of his world, to the women he liked and his girlfriend Germaine, but to his discomfort Jiena would always enter the vision. He felt acute guilt over this betrayal.

Jiena mystified him with her uncomplicated yet sophisticated aura, like a butterfly that lingered at leisure on a sunflower, but also like a swan guarding her cygnets. She captivated and confused him. As a worldly person grounded in historical as well as modern-day realities, his emotions and self-doubt surprised him. Emotionally he was in an unrecognisable zone and an extremely difficult, life-threatening situation. He felt conflicted, and he questioned his rationality. Intellectually he struggled to balance his commitment to the goals of the expedition, his loyalty to his friends and family, and his encroaching affinity with Ashaise. It was not only Jiena; it was his desire to become part of the community. What had happened to his aspirations virtually overnight was shattering to his self-image. He wondered whether he could be confident and resolute about anything again.

He stopped to admire her. Her swanlike, bare neck flowed to her well-defined shoulders, and he could see her sinuous, delicate body through her almost diaphanous clothing.

She heard him approaching but did not turn. He went closer to her and whispered her name. She did not look at him. He then reached for her hand, which she did not withdraw, but looked down at his hand on hers. She raised her moon-sized eyes with questioning sadness.

A ball in Allan's stomach dropped, and he thought he heard the thud. He spoke her name again, and she responded by lifting her other hand and stroking the side of his face as lightly as a feather.

Abruptly she withdrew both hands and turned away.

"Why did you betray us?"

"What do you mean?"

"Your people had no respect. They went to steal our lifeline, to disturb Kriziantu, to plunder and defile her sacred home.

They tried to kill the protectors and leave her bare, naked. We know what you want. You want more than what the universe provides for you. In the past you destroyed the bridge upon which we walked and shattered the lives of our children. The healing powers of the bird's egg only last as long as we nurture it. We are the bird, and it is us."

"Jiena, I am sorry. We didn't know James and Timothy had tried to leave, but I understand your sense of betrayal."

"Your desire is no different from theirs. You want the bird."

"Yes, we desire the remedy that can heal millions of people in our world, but stealing is not an option. We do not know where we are. Ashaise is like Earth in many respects—your ecosystem is not different from our own except everything is almost twice the dimensions. You live a more balanced, simpler, and richer life."

"We are in the same dimension as your home. Ashaise lies within its own shield in the sphere of Earth. Sometimes the day is long, and the moon god hides the sun god every twenty nine moon days. When that happens, anything on our highest point may go with the sun."

"You mean you can come to my home."

"Sometimes, or it could go with all the other moons and suns floating on light for eternity."

Allan's mind raced, but Jiena was calm. He reached for her hand again, and since she knew of his sincerity she went closer to him and rested her head on his shoulder. He held her close. There was a faint scent of rain in her hair. The dark-brown, soft, kinky locks framed her face and reached below her shoulders.

Allan's passion soared. He stroked and kissed her head and forehead. She nestled in his arms. The shrubbery rustled, and they were conscious that they were not alone. The keeper stood still. He looked at them with an unreadable face. In a quiet voice, Jiena asked Allan to leave. Allan looked at the keeper and went through the arch to his dwelling. His emotions reeled.

CHAPTER 17

Upon his return Allan found the team gathered outside Chris's living area. The mood was somber. They spoke in hushed tones, and the consensus was that self-protection and the retention of as much research materials as possible were priorities. Since it was very likely that James had returned to Kenya, their chances of escape were good, and all of them agreed the way out was the way they had come. There were sufficient guns and ammunition to fight their way out if necessary, but they had to be confident about the day and time when the shield would break. The two remaining security members, David Cazeau and Joe Dodd, urged that they should take a chick or an egg, or blood samples.

"It's not selfishness. It's a matter of saving lives." Joe said.

The notion was anathema to Chris, who, quite out of character, slammed his fist into Joe's jaw. The unexpected action shocked the group into silence. Allan walked in on the tense situation.

Chris's sunburnt face was crimson with anger—an emotion he rarely displayed. It was not only the absurdity of the suggestion but the dishonest actions of the other two, which compounded a difficult situation. It was the recklessness and selfishness that had cost Timothy McIntosh his life. The rest of the explorers' lives were now threatened.

They all went to their respective places, and not long afterward Cazeau began to play his guitar in the quiet of the late evening.

Chris and Allan conversed about their options. They had a keen understanding of the people, and no longer had to guess what the shadows were. They believed the only solution was to negotiate with the king on the basis that they would try to deter any further trespassing on Ashaise. It would be a challenge, and the prospects for success were slim.

The Ashais knew what the group's options were and had more than likely witnessed their recent behavior. Aatum was always a few meters away, and the keeper kept watch, just as he had followed Timothy and James's movement into the cave. The keeper knew what the outcome of an attempted escape would have been but had not anticipated that James may have successfully crossed over.

Chris had never seen Allan so tormented. He saw his struggle and understood his love for Jiena. That, perhaps, was the biggest threat to a satisfactory agreement. Or, Chris thought, it could save them. His mind raced from one problem to the next. If James returned, would his attempt be limited to a rescue? *How would rescuers get out anyway?* Chris asked himself.

Chris and Allan were aware that James sought gold and marketable artifacts, and he was not the type of person to miss an opportunity for fame and fortune.

As Chris thought about the challenges, Allan broke the silence. "Chris, I want Jiena in my life. What I feel is no fleeting infatuation. I love her."

"You don't have to tell me. But you are, uncharacteristically, impractical. You're not just in plain, old love—you're over the fence. We've just been told we cannot leave, and in the same breath that we cannot stay, which at the moment I can only interpret one way. Our goals right now should be a safe crossover to home and prevention of an invasion from a rescue mission. I understand how you feel, but you have to be realistic. Even if we can get out of here, you cannot take Jiena with you. What about this project?"

"I am committed to completing it." Allan looked at Chris. He knew Chris was also in turmoil because of what their long years of friendship meant to both of them. For eighteen years they had been together, from university to the Army and through subsequent expeditions. They had coauthored books, lectured, and now they were in Ashaise. Chris's marriage had ended after one year because his ex-wife had accused him of spending more time digging up ancient crap with his "cave twin" than with her. Overlapping emotions tugged at them.

Chris shrugged his shoulder and shook his head in frustration. "Look, man, you're not making sense. The woman has you so disoriented you don't know your ass from your head. It's foolish to think about having her, wanting to stay, and continuing to work with me all at the same time."

"We'll work on the project together and finish it. That I promise."

"How? Tell me how. You wouldn't get my e-mails here." Chris glared at Allan, who chuckled.

"You never know. I'm serious, Chris. I have to figure out a way. If only I could convince Meleke to let me return. There are always options in life, and sometimes none is good. In this case none affords me the opportunity to be in all the places I wish to be, or to be with all the ones I love, so there has to be a choice. I don't mean to sound callous. I love my parents more than my very life, and I treasure your friendship." Allan choked up. "I love you. We've been together for so many years; it's difficult to imagine life without you. That will be the hardest thing for me. It's only a dream to wish you and all the others will always be in my future."

"You speak in riddles, and at worst like a mad man." Chris threw a bag at Allan's head. Allan caught it and threw it back. "What are the chances of negotiating our way out of here?" asked Chris.

"Bad. I doubt an invasion would be successful because Ashaise lies within in a band that is a protective shield. It is within Earth's sphere but not on Earth—Nehsi and Jiena said as much. Within the band this land cannot be detected, and when the shield breaks it's for less than nanoseconds, so signals aren't picked up. Remember the map we saw in the temple? It showed a strange spot on Earth. If, as they say, the location is correct, and I have no reason to disbelieve Jiena, it would account for the long days at times, the midnight sun, and the frequency of eclipses. It appears that around the time of the eclipses there is a minute tilt of the

Earth in relation to the Sun, and anything at a high point close to the equator could be thrown off the edge either way. This is the Ashais' explanation. The tales about people going up the mountain and never returning sounded credible."

"Can we convince them we will not return and there will be no invasion to take the crystal bird?"

"I don't think so. They won't believe us. Their distrust didn't come about only because of what Timothy and James did. That just reinforced it. Embedded in their history is the story of the young Maasai warriors who slavers captured sometime in the fifteenth century. From the drawings and the timeline, the slavers were Arabian and Portuguese. The distrust is engrained in the Ashais' psyche and culture. Their physical features, language and art suggest they are not only descendants of the Maasai but also Samburu, Yoruba, and Dogon people, all of whom probably fled for their lives and took shelter in mountain caves."

Allan continued, "They believe our expedition is sincere and know we came here by accident. It's in their minds that outsiders are likely to be traitors because that's their history—a history of betrayal by tribes who were their neighbors, and by foreigners. It's the history of the continent of Africa and epitomizes the plight of indigenous people everywhere. I suggest we seek an audience with the king, but I want to be with Jiena if that is her desire."

They walked and talked about various aspects of the culture. At the early age of five years, children learned primary meditation techniques but were just as rambunctious and mischievous as healthy children anywhere else.

The land was lavish in the variety of species it fed. The people enjoyed life and valued body adornments, silks, and crafts.

Since the early Ashais were from different kingdoms and tribes but predominantly Maasai, they had worshipped many ancient gods. The god they recognized as superior to all other forces was the sun god, creator of the sun, moon, and water. They did not worship a deity in the traditional sense of devotion to a divine spirit. Their sun god was divine, and the energies of the moon and water were also deemed to be divine forces. The people revered the sun, moon, and water because these elements sustained and regulated the lives of all things in the universe.

Aatum told Chris and Allan that all life had originated as molecules in water, and some washed ashore in multiple places and divided into cells. He said animals and plants were brothers of man because all had evolved from the same energy source. This was the reason why they celebrated every new moon and the first sun of spring, and bathed their newborns in streams and lakes. Aatum promised to take them to another temple where they would see images of creation and evolution. He told the archaeologists life existed throughout the universe. The statement puzzled them, and they looked forward to the visit.

Deep commitment to the community and tradition were evident in Ashaise, as seen in the marriage ceremony. The Ashais did not accept a doctrine of heaven and hell and a god that bestowed mercy and punishment. Good and evil had to do with how well a person controlled his or her thoughts and desires, which motivated evil or compassionate deeds.

Early induction of children into the school of critical thinking was compulsory. They continued higher levels of this type of training progressively, from one stage of development to another.

"You realize, of course, they believe in both creation and evolution," said Chris. "The latter they believe is a process of the former, but certainly not in the sense that we evolved from Australopithecus or an extinct primate. They believe the first human cell was of a distinct genus, similar to all first cells that mutated over time. Who knows? Maybe it's the missing link in our origin, and it's why they believe there's life on other planets."

"Now I know who the mad one is around here," responded Allan.

"Why you don't jump in the frigging lake?"

For Chris and Allan, Ashaise was a laboratory in which to immerse themselves. They had no delusions about the might of the people—and the fate of any invader.

※

In the garden of butterflies, the keeper looked at Jiena with fatherly concern.

"They must go with the currents, Jiena."

"I know Allan is sincere and will do no harm. We're descendants of those the sun god brought here. King Mbtani and Queen Eliye came with the sun. Allan came with the sun, and he can be one of us. I think that is his intent."

"Have you tried the powers to overcome this feeling?"

"It has nothing to do with powers, so I have not tried," said Jiena. "I do not want to overcome my feelings for him. I see in his eyes wisdom. In his voice I hear the call of my being. I feel in his touch the feather of Kriziantu, and he breathes the strength of the mountains. Chinua, I do not want to drown in the deep well of my love, and if father banishes him to the currents of the sun, then I have no choice but to swim in the well of my mind. Father has said these visitors cannot stay, yet they cannot leave. I know what that means, but I ask for mercy for them."

Jiena got up from the marble bench and stood near the poinsettia tree. She turned and looked at the keeper. "Our great ancestors had mercy on Mbtani, who brought the strength of Matai and the healing of Kriziantu. They built upon foundations of antiquity and integrated their wealth. He showed compassionate strength, and they loved him. We became the Ashais. I know and will feel the warrior spirit should the visitors bring others to take away our lives. We have powers to stop them without shedding Ashais' blood. Chinua, accepting Allan does not mean the end of us, for it may be the natural path to continued development."

Jiena adored her family, and she was close to her brother Nehsi. Her parents respected her independence. In fact they had little choice once she'd made up her mind on a matter. Most often the only person who could get her to change her decision was the keeper, so if an issue arose her family was likely to seek his intervention.

"Are you saying we must welcome others if we are to survive?" the keeper asked. "That's what your lips are saying, but it's not what I read in your heart."

"You taught me to be wise, so you know my thoughts. I know that to trust outsiders could mean the end of this existence. If we're too generous, this life will be gone. We will not be the same if we share because we too will have to be gracious and accept some of the ways of other people. Our children and their children will become different, as we have become different from our ancestors."

The princess paused as if she were thinking about the implications of other visitors arriving in her homeland. She took a deep breath and paced a few steps. "I know we risk the extinction of Kriziantu. She cannot produce enough for all peoples of the world, and no one can reproduce her. While we have diversity in our land and much contentment and happiness, our powers cannot stop our feelings of love. We can only use those powers to control our desires. Allan feels the lust in his breast. So do I. That is the natural way of life."

"My little Jiena, how much you have grown like the mountain. I do not want to see you grieve. I do not want to see you like a ghost in the forest. I will be there for you when your tears fall like rain on the leaves, and I will be there when you laugh like the spring breeze, so go and talk with your family."

Jiena kissed the keeper on his forehead.

"I know you will always be there," she said. "You remember how you used to take me up into the mountains, where we sat on the Seat of God, near the crags where the klipspringers gave birth? We sang songs from the old days, and you told me stories about the lions, gorillas, and Kriziantu. I treasure those memories. One day, you will tell my children stories."

He looked at her and felt a deep ache. He smiled and kissed her forehead before she turned and left for her home. He looked in her direction long after she had gone before walking toward the mountain.

CHAPTER 18

Jennifer and the dean sat with the American consul in Nairobi and had just finished coffee when James entered, looking very confident. He had an air of importance and expectation.

After inquiring about the health of James's colleagues, the others immediately proceeded to obtain from him a detailed description of the location of Ashaise beyond what had already been said publicly. When he was through, they were no wiser with respect to the location other than believing it must have been in a north-westerly region off the summit of Mt. Kilimanjaro.

Jennifer mentioned the search-and-rescue mission and expected James would agree to be part of it. He was eager to join, and to attend all briefings. James had one request: that they allowed a botanist and an ecologist from the global pharmaceutical company Synthesis to accompany the mission. James assured the others that these people would not be at risk since they engaged regularly in research on that continent, as well as in the Amazon rain forest.

"That's a matter not entirely in our hands, as it is subject to approval of the Tanzanian government and the leader of the mission," said Hackshaw. "The leader will be Major Raymond Johnson, an American who's been stationed in Kenya for the past five years."

The American consul had told them the Kenyan security authorities gave permission for another person to join the mission. His name was Brother Caftie from the Church of New Life Missionaries. Caftie had climbed Kilimanjaro on more than one occasion.

The governments of Tanzania and Kenya had allowed three other people to climb who were not connected with the mission: a biologist from a German pharmaceutical company, and two researchers who represented the respective governments.

There was another group that no one expected. They had entered Tanzania as environment conservationists. Their goal was to prevent, if they could, any attempts to interfere with the mountain's natural environment, which was already under threat. They had worked previously with the government on a rain forest restoration project and were permitted to monitor activities on the mountain.

With the sudden influx of disparate mountain climbers, media reporters, and opportunists, the Tanzanian and Kenyan governments decided to shut down temporarily the operators providing mountain-climbing services to tourists. They closed all entrance gates leading to the summit.

Although James's story was dismissed by many, old reports were resurrected about disappearances on the mountain, fire and smoke, and an ancient god in the form of a large bird. The local people speculated; rumors and theories were widespread. It was not long before the mountain assumed mythical and sacred proportions.

Major Johnson's team gathered at the gate of the Machame Route, which had been used by the expedition members nearly five weeks earlier. Raymond advised the Kenyan and Tanzanian authorities that he would not assume responsibility for other groups and hoped they would not get in the way of his mission.

They took off at the break of dawn with the intention to reach the summit at Uruhu Peak within five days at most. Raymond had a team fit to cope with the challenges and unpredictable weather conditions on a difficult route. He did not think acclimatization time was needed. The morning was sixty-four degrees Fahrenheit, which was not unusual for late April. The temperature was likely to plunge lower than twenty degrees as they advanced to the summit at approximately 19,300 feet.

In reflecting on the team members, Raymond figured one or two might experience some distress. He would monitor them for signs of hypothermia and breathing problems. It was the main reason why he thought it inadvisable for the authorities to have included other parties, regardless of how experienced they were. His priority was finding the explorers, and he had no time for anything else. He assumed unfit climbers would be forced to abandon their attempts to reach the summit.

The noises of the forest below faded as the group climbed. The first two days of ascent along a steep path through the rain forest were uneventful, but notable for their sightings of colobus monkeys, the odd warthog, and a variety of birds including iridescent sunbirds. The breathtaking climb through highlands, desert, icy rain, snow meadows, and treacherous cliffs was both exhilarating and exhausting, but the endgame was in sight. The warmth of their tents on cold nights provided an opportunity to discuss with James the place he called Ashaise. His description of the bird fascinated the botanist and ecologist, both of whom felt an unease they could not explain.

James's enthusiasm when he spoke of his experiences in Ashaise was infectious. This keenness gave credence to his reports. His detailed description of flora and fauna convinced the scientists he had been to an unusual and exceptionally beautiful place. He did not appear to be a gullible person; he had a military background and was a hardened adventurer. The scientists reserved any skeptical comments or questions.

The leader of the mission was familiar with the climb and knew there were unexplored caves. However he was skeptical about the existence of an undiscovered civilization. He considered the possibility of a Maasai group living in a cave off a ridge plain close to the summit, but with the heavy traffic on the mountain, detection was likely.

His mind was mostly occupied with thoughts of the members of the expedition whose lives were in danger, and what it would take to free them. He felt a chill that had nothing to do with the falling temperature. He did not want to fight people who had not been a threat to anyone.

Raymond was a practical man. If any tribe or hostile group existed the strategy would be to negotiate a safe release of the men. Based on previous conversations with

James, Raymond's concern was getting out of the strange land. He had taken the precaution, and made arrangements for American troops to be stationed lower down the mountain.

"You said their lives are in danger. If that's so, what would it take to free them? I hope their god wants peace. Would they negotiate?" he asked.

"No," responded James.

The climbers had not yet encountered any other group. There were several well-known routes to approach the summit of Kilimanjaro, and Raymond surmised that other groups could have taken another route. He hoped the mountain would prove too difficult and the others would be forced to turn back.

Raymond's team resumed climbing at a pace only the fittest and most daring could have endured. By the third day they were at the lava cliff. By mid-morning igneous rock that many aeons ago had flowed like treacle down steep ridges contrasted starkly against the blue sky.

The mission's members all turned their heads upward and watched a white-neck raven with an extraordinary wingspan cruising by. She did not flutter in her passage. She flew up and away into the clouds in a manner that seemed calculated, leaving her watchers wondering where she was going.

They climbed through dense forest with mossy beards, fungi, and algae that thrived in a symbiotic relationship with vegetation and rocks beneath a green canopy. Through scrubland and desert, they continued up the obsidian-like surface.

Barely two hours of a new day had passed when mist crawled over them. The sunny, crisp sky turned suddenly to a powdered screen, ushering in a snowstorm. In the white-out conditions, the group heard Raymond advising them to stay close to each other. He led the team to a temporary shelter, and they remained there for several hours until the storm ceased. The weather worsened to a hail tempest, and icy conditions made climbing a death wish. A thunderous rainstorm took its turn.

Raymond wondered about Brother Caftie, who must have been on a regular workout plan. Caftie did not have the stature of an average missionary, who typically had a less ruddy complexion and tended to be more on the plump side. He was about six feet three inches tall, well built, and his pleasant face was burnt. Raymond looked at him with squinted eyes and wondered whether Caftie was an inform-ant for the American government apart from being a mis-sionary with a loyal flock. He summed up Caftie as one who had more than some familiarity with the mountain. Caftie would pose no problem when coping with treacherous conditions.

The storm caused an unpredicted and unfortunate delay that gave the group of researchers an opportunity to catch up with Raymond's mission, much to Raymond's irritation. Fragile weather patterns were such that conditions could be entirely different every few thousand feet.

Mt. Kilimanjaro sits on the borders of both countries, and it occurred to Raymond that discoveries on the moun-tain, may result in disputes which could easily turn into disaster. He feared problems between the two sets of local military men. Raymond understood why both governments chose to send their country's military, and researchers to represent them.

Raymond worried about the tense relationship between representatives of the pharmaceutical companies, and the possibility of an international problem. The explorers were of different nationalities—American, British and Kenyan. Raymond decided that he would focus solely on his job which was to find, and bring the explorers safely down the mountain.

Not long after the storm ended, the merry group of Eco Savers were on the same ridge as the others. Raymond rolled his eyes toward heaven and asked whoever was up there why these things happened to him.

CHAPTER 19

Chris, Robert, Springer, and the two remaining security men—Joe and Cazeau—were in the area of Allan's dwelling, where they had just consumed a morning meal of fruit, nuts, bread, and tea. By their calculation it was Monday, May 3.

It was another lovely morning. Sounds from the flowering forests caused them to remain silent and savor nature's grandeur. It appeared as though every tree had blossoms. Allan looked across at the mountain, where the evergreens were dusted sunrise white with mist curling through the lush foliage. There was a dramatic vista of light in the valley. Swishing leaves flashed earth colors under the chatoyant eyes of Ashaise's morning sun as if signalling joy with all creatures that occupied the space.

With the weight of the team's predicament on his mind, and with love for the princess, Allan did not join in on Chris's light banter. He threw a handful of nuts at Chris's head, then sauntered off to the lake. Allan knew he had to meet with King Meleke in an effort to secure their release, and eventually broach the subject of Jiena with him. Allan was not sure how to do so without complicating things. He was confident her affection for him was much more than infatuation. He was not sure what her thoughts were with respect to the future. Leaving Ashaise was, more than likely, not an option for her, Allan thought. In any event it would be necessary for him to return home to say goodbye to his family and complete the project. But other than that, Allan had no doubt where he wanted to be.

Allan sat on the ground and picked up a handful of moist soil. His mind strayed to his travels, exploration, and childhood days, and the relationship he enjoyed with Chris. He thought of home, when he and his girlfriend would sit on the balcony of his parents' rambling house discussing his next expedition. On bright nights they counted stars, laughed at their folly, and named the planets to each other.

On this morning he wondered what Earth would look like if he could see it from Ashaise. He gently dug, scraped the soil, and saw planets in grains that slipped through his fingers. The grains were tiny pulsations of life feeding greedily, and there was something innate, familiar, yet tribal in them—raw energy; ancestral flight stretching back to genesis. He smelled decaying leaves, rotting fruit, and wood on the primordial breath of the earth. All around him was renewal. A green shoot pushed itself through the birth canal of a seed on the garden floor. He became aware of large slugs that happily slimed away. Earthworms that were burrowed in the moist matter discreetly slithered to their dwellings and, he thought, a convenient grave.

Allan's mind filtered back to the garden at his parents' home. He could smell and see pesticide on the plants. He imagined, like a child, that worms heard when peopled walked on their roofs, and their babies in cocoons cried when poison penetrated their burrows. He thought of the creepy creatures dying. The dirt stuck to his skin. How complex life was. He inhaled the sweet fragrance of the shrubbery and picked up a tiny, dried seed that he buried under a light layer of soil. Would he still be there when it germinated and burst out to grow and flourish? Enough dreaming; he had procrastinated enough, and it was time to see the king.

He returned to discuss the next move with the team. Springer remained silent; Joe had one comment: "How we leave is not dependent on the Ashais' permission. They will not let us leave. We have adequate weapons to protect ourselves and get out of here."

Joe felt their approach to the leaders of Ashais should be from a position of strength. The Ashais respected courage, so the group could not cringe at their feet. The Ashais were not as peaceful as they appeared to be.

Chris told the others that while he respected the views of all members of the expedition, Joe's strategy was not likely to succeed. Further Chris did not think that by seeking dialogue and negotiation they would appear weak. Rather it would show respect. However, if all else failed, he would be prepared to resort to different initiatives. The explorers were comfortable and had fresh food to eat every day. They decided Allan would seek a meeting that day.

As the family sat on cushions around a low, round table, Jiena remained silent most of the time. Her mother glanced at her now and then and noticed her daughter's face was sad and stressed. Of course Teye was aware of the situation, but, like her husband and son, decided she would not say anything. They all knew Jiena would talk to them when she was ready.

Jiena was oblivious of the family's conversation. She focused on the mountain through the large window. When the meal was over, she broached the subject.

"You know what I want to speak about, and there's no point in waiting for the sun to set. I expect Allan will not be harmed. I understand the threat to Ashaise, but he is not a threat. Allan, his friend Chris, and the one named Robert will not hurt us."

"Jiena, we know that to be true, but there are others with misguided intentions," said the king. "We have to treat them all the same. We do not want to cause you pain, but you know none of them can stay here. We cannot permit them to leave lest they return with others. We expect the one who got through the barrier will return to do harm. I'm sure they will stay together. They will not betray their own, but us."

"I thought you were going to marry Sahure," said her mother. "It's what your father and I have been waiting for. And not just us, Jiena. Ashaise is waiting for the union. These strangers have been here for a short time. We do not have knowledge of Allan's life. What is his intention to those to whom he belongs?"

The queen left her seat and stood behind her daughter. She placed both hands on Jiena's shoulders and rested her cheek on Jiena's head.

"Think of Ashaise," the queen said. "That is all we ask of you. The strangers must leave at the next hiding of the sun. We will spare them physical harm. They will be on the invisible ship on which others have sailed across the open space."

At these words all were silent. They did not underestimate Jiena's resolve.

"I must follow the voice that speaks within me," Jiena replied, "for I have to live with myself. I will not abandon you for my own needs. These are not two irreconcilable desires. Not at all. I love Sahure, but how I love him is not the same as my feelings for Allan. Sahure and I grew up as friends, and he could be my brother, although not the same as my Nehsi."

Sahure was the son of the chieftain of Sahur and an outstanding protector. Citizens of that realm respected the young man, who had gained a reputation among the people of many other realms for his victories in sports. His relationship with Jiena had progressed over the years from childhood, and he believed Jiena would one day be his princess. He felt it was time for him to take his woman and deliver their children to the arms of the kingdom. Their union would be no ordinary ceremony; after all he was the son of a chieftain, and Jiena was the daughter of the king. It would be the greatest event since the ceremony of Jiena's parents.

Sahure had asked Jiena to be his wife. She had not refused his proposal, but said she needed time. He decided to tell his family and friends he had proposed to the princess. After Sahure's boasting about the proposal, there were expectations throughout the kingdom that they would marry—a foregone conclusion and logical consequence of their friendship.

Meleke now stood up and walked to the window. He paused before he went back to Jiena and her mother.

"We must put Ashaise first," he said. "I know you have the strength of mind to overcome the fact that Allan has to sail. You may wish to sail with him. It will be painful and difficult to forget. We will be forever sad, so please spare us the pain of separation from you."

Nehsi rose. "There may be another solution to this. I cannot bear the thought of my sister sailing on the invisible ship. I remember when we were children. I pulled her hair and threw a heap of dried leaves over her. I pushed her in the frog pond as punishment for spoiling the hunt with my friends and stealing my food. How much I would like to do that now! She's still my little sister to love and protect. If this man is sincere, he will sacrifice for her. I suggest that he stays on Ashaise but cannot be with you until we satisfy ourselves that he will forsake all ties with those he has left behind. The others can sail the skies."

"Nehsi, I know you mean well," said Jiena. "But no one can ever sever all ties with those they love if indeed it be love. The memories will always be there. If I ever decide not to see you all again, do you think I could sever my love for you? Although you sometimes make me mad, big brother, I could not stop loving you. I must shape my own destiny— that is our way. I will not be selfish and put my desires before the safety of my precious land. I do not believe Allan would allow his friends to be harmed. He would want to know what will happen to them. The same way I will not sacrifice my people, he will not sacrifice his."

"That's why they must not be allowed to be a threat to us in the future," said Meleke. "I offered a way of compromise."

"But Allan must consider the options for his friends. They may not be a threat," responded Jiena.

"Jiena, come with me." Teye held her by the elbow, and they left father and son to work out a solution. As they left the room, Aatum was waiting to see Meleke with a message from Allan who requested a meeting. The king agreed.

CHAPTER 20

Atum escorted Allan to the meeting in the Temple of the Sun, where Meleke stood by the marble column in the Sanctuary of Memories. They greeted each other.

"What requests do you bring?" Meleke asked.

"I have two requests," Allan replied with courage and strength of purpose.

"What are they?"

"I want to discuss our return home. The second request does not have anything to do with my colleagues."

"That may be so, stranger, but I am certain both matters are equally complex. I want you to tell me all that is on your mind."

Allan had no choice but to get to the matter of Jiena, much to his discomfort, although his demeanor did not show this. He knew his relationship with her was a sensitive issue, and he did not want to jeopardize his prospects for getting the team safely out of Ashaise.

"Since you insist, my king, it is about your daughter." Allan saw the surprise in the king's eyes when he said the words "my king."

"I want your daughter."

Meleke smiled and did what was his custom when faced with a challenging and audacious situation: he looked his audience in the eyes, turned, and walked away slowly as he contemplated a response. The chieftains had made a decision to which he had agreed, and it was not his intention to take action that would be tantamount to a betrayal of their wishes. Meleke admitted to himself that he liked the man standing in front of him.

This was a predicament. Jiena had complicated matters. Meleke wanted to see his daughter marry and have children. Although the king liked Sahure, he was not pleased that Sahure told everybody about the proposal to Jiena before she had discussed it with her family. Meleke thought about the disappointment in the days to come if his daughter did not marry the son of the chieftain of Sahur.

On reflection King Meleke realized his daughter had not shown the usual enthusiasm of a person in love and about to become a wife. He did not want to disappoint Sahure or his people for a man who had arrived in their land only a few moons ago, but the stranger had forced him to rethink Jiena's position. After all it was the Ashais' way for young people to choose partners. As Meleke reflected, he could not recall any time when his daughter had flirted with anyone or discussed with her parents how she felt about the future. He knew Jiena had much affection for Sahure, but Jiena had not spoken of him the way other young women chatted about the handsome men who gave them flirtatious looks and beautiful adornments.

King Meleke looked out the window. He knew he would not cause his daughter to enter into a relationship if she could not commit fully to it. He smiled because when he first had met Teye, he had told his father he'd wanted her to be his wife, and nothing would stop him from taking her.

His position was clear. When it came to Jiena's future, it was only her perspective that was important. Nevertheless he could not yield to Allan's wishes. The security of Ashaise was the urgent matter at hand, and not his daughter's love affair.

⚹

Meleke turned to Allan. "Do you always make decisions without using the powers of reason? You know this is not a suitable request. My daughter needs time to think about the matter."

"I can give her all the time she wants. I will wait."

They eyed each other. Two wills, two minds spoke the same language silently. Allan lowered his head out of respect. The king said to himself, *This man has guts Jiena admires. He can protect her. He would adore her as I adore Teye.*

"Stranger—" the king began.

"My name is Allan Cline."

"Cline, Allan, my first responsibility is to keep Ashaise safe as my ancestors have done." Meleke looked toward the ceiling's reliefs. "I cannot allow your people to return to their place. If I do many others will come. Would they not? I can only do this: I will let you all return home safely on the condition that you ensure no one returns to Ashaise."

"What are you saying, King? Am I to understand you would allow all of us to leave if I guarantee no one will return?"

"Yes. We will destroy all your treasures."

"What do you mean by *treasures*?"

"The images you have collected and other treasures. You will return with only your garments. You can keep your weapons. We have no use for such things, but if any of you try to harm us with those evil tools, there will be grief."

"What about Jiena?"

"Did she commit to going with you?"

"No, we didn't speak much, but I don't want to take her from her home and family. I want to stay."

"Why do you want to stay? I hope my daughter is not the only reason."

"I would think she's worthy of being the only reason."

"You are arrogant, stranger. Why do you want to turn your back on your world and spend the rest of your life here? Surely Ashaise is very small for you to explore, and your world has more need of you than we do."

"My king, I cannot separate Jiena from Ashaise. My love for her is my love for Ashaise. It's where I want to live my life, share my knowledge in a way that enriches a people with whom I identify, and satisfy whatever your quest is. No, I am not turning my back on my world. I'm merely extending it to a place I wish to be. I want to become all I can become here. There is much we can learn from each other. I want my children to grow up here."

"You speak passionately—convincingly."

Allan looked at him. He saw not only a king but a father. Yes, Meleke reminded him of his father, the bulwark of his community and family. When Allan's father was a young man he had participated in many civil rights marches during long, smoldering summers, leaving indentations on the scorched path of antipathy. In Allan's mind images flashed of his childhood days, when he had sat on his father's lap and listened to stories of the struggle of his people for a place in a land of promise. His father would always end with the words "remember, son, education and commitment to your goal will take you to the stars." The thought of his parents tore him apart, but he knew what his goal was. He knew they would tell him to go after it—to stay in Ashaise with the woman. He now looked at the man who held his life in the balance.

Meleke respected the man standing in front of him. Allan's engaging face had scruffy stubble from days of sloppy shaving, but the man had the courage of his conviction and was forthright and knowledgeable, with the temperament more of a leader and a warrior than a teacher. The king looked at the strong face and unkempt hair, the rumpled, white shirt unbuttoned halfway down Allan's chest. He could not understand why the stranger and his friends wore tattered, faded, blue pants. Clothes aside Allan easily could have been one of the Kushite princes whose images were in the Temple of Remembrance.

Allan's questioning eyes met Meleke's. The king felt something uncharacteristically emotional happening to him. He wanted to reach out to the stranger. His mind flashed to Meke. *Why?* He asked himself.

Allan observed Meleke's hesitation—just a flutter of doubt on the king's face. Meleke threw back his shoulder, lift his chin, and thrust his chest forward.

"If you stay, your friends cannot return to their homes," the king said. "My confidence must be justified by your actions. I have never repealed an agreement with my chieftains. If I permit you to leave, I expect you to prevent others from coming."

"You give me an option of death either way. If I stay my friends cannot return home. They must live here or die. If I go, I lose Jiena."

The king remained silent.

"I will leave with them and return," Allan said.

"No, you will not."

"I cannot give a guarantee that others will not find Ashaise. My king, in the past we have journeyed to the Moon. We have made many discoveries. We communicate with each other across seas and space. We can create successor species by cloning, so we have the technology to resurrect extinct species. Innovations in health, education, science, and technology are many. We have conquered seas, deserts, jungles, deep rivers, and the highest mountains. Discoveries have relegated fate to passions, and we have thrown caution to the winds of hope. No boundaries have been too high to satisfy the quest for knowledge. So how can I prevent further exploration? The same way we came here, other explorers may also be propelled onto Ashaise. You humble me with your high expectations, but I don't have the powers to prevent others."

The king listened intently. He had dreams for Ashaise and knew the man standing in front of him would help and not hinder his people. He felt as though he had known Allan for many moons.

"Then let it happen by the turn of the moon by chance, as you say, or fate. That's the risk we will take. But there must be no deliberate attempts. We will know. Is it your quest to conquer and destroy all living things? Why do you want more? Why do you need the Kriziantu to heal your sick people? To heal your greed?"

"Because it's the nature of man to be curious about his universe. Our curiosity and inquisitiveness distinguish us from other creatures. We are seekers. We are searchers."

"For what are you searching?"

"Ourselves. Maybe we're searching to overcome our insecurities."

"Stranger, taking more from the universe than you put back only ensures your extinction. You are hastening your death. You search to discover life elsewhere, or wherever else you can survive after you have destroyed your habitat. What you seek is already with you. Conquer yourself first. Hold dominion over yourself. When you do that you will not only satisfy your greed but you will also discover the powers in the divinity of your being."

"My king, if your children were sick, would you heal them with the cure found in the eggs of the bird? Would you not want to see them walk, see their eyes sparkle and their lips smile? Would you not want to hear their laughter as they play in the garden, watch them grow strong, and give their labor and wisdom to the survival of Ashaise?

Well, that's why we search for cures, why we seek the physical comforts of life, and why you use the bird. Meleke, your purpose in life is no different from my own. The healing the Kriziantu brings to your children is the same it would bring to the children in my home. Should I let them die when a cure is available? Yes, the goal is survival, and that means giving as much as it means taking."

"But not taking more." The king looked at Allan. "So you admit to wanting the Kriziantu. Stranger, speak to me of life, not the purpose of living, and let breath flow freely to release the burdens of death."

"What are the burdens of death?"

"Ah, I see you seek understanding and sight. It is the grief of living. That's why you must return home, never to come again…or die."

They heard the low whistles of the crystal birds as they flew over the Temple of the Sun.

Allan went back to his place. On the way he looked up and followed the flight of the birds until they were out of sight. A sequence of images flashed in his mind. He searched for a thread that linked his family, the rest of the expedition, Jiena, and the king to a solution.

"No," he said to himself. "She should not leave Ashaise. It will not be fair." He could not see Jiena in his world, not even in a pristine, rural place. He stopped and stared into the Blue Mountains, where an image of Earth appeared with its splendid oceans, forests, and creatures. He reflected on the bravery and courage of its people and their resilience. In his planet was the soul of time, melodious songs rising with the wind. In the harsh deserts there was beauty. Resources were plentiful, and creativity and innovation, from antiquity to the present day, flourished and transmuted like orchids emerging to new flowers that clung to the boughs of luxuriant trees.

He saw the struggles of a divided world, the challenges faced by its leaders, and the clashing of cultures. There was the kindness of ordinary people who rescued others in need, risking their own lives when disaster occurred. He saw a vision of the white dust of death on blue faces of hope cut down in youth by war and strife. He saw too children of war. Then there was an epiphany—the insight into his world, where everyday, selfless deeds overshadowed evil ones.

The words of the king haunted him. "Speak to me of life, not the purpose of living..." And the Blue Mountains spoke to him of life on a tiny planet named Earth, where people who contributed to others voluntarily accepted the burden of life. They were the givers who got reprieve in the simple joys of life, who forgave transgressions and were forgiven. They knew that in the crowd they were alone in decisions of conscience, and no other person could duplicate their feelings for life. No person could replicate the hunger of another person who sought salvation in the achievement of aspirations and ambition. They quenched their thirst by giving and realized their dreams by reaching higher and higher still, uplifting their selves to a loftier place.

Allan continued to speak aloud to the mountain. "Is that what Meleke meant? To reach higher and higher within oneself? Is it what they have pursued? Self-discovery through the use of the mind to think deeply, to evolve reasoning to a higher level that empowers sight?"

Allan thought his world was a place where people wondered and wandered, searching for the cause of existence and the purpose of their passage. He was living his purpose but still had to understand that salvation came from the mind's being at peace with the actions of the day. He had to accept his frailties as the ties that bound him to a higher self, the human and the God, on the boardwalk of his existence. Jiena was a part of his space but not of his world. He knew that. He also knew he had to find a way.

He looked up from his deep reverie and saw Aatum waiting for him. He returned to his place.

CHAPTER 21

Princess Jiena Eliye Djedkare was not the average Ashais woman. The strong-willed, independent thinker knew exactly what she wanted in life. Jiena had been an outstanding designer of projects in mind development. In order to create teaching platforms, she had occupied her time with various specialists who had been responsible for matters important to the kingdom's progress. The princess's procrastination about marriage to Sahure had started long before she'd met Allan, and one person was aware of that—her confidante, the keeper.

The keeper was the only person who had once stirred her emotionally. Jiena had been a young teenager with a crush on him. He'd known it, but had not exploited her. The keeper was mindful of his position in the kingdom and the trust her father had placed in him. As Jiena had matured, the childhood infatuation had given way to reverence for the keeper. She now cherished their relationship.

Meleke met Teye and Jiena in the garden. He sat with them. "I want to help you, Jiena," he said. "I have faith in you."

"Father, I will not sacrifice all of my beliefs, who I am, and my home for any union. I just told Mother it is not my wish to disappoint you and our people, but a union with Sahure will not be right. He is no different to me from Nehsi. I cannot marry him. I have to meet with him. I'm sorry I have to crush his dreams into grains of sand. What's happened between the visitor and me is natural. Although I have known him for only a very short time, I see my love becoming even deeper whether he is with me or not. It's the power of my mind and the softness of my heart. This is not to say I will never love anyone else, but there's no reason to think about that while my mind and heart are with someone else. I know the options, Father."

"No, you do not, Jiena. I have spoken with Allan. He is a good warrior. I trust him. I have given him an option: he can stay on Ashaise as long as he wishes. However his people cannot return."

"But Father, I don't know you to be as cunning as the zande. What you've done is give him a choice between his people going to their deaths—and me. If they do not return, others will come to search for them."

"He can go with them and protect Ashaise from invasion. His people can also stay here with him. They will not die, and we would ensure no others come."

"You're giving them a choice to stay against their will or sail the ship? How can that be, Father? They'll try to leave Ashaise, and they will die."

"I think your father has tried to resolve the matter," said Teye. "We're sorry there's no choice that will make everyone happy. What else can we do? This is what happens when others come to our land. We've lived in peace and learned how to survive. We've built over many moons a good life with brother creatures on the land."

"What will our lives be like in the moons to come?" Jiena asked. "Do we not have a desire to know our brothers in other worlds?"

"Yes," Meleke replied. "This is not a new thought. It's the same problem our ancestors faced. It's what we continue to explore, but we have always resolved it to one answer: we will not invite destruction. We will not harvest the Kriziantu like corn. She is an essential life source. The destruction of her domain would lead to the demise of Ashaise. We see the stars these visitors see. They want to satisfy their curiosity. We can reach them and have chosen not to do so."

"But Father, we have the power to stop them forever from coming here. We can make the currents of the sun and moon send them back across the bridge or into the ship where they would sail in darkness."

"We must not interfere with the course of nature. We have learned that. We have shielded Ashaise's light and will continue to do so. If Allan stays here, he will be one of us. His children will be ours."

"He will not allow the killing of his people."

"Do you wish to go with him, Jiena?" asked Teye.

"Giving up Ashaise forever by force of circumstances should not be an option. I will yearn for my family. Such a union will be bad for the chi. I will speak to Sahure. I will not marry him."

CHAPTER 22

The blistering cold and high altitude had taken a toll. Five climbers from among the other groups had abandoned the climb, including a biologist, two Kenyan soldiers, and two environmentalists.

Raymond's team resumed a robust pace. Before they took off to the next level at about fifteen thousand feet, he urged the other teams to turn back. Acclimatization was a serious problem for some of their members, but he refused to delay his mission for groups that were not his responsibility. He anticipated more storms and delays.

Raymond would try to distance his team from the other climbers. The other two teams had their medical people, guides, and security, so they were not his concern. Brother Caftie, however, was in excellent condition. He climbed the slopes with the energy of an athlete.

At just over sixteen thousand feet, they experienced more disasters. Numbers shrank, but all three teams advanced, which was not what Raymond had hoped for. There was increasing competitiveness between the people from the pharmaceutical companies, and, more disturbing, between the soldiers. The weak fell by the slope sides. Raymond's team suffered further delays as a couple of members had problems. They camped on a barren and depressing plateau with ominous rocks just over it. The merciless terrain became murderous when torrential hail hit them with the force of millions of stones catapulted from slingshots.

Kilimanjaro was not a mountain of extreme difficulty, but the environmental conditions, which changed suddenly, ramped up the chances for mishaps. Some climbers underestimated its treacherous nature. The guardians of the House of God were jealous angels who sought revenge for the trespass of pleasure seekers.

An environmentalist who had shoulder pain and wheezed a lot passed away on the fourth night. Every day more climbers suffered from altitude sickness and flash freezing of the skin. The senses of overly ambitious members became numb with the sight of a leopard's stiff carcass in nature's freezer.

Raymond and his team replenished their weary bodies with coffee, chocolate, and biscuits. By the fifth day, members of the three groups intermingled during rest periods. Caftie sat in the same tent with an ecologist, James, a Kenyan researcher, and Charmaine Bruce, leader of the Eco Savers team. Friendly chatter was a pleasant way to pass time while waiting for the storm to subside. The conversation was cordial, and the members got to know each other better.

Charmaine, as she held a hot beverage asked Caftie about his work. He talked eagerly about the achievements of his mission and told her that many orphaned and other poor children benefitted from his church's primary and secondary education and health services.

"And I suppose you convert their heathen souls," said Charmaine.

"Yes, we preach the gospel," Caftie said softly.

"Why indoctrinate children with your religious teachings?"

"We do not force children and their parents or guardians to listen to religious teachings, or to go to church. Christians' responsibility is to spread the word of God."

Raymond had sized up the woman, who was as passionate about the environment as the missionary was about his religion. While the conversation was cordial, Raymond sensed she was contemptuous of the fact that Caftie was there.

The atmosphere warmed up, certainly not mirroring the cold, glacial peak that stood like a sentinel against the strikingly lit sky. The hailstorm ceased as abruptly as it had begun. The mist cleared, and outside the tent there was a full moon that mocked a riotous wind.

"So you have a mandate from God to save souls?" Charmaine was smiling.

"Your words treat the role of missionaries lightly," Caftie replied. "We carry out the Lord's work. Our purpose is a merciful one—saving lives and giving love where there is a void."

"Why not show respect. After all, Brother, the disciples followed Jesus voluntarily. The children in your missionary have no choice."

The wind groaned and quarrelled.

"We must push as best we can from sunrise tomorrow if we are to reach the cave," Raymond said, dismissing the others in the tent.

For the Kenyan researcher, sleep was not a best friend. His eyes burned. He had seen death many times. A priest had rescued him as a boy of only four years. Every night, memories of his family's death haunted him. He owed his life and success to the sisters of a missionary school. The wind bellowed outside the tent.

The climbers resumed at dawn. The western glacier landscape showed distressing signs, and without warning rocks tumbled down. A local guide with Raymond's mission was paying attention to his charges. He looked down to angle his equipment, and a whooshing, rumbling sound drowned out people's voices. Just as he turned, the first rocks hit him. He could not steady himself and was soon covered with boulders that cascaded relentlessly.

The total number among the three groups reduced from twenty-four to twelve. Some of them realized an uncertain goal was not worth their lives. They went back.

※

James remembered the cave. The path to it was not immediately apparent. He saw the slanted gap that looked like a vertical crevasse on the slope. He took the lead. The teams inched their way precariously to the side, using anchored rope and prongs to pull their bodies sideways. One by one they got to the mouth and squeezed through a corridor. It was a highly unusual formation that took them in a northwestern direction along a dark path inside the mountain. Headlights were required, and all they saw for at least a mile was the sparkling, blue-green wall. The lights created a dynamic play of shadows and glowing patches of various hues.

They came to a chamber that had harbored humans thousands of years earlier. The climbers did not speak. They moved from one relief to another with dreamy eyes.

James urged them along, as time paid no respect to curiosity. The path led them on an ascent to the summit of the highest peak.

They were able to move at a pace that would have been impossible on the snow-washed surface. It was just after noon when a white, silvery phenomenon that conjured the image of the ocean's horizon on a rainy day became visible from within the corridor. A shy sun hid behind clouds.

They were now motivated to move at a quicker pace to the exit. Those who had climbed the mountain on a previous occasion realized they were on a side of it that was unknown to them. There was nothing to see but thick clusters of clouds from the mountain's crest. The climbers' silence was the language of passing clouds.

Throughout the trip Raymond had sent regular communication to Jennifer, who had decided to stay temporarily in Kenya on the border with Tanzania. Since entering the cave, he had lost contact with her.

"This is where we were when we came out from the mountain," said James.

"What happened next?" Raymond asked.

"We stood here hoping the clouds would clear. Robert Armstrong—the geographic explorer—was familiar with the mountain. Joe Dodd, who mapped the surface areas, had previously climbed to Uruhu on at least three occasions, but neither of them knew on which side of the mountain we were. We climbed from a westerly direction, so we assumed this path continued in that direction. After a few meters, we veered in a northerly direction. We believed we were at the northwestern side. In any event the clouds tumbled, and within an hour or so there was some visibility, and we walked a few meters. We continued in a westerly direction.

"Gradually the clouds parted. The sky was orange, and the most astonishing phenomena occurred. The watery-blue moon moved at an unusual pace, at least to us. The scene became dark except for the glow around the moon. It was difficult to see anything. All I remember after that was the belligerent gale that roared like a hundred lions. Almost as fast as the day turned into the night, it was daytime again, and we were in a place that looked like Eden. The tree trunks were about six times the size of the giant sequoias in the Redwood Forest at Yosemite National Park, and probably three times as high. We could not see the tops. The following day, after meeting the people who lived there, we saw many shepherds and farmers with cattle and other animals on a grazing range. On adjacent acres corn, peas, beans, and wheat grew."

"Could you repeat what happened with the sun? Did the moon eclipse it?" Raymond asked.

"I'm not sure it was an eclipse. The sky was frightening but beautiful. It turned a flaming orange-red, like the color of lava, before it darkened."

"Did you feel anything apart from the strong wind?"

"No."

"But how do you know you weren't still on this mountain?"

"It's not possible. Robert and Joe calculated that Ashaise is about three thousand square miles. There are about two million people living there."

All were silent. James did not appear to be crazy. He was convincing.

"You mentioned this phenomenon of eclipses appeared to occur in thirty-day intervals in Ashaise. By your calculation when is the next one due?" Raymond asked.

"Maybe a couple of days, or perhaps weeks. It's difficult to be certain because I'm not sure of the time in Ashaise in relation to the time here. Their days are longer than ours, but their years are shorter."

"Tell us about these people you call the Ashais. Should we expect aggression?"

"We only saw spears." said James. "I'm sure they could defend Ashaise, which doesn't have anything to do with man-made weapons. They are by no means a lost civilization in the sense that they're an ancient tribe. The fact that their mode of transport is primarily animal power is more an indication of their philosophy of maintaining a balance between man and his environment. The mountainous terrain of Ashaise supports that transportation. Having been there for a month or more, I don't think any other mode of transportation is practical in some areas. We saw automated vehicles but not like the motor car. The Ashais's vehicles were circular in design.

"Spears, transportation by animal, and you say they're civilized?" remarked Caftie.

"Oh, Brother, how ignorant some of us are! Since when are toxic vehicles, guns, and tanks evidence of civilized behavior?" said Charmaine. The others giggled.

Charmaine was quick-witted, radical in her views, and provocative, but kind and generous. On the cold, windy mountain, her snide comment with a grain of humor was a stimulant, albeit not the kind Caftie welcomed. Raymond realized she affected him more than he cared to admit to himself. He knew eventually he would have to temper her enthusiasm for engaging in verbal battles.

"They may very well attempt to leave sooner than we think, but it depends on the time zone in Ashaise," James said.

CHAPTER 23

While Allan had gone to negotiate with King Meleke, the rest of the team continued to explore options for returning home. Chris and Robert considered the implications if the king agreed they could leave, but without materials which would prove the existence of Ashaise.

There was sufficient evidence that pointed to the genetic history of the Ashais, and a lot of information had been gathered on their rituals and traditions. Although their rituals no longer embraced deities and idols of antiquity, their reverence for natural forces such as the sun underpinned their confidence. With due regard for natural phenomena, the Ashais believed people individually and collectively shaped the destiny of all things.

A couple of hours after Allan had left with Aatum, the keeper visited the other explorers. Chris, Robert, and the keeper strolled over to the lakeside. In a state of almost complete tranquility, perhaps brought on by a warm, soothing breeze, and the heady perfume of flowers, they chatted about their work, their aspirations, and the everyday events back home. The wizardly keeper sat on a rock and listened to the conversation about the visitors' homeland. In fact, he heard everything—the sounds beneath and above the water, and those in the mountains that no one else heard. He looked out to the silvery water.

Chris asked, "Keeper, do bad things happen in Ashaise?"

The keeper took a while to respond. His hesitation did not suggest he was thinking about the answer. Chris and Robert deduced he was concerned for their safety.

After a few minutes, the keeper said, "Man's intellect gives him the capacity to minimize the terrible effects of disasters. You have power over many things. When a deadly storm killed our people and animals many moons ago, it had to happen because it was the end of a cycle. Destruction is like the way you till the soil or prepare the ground for building. It is the beginning of another time, like the birth of new plants that break through the soil after the storm. Renewal after death and destruction is necessary, intrinsically and materially."

"So you have storms and earthquakes," said Chris, who made motions with his arms to simulate the shaking of the earth.

The keeper smiled. He turned his head to face the lake. "After the storm we moved our dwellings to safe areas within the mountains and among the trees that grow in the valleys. There are times when we have many storms and the earth shakes."

"But falling trees can kill people."

"They are likely to fall away from dwellings."

The visitors recalled the tour of the mountain caves, where they had seen the storage of food and other items. The Ashais stored nonperishable commodities in spacious rooms with marble floors built within the mountains. Skilled artisans covered walls with copper, silver, and gold metals and made extensive use of bamboo for furnishings. They treated the physical land no different from their animals: with reverence. Hence trees were seldom cut down. The huge trunks, like the caves, were perfect for protection. The wood from sprawling branches made furniture.

The conversation was interrupted when they saw Allan and Aatum returning. The keeper got up, placed his hand reassuringly on Chris's shoulder, then Robert's, and went about his business. Chris and Robert then wondered whether the wise and compassionate keeper had visited them at that moment to bolster their spirits.

※

Just before Allan joined them, Robert remarked to Christ, "I wonder how they control the animal population."

"I think they don't do anything. I suspect they leave it to the laws of nature." Allan now sat with them, and before he could say anything Chris asked, "What did the king say?"

Allan breathed a long sigh, shrugged his shoulders, and explained the possible scenarios.

"I could not have agreed to the condition that if we were to return home, I would prevent other people from coming to Ashaise. I can't stop anyone from trespassing here, either by accident or if it were a planned invasion. The king did say that if he allowed me to stay then the entire team has to stay. That was not an option. My impression is that the king doesn't want to harm us. He's likely to take a risk and allow us to leave but without any of the materials. Meleke was not specific, but what was clear to me, he needs time, probably to confer with his chieftains."

Chris and Robert saw a distant look in Allan's eyes, which left little doubt that he had become so involved with the Ashais, disengagement was emotionally painful.

As Chris was contemplating their plight, it crossed his mind that if the king decides to let them return home, Allan may plot, with Jiena, to stay on Ashaise. He hoped his friend would perish any though of risking death for the woman. He knew Allan was capable of taking such risks.

Robert had materials that certainly would captivate sub-scribers of his geographic magazine and the world. He imagined they would have to produce millions of copies of the magazine to meet the tremendous demand for information on the discoveries.

"What do you mean by leaving without materials?" Robert asked.

"Exactly what I've just said. We'll not be permitted to leave with anything other than our clothes and weapons. The king is fully aware that we have weapons, and how many. Attempting to escape is suicide."

Robert wrinkled his burnt, stout forehead. He stared at the distant mountain and thought of different scenarios. He looked down at the camera in his hands, turning it over several times. This writer was a deep thinker—a man for any moment, with an abiding sense of the resilience of the human spirit. He too loved Ashaise and felt a bond with the place. Robert loved to be in the company of Kiserian. He wanted his materials.

Like many thinkers, physicists, astrologers, and other scientists, Robert wondered about the likelihood of the existence of a place in the universe similar to Earth. Where was Ashaise? His mind played many different notes, and he had a momentary sense of guilt as subterfuge drummed. The stark reality of their position jolted his mind back.

"Okay, from what you've said we must leave without evidence of Ashaise." Robert engaged Allan. "Has Meleke had a change of heart? I thought we faced an uncertain fate—either the embrace of Apti or to leave on a ship, which I have yet to hear someone explain."

"Yes, there has been a slight shift in the king's thinking, but I don't want to make any assumptions about what's in Meleke's mind. He wasn't conclusive. He said he would take a risk. My interpretation is we would be allowed to return home with the clothes on our backs, on the conditions I never try to return and I would prevent any planned invasion of their country. I think he was testing my sincerity. I doubt very much there will be divine intervention."

"So exactly what's our position?" asked Chris. "I have to admit my human brain cannot fathom what seems to be an Ashais parable of some kind. It's time we advise the others."

Robert rose and went to get Springer, Cazeau, and Joe. Their attitudes were upbeat and excited about the possibility of returning home, but they regretted they would have to leave empty-handed. They could not think of a rational

basis for such a demand and were outraged at the conditions
Meleke had laid down.

"Why would he offer such a stupid undertaking?"
Springer asked. "So you would not take the woman? If these
people are as intelligent as you believe them to be, they must
know you cannot make any such commitment. How will
you prevent us from saying what we saw and experienced?
Surely people back home would not believe all of us have
gone mad or are in a permanent state of delirium. The king
is fully aware you cannot deliver on any such promise, and
I imagine it assuages his daughter's feelings. It's unfair. It's
nothing more than another way of sealing our fate here."

Robert nodded his head in agreement. "It doesn't make
sense, Allan."

"It does to the king. Springer is right. The king would not
want to hurt his daughter, but he will not make any decision
that poses a threat to Ashaise. It is exactly why they have not
made themselves known. His daughter would not want me
to perish, or any of us for that matter. I love the princess and
would like to stay here with her, but I know I can't."

"Oh, shit! Women again. Can we ever learn? You surprise me. You have a woman back home!" Robert exclaimed.

"That was until I came here. Call it fate. If I stay then you
cannot return. There is another reality; the whole kingdom
has expectations about Jiena's future husband. He doesn't
look like me so I have to get out of here or sail the sky, or go
with some mighty friends beyond the Seat of God. We must
find a way to return home. One thing is certain, and that is
they would not allow anyone back in Ashaise. They have the
ability to stop us, and I don't think any weapons we have will

be a match for whatever they have. Know this; my priority is your safe return home. I will not jeopardise your safety."

"It still does not make sense," said Springer.

"I've told you exactly what the position is. Contrary to what you think, my relationship with the princess is not the problem. She stands between our returning home and our deaths."

Allan left his colleagues bewildered.

CHAPTER 24

Springer, Cazeau, and Joe had many years of experience working in the countries of the African continent. Springer's family had vast agricultural lands in Kenya. His ancestors had been among the first generation of European settlers centuries ago. In the early days, they had been notorious traders in ivory, animal skins, gold, and slaves. Springer was not content to accept uncertainty. He had encountered many challenges in his journeys since leaving his parents' sprawling bungalow in Nakuru fifteen years earlier to study anthropology at Oxford University. After graduating he'd pursued his dream, which was to explore rain forests in countries across the continent.

Unaccustomed to a junior status on any expedition, he had been pleased nevertheless to join Chris and Allan. Other archaeologists, anthropologists, historians, and academic communities studied their work.

The pyramids in Ashaise and the exquisite marble work in the temple were revealing to Springer. He saw, in one case, a similarity in design with the step pyramid built during the reign of King Djoser in Egypt's old kingdom nearly five thousand years earlier. The Ashais' version was a structure of grander scale.

Kevin Springer was an expert on his homeland and was not astonished by the grandeur of the Ashais' temple. He looked at the ceiling. Light poured in from the upper part of the nave and bathed the chamber with its glow. The Kenyan knew the people of the continent were among the earliest architects, builders, sculptors, metallurgists, educators, and doctors just as much as they were hunters, agriculturists, herbalists, medicine men, and witch doctors.

Springer was a hunter who felt that fate had brought him to Ashaise to reflect on the land adopted by his forefathers. Like their ancestors the Ashais had innovated to create smart community structures that were fairly well protected from the elements; they had chiselled dwellings in the mountainside, and those in between trees were dome-shaped or pyramid-shaped. Mathematically designed chambers of marble and sandstone images of young warriors graced the outer perimeters of their main community halls. The Ashais' places of meditation were similar to ancient asymmetrical structures.

In Springer's travels across the continent, he had seen the sun-dried brick houses and the university in Timbuktu, and the many West African mosques specific to sub-Saharan region. It was irrelevant whether designs may have been externally influenced or not. The reality was indigenous craftsmen had built them. In Ethiopia he had seen the temple of Almaqah in Yeha and the impressive granite obelisk in Axum. Today the high priests and keepers of their cathedrals still prayed and performed religious rituals in halls that had withstood the ravages of time.

Springer had seen evidence of the Walls of Benin, which were longer than the Great Wall of China. The adventurer's escapades throughout the vast motherland had been many. Through his profession he had acquired vast knowledge of sub-Saharan civilizations. The indigenous people told the early settlers' stories. They interwove the stories with tales of bravery and enterprise.

To Springer—the wayward anthropologist—the dissecting, psychological, and physical blades of invaders, wars, slavery, missionary fanaticism, and colonization had raped the mother of man. Springer knew bigotry placed truth in abeyance. Indigenous people had entrenched their footprints. They walked the paths leading from the continent to the cardinal points of destiny.

Springer was as fascinated by the Ashais as the others were, and ready for a spoil. He had to get closer to the crystal bird because he was a hunter and an adventurer before he was an anthropologist. The whistle of the bird made Springer want to get close to her just as the roar of the proud lion or the trumpet of the magnificent elephant had drawn him to the forests at home. The threat of travelling on a ship was not a puzzle to Springer. He understood old African customs. The Kenyan knew it meant no chance of returning to Ashaise, or to his home. There had to be a way to survive, return home, and come back as a bridge between two worlds.

Springer left his place to seek Aatum, who was not far away from where the visitors stayed.

"Aatum, I wish to let you know I respect the wishes of your people," Springer said. "I like to explore our world and discover new species of animals."

"We know who you are and what you want. You must not seek Kriziantu."

"What can I offer, Aatum? What do you and your family need that we can bring to Ashaise? Look at this image of you and your friends, and here you can see a picture of my home. Surely you have a desire beyond the boundaries of Ashaise just as we desire to go to the far reaches of the universe. It's why we're interested in Ashaise. It's not only the crystal bird. I know she's as critical to your health and survival as our medicine is to us back home across the sun. I would like to see her."

"You cannot see the bird or go elsewhere. When the time comes for you to leave here, I will come for you. We cannot exchange our lives for things made by you."

There was no defense against the veiled rebuke, and before Aatum had given his response Springer had regretted his words of offer. Aatum walked away.

Springer watched him go, then went to find Chris at the lakeside. From Springer's perspective the group was in a situation of life and death and had no choice but to defend themselves. Their arrival on Ashaise had not been a premeditated action, and if there could be no reasonable compromise on the part of the Ashais, the explorers would have to get out by whatever means they could. Springer thought of the crystal bird and had no viable answer.

Chris remained silent as Springer voiced his concerns and what he believed their options should have been. Springer recognized his allegiance to the expedition and its leaders.

He did not want to act independently unless forced to do so. His steely, gray eyes looked out at the breathtaking beauty of the lake. He stroked back his light-brown hair, then rested a hand on Chris's shoulder. At that moment the birds whistled loudly as they flew over their place. As Springer watched them, the blood crept under his skin, darkening his tanned face. His eyes remained in a trance, fixed on the spot where the birds had disappeared. The hunter wanted the challenge to follow the crystal wings, to look into the eyes of the queen bird, and gently stroke her iridescent plumage.

"Unless you're adamant that I remain with the rest of the expedition, I have to go into her habitat, and if any harm befalls me then it's one less Meleke will have to worry about," Springer said.

"It's not the king. It's all of us. We should stay together. If we left without the Ashais' consent, they would consider it offensive. Everyone would be compromised," said Chris.

"They've already made a decision on the conditions under which they would allow us to leave. They know Allan cannot make any such commitment," responded Springer.

Robert was toying with his camera and still smarting over the fact that they would not be allowed to leave with their equipment and materials. "I've thought about that and do not believe Meleke is being disingenuous. He knows the frailties. Once we leave here without any evidence of Ashaise, it would be difficult to convince anyone there is a place close to earth that astronomers have not detected."

"I think most people would be inclined to believe the word of two internationally respected archaeologists, an anthropologist, and a geographic writer," said Springer.

"We would have to prove the existence of Ashaise," said Chris.

"I agree their knowledge of us is keen. Once we've gone they'll put a plan into action to isolate this place forever unless it's advantageous to its survival to do otherwise," said Springer.

Chris bent down and picked up a few flat stones and threw them one by one into the lake. The stones skimmed the surface of the water before they sank. "I believe they send seekers, and I would not put it beyond them to have gone elsewhere. There was one relief that was very puzzling. It showed exactly where Ashaise is in relation to Earth, but it also depicted space flight. We all looked at it, and I inquired further but Aatum didn't respond. Anyway that doesn't matter now. Getting out of here is all that matters, and I think Meleke has shifted his position. I've observed him when he is interacting with Allan. Unless I'm totally oblivious of body language, Meleke likes him, but his daughter's marriage to the son of a chieftain will be a momentous occasion for his country."

"I think he hopes that with Allan out of the way Jiena will proceed, in due time, to marry Sahure," said Robert.

"There is something between Meleke and Allan that's puzzling. It's a dynamic energy. It's almost as if they knew each other before now. There's some force that transcends the present predicament. We should be cautious. I believe Meleke knows more of us will try to leave, and not with empty hands. If such a scenario plays out, he will not be responsible for the consequences. Springer, I suggest you do not pursue the crystal bird," said Chris.

CHAPTER 25

A meeting of the council of elders took place in the chamber of the chieftain of Sahur. The mood was light, rather quiet, and indicative of the way the Ashais handled challenges. Sahure, son of the chieftain, sat at his father's side. The previous evening he and Jiena had met in the garden.

"Sahure, I love you very much as I love Nehsi," Jiena had said. "It's not my desire to disappoint and hurt you, but you need the love of someone who wants to be your wife."

"What is this about your wanting a stranger?" Sahure had asked.

"I love him."

"He will soon be gone. I will wait for you."

"You must understand my dear one. I could not love you as a wife would. He is not responsible for my decision. You know that."

"But had he not troubled our lives, you would have married me. Love for me as your husband would come with time. Our children would be our bond."

"No. I'm sorry for my error. I should have told you what was in my heart. I admit I've caused disappointment and was wrong to allow our families and friends to believe we would be man and wife."

Sahure had reached for her hand, which he'd placed on his face. His eyes had pleaded with her. "I want you to be the mother of my children, Jiena. I want to be part of your family, and to please all in the realms who expect us to marry."

She had withdrawn her hand. "My love for him has nothing to do with anyone else. It is him and me. It's pure as the Crystal Lake and as warm as the sun god's breath. Let me not give you more pain. Forget me, Sahure."

She had turned and walked away. He'd stood in the garden, staring in the direction of the mountain on which the strangers had arrived.

"He must go or die. I will wait."

Sahure was an ambitious man who valued the prospect of becoming a member of the king's family.

The news that Jiena and Sahure would not be married disappointed the elders. They loved their princess and held Sahure in high esteem. He committed himself as one of their outstanding protectors. Realm members predicted that one day he would be a chief protector. They did not want to separate the princess's decision from the visitor's presence. They had seen Allan at the hunters' game and expressed their amazement and respect for his prowess. Many said he was a warrior, and the elderly commented on his likeness to themselves. They also heard about his storytelling and liked him. But Sahure was their son, and they felt his disappointment.

The question of Ashaise's vulnerability resurfaced in their minds and how best to protect their land was a matter for further discussion. Since there was already a consensus that the visitors had to be dealt with, the elders turned their attention to the urgent issue of protecting their homeland from further intrusions.

They devised a plan and took it to the king for his approval.

※

The keeper led a group of protectors to the mountain, where they gathered at the Seat of God. Among the warrior protectors was Sahure. They stood around the keeper, who held his staff like a shepherd guarding the flock. They bowed heads as if in prayer; reflecting on the task, visualising its success and the preservation of their home.

Some of the warrior protectors carried assegais while others had refined devices that looked like bows and arrows. They were more sophisticated weapons than their rudimentary predecessors.

The warriors draped their red shukas over their shoulders and wore gold bands around their heads and arms. At the side of each stood a lion, and above them, seated on the rocks, were other lions. Standing on the highest rock, against an orange sky, was Matai. The beast roared at the end of the warriors' chant.

The forces of Ashaise had gathered to await the journey across the sun, and to fight if necessary. At the end of the ritual, the keeper, with his head poised like a bird focused on its food, turned and told the others to follow him into the mist. They climbed beyond the habitat of Apti, in the direction of the summit where the sun god would take them over to Alkebulan. Within the mist the shadows walked alongside their masters, unseen, unheard. The low whistle of Kriziantu added a surreal tempo to the mountain's undecipherable lyrics as the birds flew to their nests.

In the crystalline habitat, the birds fluttered from one rock to another. Mothers tended to their young, opening their wide, pinkish beaks to regurgitate plankton for their ravenous babies. Unruly young birds flew around the massive domain. The queen was the largest bird, a magnificent spectacle especially when she spread her wings. Her population of about one hundred birds had to be protected from predators.

The hermaphroditic birds were delicate, regal, sacred, and untouchable. Without them Ashaise would no longer exist. They nurtured, healed, and sustained the environment from which they fed; their spoors nourished life within the water, and they kept the temperature within the pristine environment balanced. Their eggs healed the Ashais from fatal diseases.

They were their life.

In the sun-hued valley below the mountain, two people found each other before night showed off its moonlit gown.

CHAPTER 26

llan and Jiena felt a stirring power as they walked slowly and silently with fingers entwined. The wind whirred the leaves, muffling wayward sirens in the Blue Mountains that sheltered the valley. Their bond had already reached another level—a spiritual dimension. They felt connected by an inexplicable force. There was a familiarity, which they could not comprehend. It was as though they had known, and loved each other for ages. The yearning for each other was like an unyielding tide rushing toward the shoreline—a tide which no one or anything could stem from reaching its natural destination.

Jiena remembered the conversation with the keeper and used the authority of her mind. He'd told her happiness was in the tomorrow of now and she must find it before the day fades.

She and Allan sat under the bushy boughs of a giant, flamboyant tree, listening to the happy sounds of children playing beyond the hedges. Their silence was a testimony that no words were necessary to repeal the peacefulness of the evening. It was superfluous to say anything—most of all to speak of love, for the spirits of the two had already become one.

The low whistles of the crystal birds shushed the exultant noises of the Blue Mountains. There was a song only both of them heard. They got up and strolled along the wooded bank, where they listened to water flowing in their river of fate. It was fate that had brought them together. It was fate that had made them think and move in tandem with the currents that were taking them to their destiny. The night would be the respite from shadows, time to reflect on their respective patterns of existence and the tapestries they had sewn. They listened to the music of time and, for the moment, simply touched the space of peace.

From afar the king watched. He knew that whatever the elders wished, no one could do anything to change Jiena and Allan's growing love. Whatever time commanded, Jiena would conquer her passion but not surrender to a union in which she could not be fully genuine.

Allan was respectful of her serene presence, her inner strength of purpose. His love for her was distinctive; there was a connection and a bond he did not try to fathom. She was quiet, intuitive, and wise.

Jiena's hands tightened around Allan's. She did not look at him. He looked at her and smiled. As they sat between boulders, she played with a tuft of grass beside the rocks and he slipped into a reverie wherein he travelled to his early childhood days, when the family had gone to Trinidad to spend the summer vacation at his aunt's house at the seaside. He'd spent the long days playing with his cousins behind the rambling, old, green and white house. They had romped at the shoreline, and their laughter had echoed in the wind. The opalescent, noisy ocean had been his company as he'd sat behind the old shed staring at ships sailing and wondering about their destinations. He'd seen the fishermen's shed where they'd stored anchors and oars, and containers in which they'd put bait—sardines stiff from the midday sun. The cool sea breeze had blown sand from chip-chip shells and carried out to the ocean the scent of fresh fish.

Allan felt the warmth of Jiena's hands and her breath on his face. He kept his eyes on the wide, silver foil in front of him, and memories flooded his mind. He remembered the neap tide was far, so far out to sea, leaving naked secrets of timeless sands stretching miles beyond the shore, and now he was walking out with his ankles deep in soft, brown sand. He saw a soldier crab crawling from its home, a still starfish with the sun on its back, a stranded jellyfish, and the wrecked pirogues of the fishermen.

Jiena studied his face, and he felt her fingers tracing the outline of his lips. In the recesses of his mind he saw the rambling bungalow. It was midnight, and he and his cousins were digging out warm soil. They placed dry twigs and fronds in the wide hole. They made a fire below mesh wire and placed on it the fish the fishermen had given them.

Jiena ran her fingers around his face. He smiled and looked at her.

"You are thinking of home," she said.

"Yes. The lake makes me think of childhood days when we left our home in America and went to my aunt's home on a pretty island called Trinidad, where my mother was born."

"I think you miss your family."

He smiled again at the leading statement, and before she uttered another word he held the hand that was caressing his face and pulled her toward him. Their faces were so close they breathed each other's breath. He placed his hand under her chin, and with a passionate kiss they were both lost in another reverie. They were drifting from their self-imposed safety net to drown in the sea of desire.

Jiena pushed him gently. "Allan—"

Before she could say anything else, he put his finger on her lips. He whispered, "You don't have to say anything. Unless you want to get us into trouble, keep your fingers to yourself."

She looked at him mischievously but quickly put her hands behind her back, Allan laughed. They both sat quietly, taking time for the emotional storm to subside. He then continued the conversation in a deep, husky voice with the twang Jiena loved to hear.

"Of course I miss my family, but my childhood days are long gone. I will always think of home, but it doesn't mean I want to go back except to say farewell."

"You sound as though you won't return."

"As long as you wish it, Ashaise will be my home." He said this with finality.

Their eyes held each other's for a long time, and they were about to fall in the sea again but disengaged when they heard approaching footsteps. Meleke and Teye smiled at them, and they rose from the grassy ground.

"We saw you strolling and were interested in speaking with you. Perhaps we can walk back together," said the king.

Mindful of his dishevelled state, Allan said, "Your majesties, I will take my leave."

"You need not leave, and do not call us that. You have a short time here, and we wish to hear more about your work."

The invitation surprised Allan, and he wondered whether there was a motive. In any event the king and queen moved on, looking back to see if Allan would join them.

"It is a pleasure," Allan replied.

"Why are you so interested in the past, in extracting bones and pots from the earth? How important is that to your country?" Meleke asked.

"Well, it's important to the university where I work. I research past civilizations in order to understand how they lived. Their systems of governance and social structures are important if we are to learn the truth about foundations and how we became who we are. Perhaps we may rethink how we wish to shape the future. We will always be curious about the truth of birth, and who or what the first creature on earth looked like. More recently Chris and I decided to research the African continent for evidence of literate civilizations thousands of years before written history. Ashaise is important to us. The reliefs and artifacts in the Temple of the Sun excite us. Aatum and the keeper filled in many gaps. We traced your early civilization and have made some assumptions."

"We are Maasai, and we are Kushites."

Allan was only surprised by the way the king said who they were—not by what he said. The king was emphatic, as if he felt there was no need for Allan to make assumptions. He said who the Ashais were with a great deal of pride.

"Your ancestors were courageous men and women," Allan continued. "Do the people here ever wish to know about my place, to learn about our science and achievements?"

They continued to stroll in the gardens. The noises of other creatures in the trees and the sound of water were calming.

"Yes, stranger, the desire is always there, and teachers and searchers have gone over the mountain. They take care not to be discovered. We see brothers and sisters, and they are losing themselves. They strive for places at the table. Their children do not know about the true character of the ancient land. They know not their strong foundation. Yes, we know of the greatness, but animals are caged and many are dying. Their habitats are disappearing. Do we want our children to learn more about that world? Yes, we do, but stranger, tell me, would Ashaise survive? How much would they take from us?"

Allan considered the king's question. "I do not have an answer. Ashaise is a unique place. I can only say it would survive, but economic, cultural, and social forces would change it. Change often means survival."

"So you're researching ancient civilizations, but will the children learn about the discoveries?" Meleke asked.

"That's why I'm passionate about my work—so we can write about the history of the continent and it can be taught in schools."

"That's why, my son, you must go back and write the history of our people."

Allan looked at the king and queen and then at Jiena. They walked to the bearded, flamboyant tree and stood beneath its bough.

"My king reminds me of my father. Once he took me to a playground, and I was running around with my arms stretched out. I asked him why I could not fly like an eagle. I wanted to visit the birds in the mountains. He told me that was impossible because I had no wings. My father said, 'Allan, you are human, and the eagle is a bird. You could fly, but not like the eagle. You would fly like humans do because their intellects and talents are their wings. An eagle will not want a little boy in its nest unless it's hungry.'"

Allan had his hands in his pockets. He lifted his chin and looked at Meleke as he continued. "My king, I know I cannot fly. But there are more ways to get to the sky than flying like an eagle. If you want me to write about Ashaise, I must come back."

He kissed Jiena on the forehead, graciously bowed to her parents, and went on his way.

Teye wrinkled her brow. She stared after Allan, and said to her husband, "While he was speaking, I heard your voice. I looked into his eyes and saw yours."

The king put his arms around his daughter and drew her toward him. He said, "I understand why you love him. He reaches me too. But he must go."

CHAPTER 27

The two remaining security men, David Cazeau and Joe Dodd, sat outside the group's dwellings with Springer and Robert. Allan and Chris had gone to examine fossils. Since the group had arrived in Ashaise, this day was one of the few cloudy ones. The temperature had dropped, and Cazeau and Dodd had thrown over their jumpers the shukas given to them by Aatum. Not too far from where they sat, a few animals grazed. There was always an Ashais or two around tending to the animals. If they were not busy shepherding, they were meditating.

It was midday, and as usual Cazeau was strumming his guitar while the others discussed their plight as well as the discoveries and the wealth of minerals that existed in this mysterious land. They wondered about James, and speculated on what they thought was happening at home. They felt certain a search was on for them.

Since the start of the group's problems on Ashaise, Cazeau had rarely joined in conversations except with Joe, whom he had known for many years. Cazeau was a decorated soldier scarred by the ugliness of war. His friend Joe was aware he'd had a tough time growing up in a dysfunctional family. On late evenings he could be heard singing sad country songs and strumming his little, steel-string guitar. He was friendly with the rest of the team and cracked the occasional joke, punctuated with cuss words—his trait. His black hair was always neat, and his brown eyes were dreamy and sad.

Cazeau stopped playing the guitar and looked at the others. He listened to what Robert was saying about Meleke's decision, and he interjected.

"We have to try. The time is close, and tonight will be a midnight sun, by my calculations. There are many weeks of work in these files. Since we're not sure whether we'll survive or not, we might as well try—take a chance and get some of the evidence out."

"The material is not yours," said Robert "While I agree Meleke's decision is unreasonable, it's a matter for the archaeologists to decide."

Springer shook his head. "We're not rogues who plotted a way to get here to trick and steal from them. We've made life-changing discoveries. Ashaise is testimony to the fact that man can live for more than a hundred and forty years. We can self-heal many ailments, and there are cures for fatal diseases."

"Taking away the materials would leave in doubt the existence of this place." Cazeau was adamant. "This is what the expedition was about. The goal was to search out evidence of early civilizations and tell the world. It's now much more than that. If Ashaise is not on Earth, then we've found another habitable planet—maybe an exoplanet. That is my business."

"Allan tried for the best option, but his relationship with the woman complicates things for Meleke," said Springer.

"No. I don't think so," responded Robert. "Leaving that aside, the issue is invasion and destruction of their way of life, which is a legitimate concern."

"But we also have a justifiable position." Cazeau looked directly at Robert. "It seems you're more sympathetic to the Ashais's position than ours. I came on this expedition as security for the team and their discoveries, so don't tell me about who owns the materials. I'm not prepared to be thrown off in limbo or die in the gorillas' habitat." His quiet disposition aside, Cazeau was deadly. "The intention is not to send us home with memories. That is a reasonable assumption only if they have the means to block further entry."

"They have a legitimate fear," Robert said. He had often written about the environment and remote tribes, and had a genuine concern for the fate of Ashaise should its existence be publicized. "We don't know where we are. Sure, we went up Kilimanjaro, but this can't be on the mountain. In any event, if it is there, then the authorities may see an opportunity to exploit their territory. It's easy to understand what tragedy lies ahead. Just think what's still happening on the continent."

"Listen, guys," Cazeau said. "The problem we face right now is not invasion—just the opposite. The challenge is to get out, and with an egg or a vial of the stored healing potions, or blood samples." His resoluteness was a strong indication of his intention.

"So what do we do?" Joe asked. As a security member he was conscientious about his job and did not get involved with the chatter of his bosses. He listened intently. Joe was always aware of the environment in which he worked, and he frequently paced around the dwellings. He sensed the group was under constant surveillance. The sandy-headed, strapping extrovert was always ready for a good time...and a brawl. Like the other mercenaries hired to provide protection service, Joe's interest in Ashaise was material. He could not contain his excitement every time he came across another display of precious stones and metals.

"We leave tonight," he went on, "because tomorrow will be our last chance. Let's focus on the mission. Except in self-defense, weapons will not be used."

Cazeau and Joe had long ago made a decision that they would leave to explore options for getting out of Ashaise. They would seize any opportunity that arose. If he and Joe were safe, they would rescue the rest of the team. He was ready to put his plan into action.

"I'll go with you," said Springer. "I only want to see the bird."

"I will not be leaving, and you can appreciate that I have to tell Allan and Chris immediately," said Robert.

"Sure, but they can't stop us," Cazeau retorted.

Robert didn't like the situation that was developing here. If they left they would be tracked as Timothy and James had been. The trackers would not interfere but wait for a pre-dictable outcome. Robert had to try to stop them from leaving and needed help. He had to find Chris and Allan quickly.

They had strolled about three kilometers along the lake, examining fossils and rocks. By the time Robert caught up with them and returned to the living area, Springer, Joe, and Cazeau had gone. Allan and Chris were furious.

"Where the hell are they? Where have they gone?" Allan shouted.

"They said they would leave tonight, so I expected to find them here."

"We have to get them back. Let's go now. They cannot be far. It's time someone kicked the shit out of those fools."

※

The ever present king's assistant heard the commotion and approached the men. He had seen when Springer, Joe and Cazeau left and headed toward the savannah. Allan begged Aatum to help bring them back. "I have to go, with or without your permission. We've already lost one member due to his own foolishness and greed, maybe two. I don't want to hear about three others dead. I have to get them."

"You must not go," Aatum said. "We do not want you harmed."

Allan said, "If you won't stop them, I will. Why are you allowing them to go to their deaths?"

"Allan, no!" shouted Chris. "I'm coming with you."

Allan took off like a bolt of lightning, ignoring Aatum, who knew that protectors would hold him. But he stopped Chris and Robert. He called protectors to guard them. They appeared within minutes.

Allan moved with speed through the gardens. He made his way to the foothills of the mountain via the path where the keeper had taken them not too long after they had arrived. It led to the Seat of God. As he made his way up, he took a wrong turn at a fork and deviated from the track. He was always within reach of the protectors who were just about to stop him when he stumbled and fell through a sink-hole, plunging forty feet into darkness, hitting his body several times before landing at the watery bottom.

"Go now. You must hurry," one of the protectors said to his colleague. "Let Aatum know what has happened."

The protectors could not see anything as they looked into the black hole. Aatum arrived within a short time with others who were healers. After working for well over an hour, they lifted Allan, unconscious, out of the sinkhole. The men placed him on a stretcher-like piece of equipment and carried it to an auto-carriage.

The blows had bruised and torn Allan's skin, exposing his flesh. A few ribs and his left hip were broken. The jagged walls of the sinkhole had lacerated his face from forehead to chin, from cheek to cheek. They observed several marks on his swollen left calf, trailing down to his toes.

They took Allan to a pyramid called the Temple of Healing. The helpers laid his unconscious body on a narrow, firm bed in a large, columned room furnished with chairs and medical equipment. Stacked on rows of shelves were jars of marble and ceramic. They left him in the care of the physicians.

"Will he see the sun?" Meleke asked Aatum after he advised the king of what had happened.

Aatum's face showed grave concern. "He is now travelling in the light. The healers worry about the poison. Deadly scorpions stung him."

"We must tell the one called Chris. Does Jiena know?"

"No. I will go to his friends. The healers can mend the bones, but the poison is strong."

Aatum immediately went to get Chris, who was sitting with Robert outside their place. They knew something serious was amiss before Aatum had said anything. He told them what had happened. "I will take you to him now, but he is in the light. The healers may bring Allan back."

Chris's sunburnt face was the color of ashes. During the short ride to the Temple of Healing, he remembered the times he'd had with Allan, which was most of their adult lives. They had faced adversity before now, alone in places torn by civil strife and during military action. This was different. He did not know exactly where they were. Chris grinded his teeth and squinted his eyes. He bowed his head and stared at the ground.

Robert placed a hand on Chris's shoulder. The changing situation and Allan's condition had caused deep anxiety.

Chris lifted his head and stared in space. He saw himself and Allan together, working, partying, at family dinners, dating and sharing women, comforting each other in downtimes, and living life freely. They were successful archaeologists. The depth of their bond was based on abiding love only the two men understood.

Chris turned to Aatum and said coldly, "I'll not think negatively, but if the worst happens to him, and if the Ashais don't kill Springer, Cazeau, and Joe, I will."

Aatum looked at Robert.

When they arrived a protector permitted them to stand a little way from the bed where healers worked on Allan. One of them dabbed a solution over bruises on his swollen face, which was mostly covered in dried blood. With expert fingers another healer gently probed other areas—the ribcage, neck, hip, groin, and legs—with circular movements. When he was through, the physician lifted Allan's body with the help of the other healers. They wrapped him from neck to hips with strips of long, broad leaves. From one end of the bed to the other, they placed a clamp. Chris and Robert assumed it was a device to prevent him from trying to move.

The healers applied large amounts of cream and compresses to the leg. They took up an instrument that emitted steam and moved it over Allan without touching his body. Thereafter they covered him with a light, cotton cloth. Chris went closer and gently rested his hand on Allan's forehead, which was hot.

"He is strong. We'll know how well the medicine has worked by sunrise. We'll be here with him until he is well," one of the healers said.

Chris told Robert to go back to their dwelling area in case any of the others returned. He assured Robert he would not leave Allan.

At dusk Jiena came into the room. Chris saw her enter. She acknowledged the healers and took off the shawl that covered her head, letting it fall over her shoulder. Jiena then turned to Chris. She had effortless grace and humility, and a face that caused him to stare at her. He had chided Allan for getting giddy over a woman, but as she spoke he understood why his friend had gone over a hill. It was not only her beauty and grace.

She said, "I share your pain and worry."

"Thank you," Chris said, bowing his head slightly. "He speaks your name often. I see why."

Her lips parted slightly into a beguiling smile. "You must tell me what he said." She moved to where Allan laid. As she saw his bruised, battered face, her eyes welled.

"I will stay with him." She gestured to the healers, who got up and moved to the other side of the large room.

"No, don't go," she said to Chris. She saw the anguish on his face. "You must stay."

Allan was still unconscious, so they chatted quietly. As somber as the mood was, she made Chris laugh several times. Her humor, her ease, and her light but witty conversation charmed him. He talked about his friendship with Allan, the places they had been, and the experiences they had shared. He felt her compassion.

They turned and looked at Allan. He opened his glazed, half-dead eyes.

"Allan," Chris said. He squeezed Allan's hand. "Can you hear me?"

Allan's eyes closed.

Jiena moved closer and bent over to speak, though she wasn't sure whether he heard anything. She caressed his forehead. The fever raged. She looked around for the healers, but they were already upon Allan. They knew the phase. His body was reacting to the poison as muscle spasms began. He frothed; his nose bled; he breathed rapidly; and with swollen throat glands he rasped. The fever raged for hours. The healers moved with nimbleness and ensured medicine was flowing intravenously.

It was near dawn when Allan settled into a deep sleep, and Chris left to find out whether Robert had heard anything about Springer, Cazeau, and Joe.

CHAPTER 28

Springer, Joe, and Cazeau had made their way to the lower mountain forests. They thought the warrior protectors who guarded the communities against animals that wandered from their habitats would not see them.

Ashaise had been a society free from external threats prior to the expedition's arrival, but its young men and women trained intensely in self-defense to protect their realms in the event of external danger, and if any internal threats emerged. A principal chieftain directed their operations.

The king approved all crucial decisions affecting the safety of citizens. He seldom disapproved proposals made by the realms. If a disagreement occurred, he would convene a meeting of chieftains for a resolution. Such consultation could be extended to community meetings if necessary. Realm leaders and chieftains had to justify their decisions to the king and citizens.

About a hundred moon years earlier, the chieftains had been on the brink of rebellion against the principal chieftain, who had wanted control over all the realms. He'd perpetrated initiatives that had divided realms. He'd wanted no intervening layers to the king but made a serious mistake when he'd ordered the capture of a bird for his personal pleasure. That was a sacrilege.

The keeper had forcefully demonstrated his faithfulness to the vow he had made to the king and citizens. Infidelity in that role was an evil that led to self-destruction. The governing chieftain had no discipline of mind. He idolized power and material things, and the keeper told him self-indulgence was not a virtue. While the principal chieftain came close to causing considerable disruption, he failed in his nefarious mission. The chieftain, whose name was Leboo, wanted the Kriziantu to show he was above all others.

One evening, as the sun was setting over the Blue Mountains, Leboo called his soldier warriors and gave orders to capture the bird. They mounted black lions and took off to the habitat of the crystal birds against the keeper's advice. The warriors captured a bird and took it back to their chieftain's place, where he ordered a cage to be built. The bird refused to eat and drink. She whistled a low, grieved sound continuously, which the flock heard, and they came to her rescue. Chieftain Leboo died in their claws.

Within the dense forest, though the rest of the party felt quite safe, Springer was anxious. His conscience nagged him. The hunter and adventurer had succumbed to shame because he was not a crook. Springer was a respected anthropologist who valued the relationship he had with his colleagues. Many evenings he was in their company either for a meal or to review research materials, and went to sleep enlightened.

It was Springer's sense of insecurity, and the passion to hold the bird, that motivated his present behavior. He loved the Ashais and could not hurt them. In any event it did not matter that he made no secret of the fact that he wanted to learn more about the bird. Springer knew now that he could not betray the Ashais and his colleagues.

Springer had never experienced such a burden of self before. He knew it was more than likely that the Ashais protectors had seen them. That was not relevant now because it was the first time in his life he felt a sense of responsibility to someone else. Instinctively he stopped. His behavior perplexed the other two.

"Guys, this is as far as I'm going. I came as a member of the expedition and cannot jeopardize their lives."

"What the hell?" Joe said. "We've come this far and will not go back. Go back to what? We've served the purpose of providing security as laid out in the contract."

"But you made a commitment to Allan and Chris."

"We did, but there's no more expedition because Allan wants to stay here. To whom did he make a commitment? And Chris would leave without anything, so our commitment is to our lives, those we left back home, and America. We are not abandoning them. Once we get out of here we'll return for them."

"Allan cannot stay here. He made that clear to us. Chris and Allan would surrender all gains of the expedition to save our lives. Sorry guys, but I'm going back."

"I didn't think you're a coward, said Joe."

"I am not a coward, asshole. This has nothing to do with cowardice. It's about people I respect. This isn't about who we are. My interest is the beautiful creature, to get close to it and touch it. I will not harm the bird, nor will I harm Ashaise. I love this place and can live here easily. It has everything I've wanted out of life. There's another way, and I urge you to turn back. I don't think weapons will be of any use. The very fact that Meleke would allow us to leave with only the weapons means these people are not intimidated by guns."

"No, I am going ahead," Joe said.

Cazeau's body language indicated he was continuing. It was obvious the two would proceed with the plan. Neither of them felt taking an egg or interfering with the precious creature was in any way tantamount to deception and theft. They had fought for their country and had no obligation to Ashaise. Fame and financial gratification at Ashaise's expense was not an issue. How they would return to get the archaeologists out they didn't say.

Joe's goal was the establishment of an international security company. Ashaise's gold was the route by which his dream could be accomplished. The celebrity status and notoriety they would win by giving to their country a substance that could revolutionize medicine and save lives would be greater than their military awards.

Springer walked a little more than twenty meters, then stopped suddenly and looked around. His hunter's instinct was at work. He sensed he was not alone. He had heard stories about lions, and now he heard his heart pumping. He walked slowly. Out of nowhere, as far as he could determine, a warrior stood in his path.

"My God. Where did you come from?" Springer asked.

"We understand your decision not to pursue the foolish plan. It's unfortunate the others did not have your sight."

In their six weeks in Ashaise, Springer had not seen any of the warriors in clothing other than their signature white or red shukas draped over one shoulder, except when they were at the wedding of Omeke and Lelite. This soldier was nearly eight feet tall, with atypical reddish-brown hair. He had light-brown eyes and wore a short, black wrap. His impressive appearance was intimidating, if not threatening, as he looked down at Springer with amusement.

"I tried to convince them," Springer said.

"We know," the warrior replied.

"How long have you been following us, and where are the others?"

"We followed when you left the dwellings." As he said this, three warriors, similarly dressed, appeared from nowhere.

"What will happen to my colleagues? Can't you go and get them? You know they're in danger."

"We did not send them to danger. They are traitors. They are on the wrong path to the sun and the birds."

"Are you saying they've gone the wrong way?" The soldier did not respond. "Please help me bring them back."

The warrior looked at Springer with laughter in his eyes. He did not say a word. He moved in the direction from which Springer had come. The other soldiers followed, and so did Springer. He observed that one warrior was a woman.

They began to run, which Springer did not appreciate because he moved like a tortoise compared to his athletic escorts. They were as light and sure-footed as ibexes on which the Ashais travelled long distances over rocky mountains. Like spirits of the forest, they moved without sound, and Springer began to pant, feeling slightly dizzy and ashamed. He could not keep up at their pace on the steep slope. The soldiers knew that.

The grinning soldier stopped and looked back at him. Springer swore under his breath. He was a fit man by any standard, accustomed to going days without sleep and traveling long distances while tracking animals in the jungle, but this was too much. The others scaled rocks like high jumpers, almost flying over the mountainous terrain.

Springer realized there was something else unusual about the warriors. Every now and then they seemed to have vanished but then were immediately visible again depending on the angles of their bodies in relation to the sun and vegetation. Springer recalled how the three others had appeared from nowhere, and also what Chris and Allan had told the rest of the team about the white body cloth that the keeper had given to them in the crystal cave. As they temporarily slowed, he observed the sheer cloth and cream that plastered their skin. It reflected everything around them.

Springer's pulse raced. He didn't have time to think of the many uses of such an innovation. The military came to mind first, then the unprecedented advantage of any commercial enterprise, individual, or nation holding the rights to such camouflage material. What was it? Springer recalled the strange, shadowlike movements he and the others had seen from time to time.

The warriors picked up their speed again as they entered the mist. Springer stopped as it occurred to him that between the time he had left his colleagues and the time of encountering the soldier, Joe and Cazeau could not have gone very far. He called out to the soldiers.

"Ashais, where are we going? They would not have come this far."

"My name is Knufu."

"Wait, wait. I don't understand. I thought we were going to get them to return to their dwellings until you're ready for us to leave."

"Did I say that?"

"What do you mean? Where are we going?"

"You are not a traitor," the warrior replied. "You inner voice guides you. It's a powerful voice. I'm taking you to a place that is important to you."

"Knufu, I want to see my friends. Please help me find them. I must save them."

"I do not know where they have gone. Others will know that. It's useless for us to try to find them now. We stopped seeing signs of their feet when we reached the clouds. It's likely that they were taken."

"Who would have taken them?"

"My people or the lions. We're going over the mountain, back to your dwelling."

Springer looked to where Knufu pointed. It was the highest of all the mountains he had seen. Although he was in turmoil, feeling a deep sense of guilt as well as anger, he was also grateful. There was nothing he could do other than try to pursue his friends on his own. He knew the folly of that. To be part of the expedition was similar to being on a hunt, and hunters worked as a team. There was trust and mutual respect. There was satisfaction in capturing the quarry. The pleasures of conquest were mutually felt. There was learning about each other, and enduring relationships developed.

Springer felt sorry; he was deeply concerned and had a feeling of impending tragedy. He blamed himself. *What a fool I am. Why did I agree in the first place? Why did I encourage them?* "Knufu, can we go and find out what became of them?"

"Come with us."

Springer looked around and contemplated going in search of the others, but he had no idea where to start. He said to himself, *If nothing bad has happened, Cazeau and Joe will be deep in the forest. Protectors will be following them every step of the way.*

"They may be safe" said Knufu gently, "unless they stepped over to the place where the lions dwell, or where Meke dreams."

Joe and Cazeau continued to climb and found themselves in thick mist. They proceeded with caution and hoped they would soon arrive in the area where the birds nested. They thought it was possible to climb the mountain within a short space of time and pass the gorillas' habitat without incident. Finally they would get to the place and await the next eclipse. They predicted it would occur within a couple of hours. It crossed their minds that they may be watched, but during the last few hours they had seen no signs of anyone. They often stopped to survey their surroundings and thought that in the misty mountains it would be difficult for them to be seen.

They did not realize the path led to a fork, and at that juncture the other path was barely discernible in the sunlight, and far less in the mist. It took them to a place where they saw many animals grazing and drinking from a stream that ran between mossy rocks and a variety of weeds. While taking in the landscape, they saw Meke sitting with his legs crossed on a boulder, among the animals near the stream. The two men did not know where they were, and they made their way to the boy.

As they approached, Meke was still, as if asleep. He heard running water, the breathing of animals, and the noises that the creatures made to each other. He heard the flutter of butterfly wings, so keen was his hearing. He knew the smell of stream water, the scent of each species of animal, the call of different birds, and the scent of strangers. He did not move. He kept his eyes closed as Joe and Cazeau approached.

"Hello. Where are we, little boy?" Cazeau inquired.

Meke looked at them with expressionless eyes.

"We need you to show us how to find the place where the birds fly and the mountain where the moon crosses the sun," said Cazeau.

Meke did not answer. He closed his eyes. From the early age of seven, he had commanded the obedience of animals. The beasts knew him as they knew the keeper. His fearsome protectors, Zete and the camouflaged warriors, were always near him.

Meke did not move. He knew the strangers should not be where they were and sensed they meant mischief.

"Show us the way, little boy," Joe said. "You must show us the way to the eggs."

They had not seen Zete or the lions; the latter were always shadows. Joe raised his voice, and in frustration he and Cazeau approached the boy. They heard a deep bellow, turned around, and saw the bull nearby. They wondered why they had not seen it before.

They had not realized how cold it was. Only a few hours earlier the temperature had been warm. They had become accustomed to the frequency of climate changes in Ashaise. Within a couple of days after their arrival, it had been obvious there were several time zones, depending on which side of the mountain they were on.

The cold temperature was not the only thing that sent a chill through the two men; so did fear. They moved closer to the boy. The bull lowered its head and moved toward them. The lions moved, and the men took out their guns. They did not see or hear Zete's approach, such was its speed. They felt the force by which the animal raised them off the ground, and within seconds of landing on rocks, something dragged their bodies under the crystal waters.

Meke remained with his eyes closed. Zete lifted his head to the boy, then went beyond him and sat under a sprawling mahogany tree. The lions bounded up the rocky mountain, where grazing goats scampered.

CHAPTER 29

Their time on Ashaise was coming to an end, although they did not know exactly how much longer they had to wait before the next moon would cross the sun. It would be the moment to return home—or somewhere else where they may take their last breaths.

Chris and Robert were in a melancholy mood as they contemplated Allan's state and the fate of Joe, Cazeau, and Springer. They regretted not taking seriously the conversations about members going off on their own.

They were now alone, chatting while strolling in the fields where cattle grazed. Given the recent events, there was no longer certainty about leaving. There was no doubt in their minds that they loved Ashaise and its people, as well as the Ashais' moral perspectives on life and justice and their fascinating history. If the explorers got out, they would cherish their experiences here.

Meleke was an intriguing character. He had the power to do as he pleased, yet he never used his position to achieve aims while governing his kingdom. Rather he skilfully used referent power and gained the confidence of the people to accomplish his ambitious goals.

Allan and Chris had carefully documented and coded their discoveries. These findings had even more significance in the context of their work in Ashaise, since records in the Temple of the Sun and the Temple of Remembrance depicted Ashaise's earliest inhabitants as having arrived more than twelve thousand years earlier than Allan and Chris had originally thought. The archaeologists had unearthed, in a cave between Calem and Sade, human fossils they speculated to be older than anything previously discovered in Africa. They had no way of dating the remnants, so their experience was the judge. They felt it would be a serious loss to leave without their photographic and electronic materials.

"Although there is not much documentation on the pre-history of the continent, the temples here have substantial depictions of daily tribal activities and structures unknown to us before now," said Chris. He tried to find the words to describe the society. He looked across the lake as he conversed with Robert. "While this is a developed civilization, it has an aura of antiqueness and rustic charm. The best description I can come up with is 'unconventionally modern and urbane.' We saw irrigation systems, practical storage units for perishable supplies, and skilful use of precious metals for convenient living. We're witnessing the efficacy of their medicine and healing skills as the physicians make Allan well."

Chris found the structure of governance in Ashaise interesting. It was a kingdom, but anyone could aspire to be king once they attained the required levels of insight, which the visitors did not fully grasp. The system went back to the days of antiquity, when Tariku and Asefa I ruled. A son of Meleke may not succeed him. Popularity and heritage did not enter the equation.

The Ashais elected chieftains solely from among those who served the realm and who had proven they could lead the community. They valued education, agriculture, history, science, and medicine as building blocks of society, and, of course, they maintained the oral tradition of storytelling.

"Aatum said storytelling helps children to know about their people and life, and keeps history alive. It also creates understanding and love between generations," Chris explained. "The children respect their elders. When people speak to each other, they are peaceful. I wondered at the time whether Aatum sensed division in our group and was sending a message that we must talk with each other. He must have known we had argued."

Robert smiled. "Of course he was saying it is trusting relationships that count and I don't think he was necessarily speaking about words. He referred to our actions."

"It's obvious that robust competition plays a part in the development of their realms, so perhaps he was also saying you must communicate with your rivals. They're always sending us subtle but loaded messages." Chris chuckled.

"I think they've reached this far because there's no dysfunctional competition for power. There's a tradition of remembrance, but not in a sense of sadness, rather in a spirit of renewal. They are always on the alert for the unexpected or inevitable."

"I want to examine the strange drawing again, which has to be a map, and hope to get an opportunity to study it closer. I've seen the one that shows Earth eons ago as one land mass, but I haven't figured out the other one."

"I would hate to see harm come to the Ashais. I would want no part of that."

"I wonder what they would do with laptops and cameras," Robert said.

"I'm not sure they're interested in these things. On the other hand, I wouldn't put it past them to replicate such devices." The two men chuckled.

"What do you think is their dark side? I sense something scary, but I can't determine what."

"I know," Robert responded. "They have an air of power, almost invincibility, yet we've experienced only humility. I can't say what it is, but I don't think we're the first outsiders since Mbtani nearly six centuries ago. The question is what happened to other intruders. The Ashais protectors could have stopped James and Timothy rather than allowing them to walk into danger."

"It's more than that. There will always be good and evil in all societies. For the length of time we've been here we haven't seen any prisons. So where do they put people who commit crimes? Surely not all of them absorb the mental development thing. There must be bad people. We haven't seen physically challenged people either. Where are these groups?"

"That's a good question." Robert shrugged. "We haven't seen all of Ashaise."

As he said this, they arrived back at their dwellings, and they heard animals approaching. At the far end of the path leading to their dwellings was Springer escorted by four warrior soldiers. Except for one, all were half naked. Robert and Chris had not seen any Ashais dressed like that before. To the men's astonishment, they were riding black lions.

Springer and the warriors strutted along the pathway toward Robert and Chris. The warriors told Springer to dismount. After he had done so, they sped off like phantoms, disappearing literally within seconds. Not too far away, Aatum watched.

"What happened?" Chris asked in a subdued but sharp tone. Springer related the decision Joe, Cazeau, and he had made to leave in anticipation of the next turning of the sun. They had hoped to get an opportunity to retrieve an egg, not necessarily in the Crystal Cave but where they had seen the birds resting near the Seat of God. He had reconsidered his actions, having realized the danger in which he'd placed the two archaeologists. He felt an affinity with the Ashais people, who were similar to those in his homeland of Kenya. He felt a deep sense of guilt.

"I pleaded with Joe and Cazeau, without success, to return. On my way back, a warrior soldier—the front rider who was just here, by the name of Knufu—came out literally from nowhere. Thereafter three more appeared. Friends, among all the amazing things we have seen in this place, the most incredible one is the warriors camouflaged their bodies."

"So what? Who cares?" Robert asked with exasperation.

"Listen, guys—"

"Don't tell us any crap about listening. I expected better from an anthropologist, but my judgement was wrong. The fact that our lives are at risk means not a damn thing. Frig off," Chris exploded.

"I'm sorry, truly sorry. I lost all sense of reason. I suppose it had to do with my desire to get close to the bird. Please believe me when I say I had no intention of harming you or these people."

"What happened to Joe and Cazeau?" Robert's tone scolded.

"I don't know. I asked Knufu to stop them. At first I thought he was going to do just that. We had gone a considerable distance, and I realized we should have caught up with them within minutes. Where's Allan?"

"Why should you be interested?" Chris turned his back, walked away, and spit out the words: "He left to bring you traitors back and fell into a sinkhole."

Springer approached Chris. "Is he—"

With a sudden swing, Chris knocked Springer to the ground, then levelled two brutal kicks in quick succession at the man's left side. Chris was no longer on Ashaise and did not see Springer. He was in the desert seeing an enemy. Rage drove him to pull Springer from the ground and slam him down for a second time. Robert tried to stop Chris, and just as Chris was about to take the man out, Aatum arrived and restrained him. Chris pulled away from them and walked to the lake.

A couple of hours later, Chris returned and went to Robert's room. "I don't think Allan would want to know we're fighting," said Robert, and he put his hand on Chris's shoulder. "Springer has asked for forgiveness. He returned, and that's what matters. We know he's not a thief or a mercenary, just a messed up anthropologist with the attention span of an ant."

Robert took up a jug and poured water into a silver cup. He drank and put the cup back on the table. He looked at Chris, who stood near the window. He said, "Joe and Cazeau played the Ashais' game and are probably dead. The Ashais knew it was not time for a crossover. They saw an opportunity to get rid of those among us who they do not trust. It's a process of elimination. By the way Springer has asked to see Allan."

Chris remained silent for quite some time. He looked at Robert and smiled. "I'm not sorry for kicking his ass, and will not allow him to see Allan. Anyway the healers would not let him near the temple. I'm sure that's an order from Meleke. The healers have become overly protective of their patient. There is something about Allan and Meleke I don't understand."

CHAPTER 30

Allan was not fully aware of his visitors. Meleke had entered the room once before and found a teary-eyed Meke at Allan's bedside. He had lifted the boy.

The healers said Allan's condition was improving, although he convulsed and had fever. He was delirious and thought it was his father standing near the bedside. He called out to him: "Pa, Pa." He tried to raise his body but could not, and reached out with one hand. He thought his father had held his hand and wiped his forehead. He fell asleep.

Meleke handed the healer a wet cloth, turned to Chris, and said, "The Sun god shines on him."

Chris looked up at the benevolent, dimpled face of the king. He thought of a tall, ancient priest standing in a temple, looking toward the sun. He felt the force of Meleke's personality: kind, congenial, and trustworthy. He was a child again in the safe arms of his father. Chris sensed warmth flowing through his body. Any fears he had vanished.

"You're the same height as his father, and you look like him too," Chris said.

Meleke turned his head to the side and cupped Chris's chin. "I have learned from Aatum that Allan's friend is also a soldier." The king smiled broadly. "We will watch the one called Springer. Do not hurt yourself anymore. Come to my home later, and bring the other two." He patted Chris's shoulder.

Two days later Jiena sat at Allan's bedside. He awoke and asked for water, which she took from the healer and gave him. As she was doing this, Meleke and Teye came in and stood at the other side of the bed.

"Has the poison gone?" Teye asked her daughter.

"The sun god smiles on him."

Meleke moved closer and studied the patient, whose eyes looked distant. "Stranger, why do you want to die in Ashaise?"

"Father," Jiena said with surprise in her voice, "how can you say that?"

Teye laughed because she understood the positive current between her husband and the man from across the sun. Meleke had a mischievous look.

"It is where I will die, my king" was the barely audible, raspy response.

"So you are well enough to be defiantly arrogant." The king's voice became gentle. "Are you still in pain?" He bent to hear the answer.

"There is only one thing that would ease my pain."

Meleke stood up fully as he looked at the man who defied death. "You must go home. You know that. The bruises are almost healed, but the broken bones will take a few more moons. The healers tell me you want to get up. I do not want to send you home with broken limbs. Rest, and take your medicine."

Allan smiled at the caring words and looked at Teye.

"We will take care of you," she said.

The healer came and told the visitors to leave. Meleke obeyed the order.

Two days later, when Chris and Robert visited, they expressed amazement to see that most of the scars and scratches on Allan's body had disappeared. He had experienced the power of medicine from Kriziantu. He was cheerful and eager to know all that had happened. They met him sitting in a small garden area within the Temple of Healing.

"We know how much you're in love, but did you have to fall into a scorpion pit for her?" Chris asked with a laugh.

Allan looked around to see where the healers were. He attempted to get up to cuff Chris's jaw. But he was too weak; he gasped in pain and almost fell off the chair. Laughing, Chris helped him and waved to the healer who stood nearby. The stern woman, with a face like an eagle's, showed her displeasure. Were it not for Allan's insistence, she would have thrown out the two men.

To compensate for not being able to get at Chris, Allan told him to eff off. The healer heard loud laughter. She gave them a cutting, sideways glance.

"You think they understand that," asked Robert, grinning.

"I'm sure they do," said Chris. "They've been around us for a couple of months. I've seen Aatum laugh after Springer used it."

"When will you leave here?" Robert asked.

"I don't know. They won't tell me. The problem is the hip. Okay, guys, now I want to know what happened."

Chris looked at Robert and said, "Springer returned the same day."

"What about the others?"

"We're not sure. From what Springer said, they got lost and the protectors refused to help them."

Allan turned away. Chris walked a few paces and touched Allan's head. He spoke in a subdued voice. "I'm sorry. It's hard to accept their misfortune. Springer is remorseful and blames himself, but they made a decision."

The healer saw a stressful situation. She was protective of her patient. She ushered Robert and Chris out.

Meleke returned late that night. Allan should have been in bed, but he continuously resisted the healers' advice. Their patient stood on the nearby balcony, looking out.

The king approached. "You are as stubborn as Zete."

"I want to walk," Allan replied. "Will you walk with me?"

They searched each other's eyes and faces. Meleke looked around for the healer who was watching. She gave the king a stern look. Meleke cringed. Allan laughed and appealed to her. She said they could go, but kept them in view. There were two other healers hovering around.

Allan limped alongside the king. Meleke had gone to the temple that morning and reflected on the life of Mbtani. The temple of remembrance was his sanctuary—the place where he found inspiration. It made him a well overflowing with compassion. He thought the stranger held a resemblance to the revered ancestor. Meleke considered Allan curiously.

"What can I do for my king?" Allan almost whispered.

"We need new ideas for Ashaise to grow. You would be a good teacher, stranger." He held Allan's elbow to help him along. "It's not that I want you to go—no more than I want to cause my daughter pain. But you must leave Ashaise. The one called James would help your people to come for you and the others, and the bird. They will never return to their homeland. But, your people will not give up trying, and we would have to defend ourselves. You would have to be a warrior for either Ashaise or your people."

"Isn't that my decision?"

"Yes, but let it be made when you return home."

"Will you let me come back?"

"If it is possible, it will happen."

Allan smiled. "You mean it's not likely."

"We have to take measures on the other side, and if Ashaise shifts I do not know what the chances would be."

Allan considered his words and thought better of questioning him on the measures. He had not seen the keeper and wondered where he was. Allan stopped. He saw the hallway rising toward him as they walked; the pillars were shifting, and the room was spinning. He shook his head and put his hand to his eyes.

"You will return to the others soon. Do not stress yourself," the king said, looking at Allan in a fatherly way.

"My king." Allan hesitated for quite some time. "I will teach my people." The words were hardly spoken when he collapsed. The king held him, and the healers went to their assistance.

Over the next few days, Allan's skinny body strength-ened. Chris, Robert, Springer, and Aatum spent most of their time walking, running, and exercising with him. Jiena and Meke occupied the remaining time.

Twelve days after the accident, Allan returned to his place. His progress was rapid, and it was not long before he was back to his normal routine, except for a slight limp the healers told him would go away eventually.

Springer re-bonded with the others. They understood the urgings of the wayward adventurer-anthropologist. They liked him and respected his work.

CHAPTER 31

I n the cave on Mt. Kilimanjaro, the rescue team and members of the other group waited for an eclipse or for something to happen. Raymond had checked the prospects for such an event before he'd left base, and according to astronomers it would not happen. Twelve hours passed, and the thick mist did not clear.

He did not think the time was right. He observed nervous movements around him. There was one situation that made him walk a little way ahead of the others. He thought he had seen movements that did not seem to be a cloud formation. The movements appeared to be within clouds, as though people were walking in a line. He dismissed it as fatigue or a hyperactive imagination.

There was no use standing in the blistering cold, so they went back inside the cave and settled down for the night. But the inquisitive Charmaine would not let anyone rest. She looked around and pulled a chocolate bar from her pocket. She slowly pulled away the wrapper and was peeling away the silver foil before resuming her conversation with Caftie. Her dark eyes smiled inquisitively. Caftie liked her healthy face. It was like the mountains after heavy rains or early spring. She started the entertainment for the rest of the team.

Raymond observed how Caftie looked at Charmaine when she was not aware. While chewing the chocolate, she smoothed the dark-brown, cropped hair from her forehead and loosened the scarf around her neck. Her attractive face, burnt to the color of whisky, had a tomboyish, mischievous look. Raymond concluded there was something more than Caftie's religious work that attracted his attention.

"So why is it that wherever there's religious fervor, there's also superstition, deprivation, and crime?" She posed the question in a nonchalant way. It was possible to hear a falling snowflake. The group was quiet as they awaited Caftie's response.

"It's the other way around. Wherever these things exist, the church will be there. We do good deeds rather than dwell on the ugly and profane. Hold a piece of crystal to the sun, and what would you see if not a reflection of the environment around it?"

"Oh, well." Charmaine got up and walked a few meters toward the pathway. Raymond watched the inquisitive woman intently and hoped she would not go beyond the second chamber. While it was not within sight, it was within the boundaries of loud noise. He would hear her call.

James chatted with Raymond about Ashaise for most of the night. It occurred to Raymond that Charmaine had not returned. He had not heard any movements during the past hour. Raymond and James went to investigate, and she was not in the second chamber. They proceeded as far as they had gone earlier in the day. They called her name loudly. There was no response. The soldiers prevented the other climbers from following Raymond and James.

"Where could she have gone?" Caftie asked.

"Something has happened to her. If Charmaine were within the areas of the two chambers, she would hear our calls. I don't think she's the type to wander off without thinking, or without concern for the rest of the team," responded Raymond.

Charmaine had strayed a little beyond the third chamber, where the party had discovered new drawings. There was little visibility. There were many arteries in the cave. Unless a trespasser followed an identified path, it was easy to wander along another one, especially in semi-darkness. She took the wrong way and realized her mistake when sufficient time had passed and she had not reached familiar chambers. She saw none of the reliefs and drawings she'd seen earlier.

Raymond had a responsibility to the mission, and having spent the last hour searching, he had to return to his team. He intended to send soldiers to get Charmaine. Since James was the only person who knew what had happened on the summit, he too had to abandon the search and return to the group.

"I believe she has wandered too far to hear our call. We have lost her," said Raymond.

"If she has lost her way, I will find her," Caftie said.

"I will send a soldier with you," Raymond said.

Raymond saw Caftie in a different light. Caftie showed gumption—though Raymond still believed he was an agent.

Caftie had grown accustomed to Charmaine's probing. He wondered what had traumatized her in childhood. He saw her contempt more as a call for help, to purge some demon or other. He liked her. She was an attractive, spirited woman who needed to be saved. He took his belongings and, armed with headlamp, went after her. He dismissed the security soldier, as he was a necessary member of the rescue mission.

Neither Caftie nor Charmaine returned by the following morning, and in the Eco Savers camp her colleagues voiced their fears. Caftie traced her steps to the mouth of one of the arteries and took that path. For three hours he followed the winding passage, which led to a series of chambers of stalagmites in stunning formations and colors. The stream widened to a still pool that was as clear as glass.

Near the stream he found her headlamp. His pulse raced. The battery was dead, and he thought she would have left it there deliberately for her searchers. He called her name as loudly as possible and was certain he heard a faint response. Charmaine was on a parallel path, but neither of them could know this. They were now both running in the same direction, calling out to each other. The path curved, and he called her name again. The response was clearer. He kept running and calling but heard no further sounds. He stopped and walked several steps back in case he had gone too far ahead of her.

Charmaine no longer heard Caftie because she was running in the dark and fell over a large rock, hitting her head so hard she was stunned and disoriented. She pulled herself up and crawled around for quite some time before she heard his voice again. It was the voice of a person who was deeply concerned. The voice reassured her.

"Brother, Brother," she answered.

Caftie ran forward again, and to his right was another passageway. He wondered which course to take. Then he heard a noise and ran through the passage to his right, in the opposite direction from which the sound had come. Charmaine's voice became louder and more desperate than before. He was going in the right direction.

It had been eighteen hours since he had left the other members. He found the woman who for the past few days had taunted him. She was sitting on the ground with a broken ankle, bruised forehead, and busted lip. She was grateful he had found her, and he would not let go of her.

"What took you so long, Brother?" Charmaine asked.

He ignored her, as he often did, and lifted her up to a warmer and more comfortable place in the chamber. He bandaged her ankle and cleaned her face.

"I don't have a clue how to get out of here, but we will, by the grace of God, so you'd better start praying."

"Are you asking *me* to pray?" Charmaine asked.

"Yes, and very fervently, my child," Caftie replied.

She winced at the pain shooting through her ankle. He tried to make her comfortable.

"I need to look around to see if I can find something to make a brace for you, so don't try to move."

Caftie returned about fifteen minutes later with a smooth, three-inch shard of stone, which was the only thing he could find that was useful to keep her ankle from further damage. He tied it in position with strips of a towel from his backpack. He then propped her head, and they rested for a few hours.

Caftie struggled to support Charmaine as she hopped on one leg. They heard running water and decided to follow the sound. They walked for a couple of days and satisfied their hunger with biscuits. It was gruelling over the rocky floor of the cave. They crawled on their stomachs and sides, dragged on their bottoms, and squeezed through small tracks at the side of the stream as they followed its course. With Charmaine on his back Caftie crawled, then waded through water. They sweated in chambers filled with the detritus of bats, and where spiders thrived.

At the end of the third day, there was light—a sliver at first in the far distance, and as they got closer it bathed the cave. They followed the light. It took all of Caftie's strength to hoist himself with Charmaine on his back and get on a shelf before crawling out through a space the size of his body. They had no knowledge of where they were. The dense forest received them, and perhaps it was the first time he felt fear, but not because he was in the rain forest. His work involved going in the jungle. It was because of Charmaine. All he had was a knife and a prayer for protection.

Caftie found a small clearing and placed her beside the trunk of a tree—after a careful search for crawling creatures. He looked around in an effort to get a sense of where they were. He worried about her swollen and discolored ankle. The infected cut on her fevered forehead oozed. He could not risk wandering too far away from her.

In a faint voice, she said, "Just imagine, of all people to get lost with, I get God's messenger."

He grinned. "Shut up. I came to find you because I realized I would be lost as well without you. I prayed you were safe, and God answered my prayers."

"You mean it was the Lord's will?"

"How would I have found you without Him?"

"Shit, the holy messenger found me."

Caftie wiped her wet face and kissed her gently. She smiled.

A heavy rain drenched them. It poured for more than ten minutes. There was nowhere to take shelter. When it ceased Caftie lifted Charmaine's trembling body and made his way through the slush until he came to grassland where he lay with her, exhausted. He vaguely heard the voices of game wardens. They lifted the two people into a jeep, which moved at full speed to a lodge on a reserve.

They had exited the cave in the forest of Kenya.

CHAPTER 32

"Tomorrow they will leave," Nehsi said as he sat at the table, over a meal with his parents and sister. He looked at Jiena for a reaction. There was none.

She picked at nuts in a marble bowl and said to her father, "You said no harm will come to him, but as I sit here I sense his anxiety. I can feel his energy because he is sincere. He does not want to leave."

"We know that, just as you know I will not harm him. He's thinking up a scheme to stay. That's what he's anxious about. He doesn't know what my response will be."

"What will you do?"

"I will not allow him to stay. You know that once he leaves—once he's forced to leave—he will try to return."

"Yes, I know that's in his mind, but it's better that way because his emotions are raging rivers. His parents, his friend Chris, and his work are his life streams. He must close a part of his life. You do not intend to allow him to return, do you?"

"We will deal with that if and when the time comes, my child," said the queen. "Tomorrow let us take them into the mountains where the birds gather."

"They would like that. Yes, let their last sightings be of the crystal birds."

They rose from the table, and Jiena said, "I hope those across the sun who are searching for them do not confront Sahure."

"I hope not my little Jiena," the king replied.

※

The four remaining members of the archaeological expedition were sitting by the lake. Emotions were mixed. They grieved Timothy, Joe, and Cazeau. The soulful strum of a guitar could still be heard in the wind. They felt guilty because they were principled. Fear receded to its restful place in the brain. They would not die. They would not leave with their well-earned prizes. The enigmatic Ashais were under their skin, tugging at their core, stealing their love. Yet in grief they could not understand why the sun god's people did not prevent the misguided soldiers from engaging death.

"As long as the Ashais feel threatened, they will retaliate, preferably allowing the enemy to select his own method of death." Allan hesitated. "I have a special request."

"What's that mate?" asked Robert.

Allan took a deep breath. He was not quite the same person who had left the Rift Valley nearly seventy days earlier. He was often in deep thought. To some extent they were all more reflective than before. But his change was more evident.

The previous night Chris had said to him, "The person I knew a couple of months ago is not quite the same. He's grown into someone else. He seems to have found himself. He's left me at home. I'm not seeing an archaeologist anymore. I see a person who's ready to leap to another level of his existence. I'm not sure I can reach you."

"You will always reach me, Chris. You're in a place within me where nobody else can venture." Allan had placed his arm around his brother, friend, and confidante. He'd drawn Chris close, and they'd held each other. They'd known fate would take them to separate realms.

They'd had agreed on the subject Allan was about to broach with Robert and Springer. What mattered to Chris was that their lives would be spared, and the crossover would be safe. They did not hide their disappointment that the medicine, which had cured Allan, would not be available to sick people back home. They could not pretend the substance to produce camouflage material was not in the forefront of their minds. They discussed the significant strategic advantage it would give their country in warfare, and against terrorists and criminal gangs.

"We have an obligation to America," Allan said. "And I feel I have an obligation to protect Ashaise. Even though it may survive, I fear disaster for these people. It's a moral dilemma."

"There's one thing to factor in: we do not know what the camouflage substance is. Knufu did not tell Springer. I doubt they would tell us. We can't ask about that now," said Robert.

"No, we can't, not if we want to live," Allan acknowledged.

"Look, the reality is I don't see how we can talk about camouflage material if we don't have a clue what the substance is. I think we'll cross that bridge if we have to."

They agreed silence was the best option. Allan looked directly at Robert and Springer.

"Can we agree not to reveal anything about Ashaise when we return? Because of your work, I know I'm asking much, and it may seem to be an unreasonable request."

"You know you don't have to worry about me," Robert said. "Frankly I've thought about things and don't care much anymore about having to leave our materials behind. What matter are our lives. There are enough materials in the caves in Tanzania and on Kilimanjaro to cause a sensation. My only concern is not having a sample of the medicine."

"What about James?" Springer asked.

"If he returned home then a mission is already looking for us with his help. I'm sure the warriors, perhaps with the keeper, are on the mountain," Allan replied.

"What are you saying?"

"I have no confirmation, but they must have left the day we saw no sun. The keeper did not come to the Temple of Healing, and I wondered about that. I had not seen him for a few days before that, and he has not visited us since."

"They will stop whoever is there," Robert said.

"You have my word." Springer said. "But I wish they would give us the medicine and information on the camouflage material."

"Springer, forget about that," Robert thundered.

"I will. I don't want trouble for Ashaise." Springer replied.

As they were about to get some beverages, Aatum, who always supplied them with wine and anything else they needed, approached and asked Allan to go somewhere with him.

"Where are we going?" Allan asked.

Aatum grinned and said, "To a place."

Allan did not know what to make of the request, but the cheery mood of the king's assistant put him at ease. The others shot knowing glances at each other, and Chris said, "I'm sure the lady wants to see you," at which there was laughter.

They travelled by horse and arrived near the king's dwelling, but it was a much smaller, two-tiered structure with the trademark marble columns surrounded by a garden of a variety of ferns, flowering plants, and shrubs. There was a long path leading to the king's house. Aatum left Allan at the bottom of semicircular stairs. Allan entered a spacious room that was beautifully tiled, and which flowed to an indoor waterway with rocks and plants. Allan stopped and looked around. He walked across the room to a terrace.

Jiena was standing against a column. Her pale-yellow silk, shuka gown flowed classily to the floor. She wore no adornments and looked stunning. She smiled.

Allan caught his breath. Jiena held out her arms. He walked, with a slight limp, slowly into her embrace. His arms were a forest vine around her body. He rested his head on hers, and they stood entwined for a long time. He lifted his head and looked into her eyes, which were like lakes where sunlight played on the calm water. The strength he had lost due to his illness surged through every fiber of his body. He trembled in her gentle arms.

"There will be a midnight sun, and it is your last evening in Ashaise. Will you stay with me?"

CHAPTER 33

Chris, Springer, and Robert, followed by Aatum, went to the mountainside. There were geodes and coral stones scattered everywhere. The men showed little interest. In Ashaise they had seen many elements that would constitute untold wealth at home.

The explorers' interest was in the statues built across the mountain, all facing the rising sun as it made its journey to the west. These were massive structures, and built from obsidian—a feat the explorers thought impossible without modern-day technology. Artists had made sculptures of adults and children among lions, birds, the first Zete, and other animals. The marvellous works of art were in recognition of achievers who had brought value to their realms.

While the rest of the team studied these edifices, Allan strolled alone, thinking about the last evening with the woman he loved. He had walked far from his dwelling but was not concerned. He knew someone would be watching him. He had become attuned to the people and loved them more every day.

He heard footsteps approaching and turned to see Meke on Zete. Allan smiled and held out a hand to the thoughtful boy. The half-mad bull grumbled, but Allan took no notice. He stroked Zete's forehead and touched his fierce, antler-like horns. Meke squeezed Allan's hand.

"I came to say goodbye," Meke said.

Allan saw the boy's angelic face smiling up at him. Allan's eyes welled, and he bent and swung the boy in his arms, holding him as tightly as a father who was about to leave his son. Zete bellowed a little louder, again protesting the closeness of man and child. Meke looked over Allan's shoulder at Zete as if to say, "It's okay, I'm in safe hands."

Allan and the boy chatted and walked to the dwelling area.

"You will return," Meke said.

"Yes, I will return, son. I will return."

"You will be safe. We will protect you," said Meke. Allan understood that to mean Zete and himself.

"I know you will, and you will take me to your mountain and show me the way of the creatures there."

The child looked into his face, then hugged him again and wiggled down from his arms. Zete knelt, and Meke mounted the beast; he called Allan to mount too, which he did with one hand around Meke's tiny waist. With the other he held the reins with the boy. They rode off to the garden of butterflies, where Allan chased the oversized creatures as though he were a child again.

When the time came to say goodbye, Meke was the shy, quiet little boy Allan had first met some weeks earlier. They walked slowly back to the dwelling place where Meke stood for a while, looking at the man he'd met only a short time ago. He threw his arms around Allan's neck.

The others had returned and were sitting on the rocks under the trees. The boy looked at them, then at Allan again. He mounted Zete and went on his way.

※

The royal family came for the visitors on black lions. The last four members of the expedition watched as they approached astride the magnificent beasts. Aatum called to the group to join the party. They were each provided with a lion. In the least, the beasts were intimidating. They hesitated at the prospect, but Aatum reassured they would be safe—safer than on a horse or any other means of transport.

"Where are we going?" Chris asked.

"To your home," Meleke replied, "but first we wish to show you the summit of the Mountain of the Sun, where the Kriziantu rest under the sun god's eye. We thought it would be a befitting gift to you—a memory you would treasure. Aatum will assist you with the lions. Do not be afraid. We train them well, but remember they are still wild beasts. Be gentle."

"Be gentle!" exclaimed Chris. "How do we get on them?"

"They will yield as you hold the reins and stroke them," Aatum said.

Gingerly they walked around the lions and, assisted by Aatum, mounted, except Chris who could not mount because for some reason the animal did not sit. He repeated the action, but still it did not yield for him to get on its back. Aatum spoke to the creature, and only then it yielded.

Chris mounted. The lion roared, threw him off, stood over him, and growled in his face. Chris had seen death during warfare, but nothing had prepared him for this horror. Then the lion moved from over him and yielded. Chris was dazed and not sure what he'd heard.

It was laughter—Allan's. "I always thought animals love you. Stroke it gently."

Chris shook his head, rose from the ground, and apprehensively approached the waiting lion. He mounted, only for the glorious beast to take off as if chasing a gazelle. The others heard Chris's screams as the lion playfully bounded ahead of the others.

He barely heard Allan's voice. "Just hold on. It loves you!"

After a while the lion slowed its pace as if waiting for the rest of the party to catch up. The beasts bounded up the Mountain of the Sun at a heart-stopping pace over rocks, fallen tree trunks, and patches of pretty shrubbery. It was an exhilarating experience for Springer, the hunter, but a nightmare for the other three.

Jiena rode close to Allan. Her shawl blew in the wind—an image of wings as she sat astride Matai. His blue-black mane was also like wings at the sides of his handsome face. The group pelted up through the caliginous depth of mountain forest, where an orange sun peeped through the trees. The wind's white noise was a soothing sensation as they scaled the summit over which the birds gathered. The crystal birds whistled. A creeping, red sun attracted the expectant party.

They slowed their pace and stopped at a place called Rocks of the Moon. There was a plethora of round, smooth boulders the color of the full moon on a clear night. All members of the party dismounted, except for Chris whose beast refused to yield. He attempted to jump down, but the playful lion suddenly moved. Chris fell, hitting the earth with a heavy thud. The beast's tongue, which was much larger than Chris's head, licked and left a slick of saliva on his frightened face. Laughter went with the wind over the trees.

The dumbstruck visitors stared at a scene just below them. Springer was dreamy, while Robert was drowning in the landscape without his camera. Chris and Allan were like children again, moving from boulder to boulder to absorb every angle of the panoramic setting. The iridescent bodies of the crystal birds against the soft, golden sky, and the black lions created an enthralling scene.

After he'd climbed over boulders and walked around with Chris, Allan went over to Jiena and stood at her side. He kissed her on the forehead. She rested her head on his shoulder—actions that were not missed by her family. The king saw the worried look on Teye's face. She reflected on Sahure and felt sorry for him. He had asked Teye to intervene. She had told him that once her daughter had made up her mind on any matter, there was little chance of anyone convincing her otherwise.

Sahure felt aggrieved by the stranger. As disciplined as he was, with strong powers of mental control, it was still a struggle for him to contain his negative feelings for the stranger. He trusted himself to conquer his wicked thoughts; nevertheless he hoped he had no encounter with Allan.

Teye watched her daughter, who had both arms around Allan's waist. Teye knew that in his absence Jiena's love for him would only grow. The king held Teye's hand and gently interrupted her thoughts.

Meleke said to the visitors, "The time has come to go to where the moon crosses the sun. It will take you within her light to your homes. We will first journey through realms to the Chamber of Life, then the sun god will take you to your loved ones."

The group admired the landscape for the last time before approaching the obedient lions to journey down the mountain. The descent was no less spectacular than the ascent. Each one of the visitors felt a heavy burden of loss.

Chris took mental notes of rocks and boulders, flora and fauna that were prevalent on the mountain. Every now and then they came upon individuals in deep meditation sitting on rocks by streams and rivers and under trees. Whatever the chosen spot, they faced the sun.

The Ashais went about their daily business. Those who travelled distances from one village to the other rode on various animals, and the team observed the care given to the beasts. They were curious about how the Ashais dealt with animal waste, but soon they found out. There was a system, but they could not determine the materials used for its construction.

They passed a number of villages they had not seen before and marvelled at buildings in the Valley of the Moon with smooth, flowing passages, linking domelike houses with sky-view ventilation. This was where some families lived to take care of their elderly and physically challenged relatives.

They passed the realms of Sahur and Calem before arriving at the Temple of the Sun. They enjoyed a meal of green and root vegetables, fish, and sweets. The conversation was light and carefree, but the strain of departure and the denial of an opportunity to get access to the cure for intractable, life-threatening illnesses hung like a wet veil over the gathering.

The hue of sadness was visible on each face; no warm smile could mask its transparency. Ashaise was a magnet. The blend of tribal attraction, rustic modernity, and unaffected quality of life was a psychologically addictive concoction. The guests' melancholy affected their hosts.

As they sat on mats around a table, Allan reflected on their earlier dilemma and the regrettable actions of the security team. He figured that greed, or weapons of destruction or trickery, do not achieve anything in the long run. Rather, kindness, respect, generosity of spirit, and the mutual love of all things under the sun bring beneficial results. He said to himself, *There is immortality after all—immortality of the force that binds all people of goodwill.* He felt friendship in the room where the sun poured its light on the humble meal they shared.

"My king," said Robert. The salutation came naturally. "In our research and study of your way of life, we have not seen bad things. So tell us, are there evil ones among you? When citizens commit crimes, what do you do with them?"

Meleke sipped tea made from the leaves of trees that grew in the Valley of the Moon. Its perfume was mild, the flavor nutty and a little bitter.

"They have a choice if they admit they wronged other citizens. They can choose to spend moon years redeeming themselves by protecting our land. Depending on the seriousness of their wrongdoing and willingness to strengthen their minds, they can work among the animal brothers. It is difficult for them not to admit guilt because we will know. All citizens of Ashaise know that—even the children. If their minds are maladjusted, and there is no remorse, we will treat them as dangers to others. They will be sent away from society forever."

"That means you kill them."

"No, we will not take lives of others, unless in self-defense. Evil people are the instruments of their own deaths. We send them away, and they can live if they compensate society and develop powers of self-control. We will not allow the innocent to keep them fat. They cannot come back among us. We send them beyond Apti's habitat, to the Valley of Twilight. They more than likely will survive as long as they do not try to return."

"What did you do with others who came before us?"

"It depended on their intent. If they intended evil, they died. If they acted out of fear, they were sent on the invisible ship to sail the universe."

"Meaning they also died?" asked Robert.

"Maybe," said the king. "With the will of the sun god, they may have survived."

The visitors contemplated the king's responses.

"I respect your honesty," said Robert.

"That's all we strive for, brothers," he responded with a twinkle in his eyes. They all saw it, and it made them laugh.

"Come with us to the Chamber of Life," Meleke said at last.

Enthusiasm surged, and like children who were promised a treat, the visitors jumped up from their dining seats and followed the royal party. Allan and Jiena strolled behind, savoring the short time left.

In the pyramid they entered a long pathway to the Chamber of Life, where models made of clay, gold, marble, and other materials depicted the Ashais' beliefs about the creation of a diverse universe. It certainly was not the big bang the visitors had in mind.

The first series of images depicted cells which emerged from cloudy substances—gases, which had split into millions of particles of light. The next models illustrated interplays of the particles of light and gasses, creating in turn millions of liquid sacs. The next relief showed an expanded sac wherein they saw formations of ice flakes, then crystalline rocks, and a powdery element which looked like sand. Each sac became a star. The scientists illustrated suns and moons as stars of hot gasses and ice respectively.

Sequentially, similar to frames of film, the next scene showed the surface of a star covered in ice, some of which melted, and water washed upon the sand. The water receded to reveal molecules. The Ashais scientists depicted these molecules as tiny cells from which burst various forms of flora and fauna as the light crossed over the panorama of water and sand. Among the many drawings, figurines, and other models were creatures of the water that also flew; some evolved to beasts of all sizes and species known to modern man as prehistoric creatures.

The models went on to show how fish evolved to reptiles and winged creatures, and as they cohabitated and intermingled more species emerged. The penultimate frame demonstrated the wind pushing the water to the sandbanks, from which other creatures emerged. These were the earliest ancestors of man that evolved and mutated over time to become diverse species of humans.

Meleke responded to the visitors' questions and said that primates were the closest relatives to man, but humans were a unique species. The Ashais watched the explorers' facial expressions as they scrutinized the exhibits, stepping back and retracing their steps to make sense of what they were seeing.

Interestingly the Ashais believed man had evolved in his diversity, as had other creatures. They believed all species came from water and the sun in union with the moon created water. The king said that water generated minerals, metals, stone, cave systems, and the entire natural environment.

The end of the exhibition was quite formidable. It was elegant and inspiring in its height and expanse. It was the sea in the formation of a tsunami washing everything off the face of the land, followed by the sun's rays absorbing the water, leaving space, then darkness. There was nothing to say.

"So you do not believe the universe, all this that you have shown us, came about by the design of some great being? Robert asked.

"You mean what or who you call God," Meleke replied.

"Yes."

"We believe in the supremacy of a force greater than man, and that's no different from what you believe. We do not think of the sun god as a supreme being of flesh and blood. We believe our sun god is all forces of the universe. Man is a god creature who loses his godliness when he disrespects himself. One's interpretation of God does not matter. It all comes down to the same thing: our significance in the scheme of things, which is to be a worthy force among all the forces."

"Come," said Nehsi gently. "The moment of your departure is close, and we must leave."

Allan asked, "So you believe everything came from the sea and the earliest predecessor of humans was a human molecule that mutated."

"Yes, we do," said Meleke, "and that's no different from the earliest predecessors of each group of animal species. What is the relationship between the tiger and the leopard, the lion and the hyena, the dog and the wolf, or the swan and the duck? What's important is that we all came from one source. Believing that man evolved from Apti suggests that there is nothing else to believe until your next discovery. In your world humility is like the desert. The animals are treated as dispensable things, but they know of the seasons, when the earth will tremble, when the rain will come, when the desert storms will blow sands that will travel around your world, when danger is near, and when they will die. They hear the call of their young from across the mountain."

"But that's instinct."

"It's more than instinct. It's a different level of intelligence. They are cunning, which means they think in their own way. They prepare for danger, build their shelters, store their food, and plot to entrap you as well as protect you. They have unique cultures within groups because they transmit behaviors across generations just like we do, and they have great memory capacity. We have powers of thought, reasoning, and creativity. We see the caterpillar emerge as a butterfly. We did not evolve in the sense you believe, but we evolved from one stage of our existence as human molecules to the next, just as we are continuing to evolve to fulfill our godly potential. You have to go to the temple within you to find your powers."

"I have one more question," Robert said. "The king and his people know much about us and the universe. What are your thoughts on the future of mankind?"

Meleke's eyes danced. He reached out and gently touched Robert's face as if Robert were a child. "We do not know the future, but we are creating it now. How we align the vision we have for a livable place with intelligent actions is what the future of mankind will be. It is all we can do to perfect ourselves. Nature will determine the rest."

Outside the temple, on a site upon a mount, the visitors saw astronomical instruments and other telescopic apparatuses. Chris reminded his group of the drawing they'd seen in another temple, which depicted something that looked like a space vessel. They now scrutinized the instruments. The status of the people on the strange land and their achievements thus far now made more sense to the visitors.

They left the museum and made their way to the Fountain of the Sun, where water gushed and fell on the mountainside. The breeze was cool, the various moods of the day in remission, and there was sadness. The visitors wondered about the future.

They spent some time on the shelf, conversing about life and theories of creation and evolution. So deep were they in the stimulating topic, they did not notice the time except for Meleke, who allowed them to indulge a little more. He too was in thought about the future of Ashaise. The Ashais knew the infinite size of the universe and had discovered that life existed in many worlds. They often discussed this on evenings when the realm leaders got together with the dreamers, storytellers, artists, doctors, and scientists. Meleke reflected more on this as the visitors were about to leave.

The ecosystem of the mountain, which the Fountain of the Sun showered, reenergized the mind. Colorful birds squawked, deer strutted by, and pygmy marmoset monkeys watched with interest the humans who had stepped into their world. Allan wandered off. He strolled slowly in deep thought; snippets of his life played out in this mind. He had the audacity to think about a plot to stay. He knew Meleke was right: they all had to return home. He felt that if he had more time with Jiena it would be easier to convince her father to allow him to return.

Thoughts of the members of the expedition who had died and his own mortality occupied Allan. He looked up at the fountain, then returned to Jiena's side.

Kiserian joined the party. She went close to Robert. He smiled.

The group had now passed other villages, which Chris and Allan had seen when the keeper had taken them to the crystal cave to see the nesting birds. Once again they were mounting the animals to travel along a steep mountainside. It was of speechless beauty, covered with the brilliant-yellow petals of massive poui trees as far as the eyes could see.

On top of the mountain, they looked into a fjord on which sailboats glided to the place where the Ashais fished and harvested pearls. The party watched the boats sail on the horizon and around islets. Diverse groups of animals drank at a stream; some roamed in herds, others in prides or troupes, or they climbed trees as the leopards and jaguars did.

The expedition returned to the familiar path where the moon embraced the sun and went into the mist. Their visibility of each other became increasingly dim. Allan was conscious that Jiena was riding close to his side. He looked at her slender form shielded in soft mist. She looked at him and knew he was mulling a plan in his head. He did not have to reveal it to her. Still her heartbeat increased because she had to be prepared. He seemed confident.

Out of the mist the party emerged to where Apti and her troupe enjoyed all the land offered to them. The babies held on to their mothers. The parents played, screamed, and grinned with the young ones, which were also on the receiving end of loud rebukes from annoyed fathers who tried to rest within the dense foliage.

Allan stopped to admire the closest relatives of humans in the majesty of their green castle. He became aware of a stealthy moon just peeping from behind the Seat of God. The group looked at the moon—the symbol of their fate. Slowly they continued the journey. The birds whistled low as they flew overhead. The one that led the flock somersaulted as if to say, "See us now, my friends, for you will never set eyes upon us again." They circled and flew higher and higher beyond the rolling, white clouds.

The mountain upon which the party had landed over two months earlier was visible. Apti's bark was like thunder as she watched the expedition's progress to the mount. The group stopped, and Allan looked directly at Apti. She looked at him, then turned her eyes to the clouds where the birds had disappeared, then back at him. She lowered her eyes, turned her head, and looked up. This time she gave him a sideways glance. She sensed his intent.

Allan was uneasy and turned to face the mountain. He had reached the short avenue of olive trees through which he had to pass to begin his first steps toward home.

Meleke stopped and turned to the group. This was where the royal party would leave the visitors. He felt the burden of separation from these people he had come to respect—especially Allan—but kept his proud head aloof.

From beyond the huge, white boulders emerged Meke on Zete. In one hand he held a silver object. The king told the visitors to dismount. Aatum approached each in turn. He ensured they had no physical materials or evidence of Ashaise. Satisfied that they were not hiding anything, he bowed and moved back to his lion.

Chris, Robert, and Springer said goodbye to Aatum and each member of the royal party by placing a hand on each one's shoulder in the Ashais way. Kiserian went to Robert. He embraced her and for the last time looked into the face of the world. He kissed her.

Allan placed his hand on Aatum's shoulder. He went to Teye and kissed her gently on the forehead. She touched his face, and he saw her tears. He then embraced Nehsi. The next was Meleke, who reached out and placed his hand on the side of Allan's face. Allan put his hand over Meleke's.

"Go with the sun god, son," the king told him.

Allan's eyes welled before he quickly turned away to Jiena, who handed him a thin, gold chain with an obsidian pendant and a short feather of a crystal bird. He held her close before taking the gift. She fixed her eyes on his, staring long into their dark centers, then shook her head from side to side. He read the message and knew his plan was risky. Jiena kissed him, walked toward Matai, and mounted the splendid beast. They sped off ahead of the party. She did not look back. From the Seat of God she watched him.

Meke, the child, held out his silver object. He placed it in the hands of Allan, whose eyes overflowed to a blur. Meke left with the king and queen. Thereafter the visitors walked up the mountain, where they awaited the crossing. Before they reached the summit in the progressing darkness, Knufu and his soldier warriors in full regalia arrived to escort them to the top. Allan handed the vessel to Chris.

CHAPTER 34

On Mt. Kilimanjaro Raymond Johnson, members of the rescue mission, and other climbers were waiting for something to happen in the sky. Charmaine and Caftie had disappeared in the cave for several days, and it was unlikely they would return. Raymond could not have known they were in Kenya and had already contacted Jennifer Stephens and the dean.

The sky was a reddish brown. From the mouth of the cave, Raymond and the others looked down on grumbling clouds. Something caught his attention. Raymond thought he had seen moving shadows in the thick mist, and he went ahead as far as it was prudent. He heard his own breathing as he stood surveying the clouds. He put his hands out behind him and gestured to the members of his team not to proceed.

A tall silhouette in the curling clouds moved. After a short time, he saw more silhouettes in a row. At the side of each was an enormous beast—a black lion the likes of which were unimaginable. The men came from the clouds, and slowly approached the figure they saw standing before them until they were within two meters of Raymond. He shooed the others back into the cave. The soldiers responded to the command and sent the others back. Two soldiers remained a short distance from him in a protective posture.

Raymond took in the misty scene, which included six of the tallest men he had ever seen. They wore red shukas. The keeper walked forward and lifted his spear, though not in a threatening manner. The action cautioned Raymond and the soldiers not to proceed farther.

"Who are you?' asked Raymond.

"We are the people of the sun god. You must leave the House of God."

"We came to find our people. Do you know where they are?"

"They are behind the sun and will soon be here."

"Where do your people of the sun god live?"

"We live behind the sun. Send the others away and you may wait for your people."

Raymond turned to the soldiers. "You are to leave immediately with the rest of the mission and return to base. I will wait here."

The soldier said, "We cannot leave. Our orders are to protect you and those we came to find."

"You have no choice now. Leave immediately." As Raymond gave the command, the keeper slightly raised his assegai, and a beast moved forward, to the consternation of Raymond and the soldiers. One raised his gun and aimed before Raymond could stop him. The beast lunged. The soldier had no time to scream before clouds shrouded his lifeless body. Two warriors passed Raymond and entered the cave, followed by lions. The rest of the team rushed back to the safety of the cave.

The warriors recognized James, who had placed his back against a rock. He was speechless. He could not leave—not now that he had seen the people from Ashaise. The presence of the Ashais on the mountain saved the team from the result of a crossover to Ashaise. He had hoped the search would end on the mountain. James knew if they had crossed over to Ashaise they would have died there. This was his evidence. He had to take a picture, and he went into his bag for the camera. As he took it out, he did not see from where the arrow came. Raymond rushed over to James. He looked at the Ashais soldiers. Raymond knew then, the wrong move meant his death.

The Ashais chased the other team members for several hours along a winding path, then left the lions to continue the job. The soldiers indiscriminately fired several shots. The warrior protectors returned to where they had left Raymond and the keeper. The moon crept closer to the sun, and the aura of dusk colored the day.

Raymond moved away from James's body, and turned to the keeper. He resumed the conversation with the keeper but got no more information than he had before about the land behind the sun. Daylight dimmed. The keeper motioned Raymond into the cave and turned his slender body. He and the other warriors disappeared into the clouds. Sahure stood in the shadow, not far from Raymond.

※

From the Seat of God, Jiena watched the man she loved climb the mountain. She held the shell he had given to her. Allan and the others had reached the top and were watching the moon, which moved like a balloon in the wind. Jiena saw him as he turned and looked toward the Seat of God. She smiled because he knew she would be there. The moon approached, and the sun's white glow circled it. It was night. The wind blew.

During Allan's conversation with Meleke, when they had stood on the balcony of the Temple of Healing, Allan had realized Meleke would not let him return to Ashaise. He had felt the Ashais would try to make it impossible for anyone to find their land. He had thought deeply about his life and knew he would never be happy unless he returned to the mystical place. He had wanted Jiena. The only option had been to find a way to stay. He had been prepared to risk his life for her.

Allan knew he had to fulfil obligations. The project with Chris was too important to abandon, and in any event he had to consider his parents. Once he had a little more time with Meleke, he felt, he could convince the king to allow him to return. He made a decision that he would climb the mountain with the rest of the group. Just before the pivotal moment, he would throw himself on the ground. He would roll down the mountain far away from the force that would pull them across when the shield around Ashaise broke. He prayed he would not end up in Apti's habitat. Jiena had tried to warn him that his plan would fail.

The group had reached the summit, and just before the critical moment, Allan tried to throw himself backward. The strong hands of Knufu pushed him forward.

Jiena stayed on the Seat of God, where the keeper found her. She wept in his arms until dawn.

CHAPTER 35

They landed on Mt. Kilimanjaro and wandered through the clouds. Raymond and a lion stood at the mouth of the cave. Sahure was in the shady corner.

Allan, Chris, Robert, and Springer did not know who Raymond was. The scene, with a soldier in familiar fatigues and a black lion, astounded them. They looked around, and Allan saw the warrior who moved forward and stood a short distance from the group. The two men studied each other. Allan held the eyes of the person before him. He knew instinctively that it was Sahure. The other three men figured out who the warrior was and watched.

Chris angled his body so he could see Sahure's every move. Allan was speechless as he looked at the beautiful figure. Sahure's eyes did not blink as he looked at his rival. Allan saw Sahure's hand tighten around the assegai. The warrior's chest heaved, and his jaw clenched. Blood rushed to Allan's face. He had once been a soldier and trained to kill, and was acutely sensitive to danger.

As he processed the standoff, Allan saw a slight movement in the warrior's eyes. It crossed his mind that the Ashais were masters of their emotions, though he was not sure about Sahure. The enemy had to make the first move, and the Ashais would be ready. They would be fast, accurate, and deadly. It was unlikely that Sahure would make an aggressive move except in self-defense, but Allan figured the warrior would not need any excuse. Intuitively, he knew that the wrong move meant possible death.

He took comfort that close by were two war veterans, a hunter, and an armed soldier, but he would not make the mistake of underestimating an Ashais warrior with a lion. Sahure would have calculated the odds. Allan could not be sure whether there were other warriors and lions.

He kept his eyes fixed on Sahure as he took a step closer to the warrior, stretched out a hand, and rested it on the warrior's shoulder—the Ashais' sign of peace. Allan bowed his head, overwhelmed with a feeling of despondency, almost grief, and emptiness. Something had gone. He had gone. He was no longer the Allan Cline who had left earth's realm over two months earlier. He removed this hand from Sahure's shoulder, turned, and walked to the entrance of the cave.

Chris held the silver urn Allan had given to him. He knew why his friend had done that. He placed the urn inside his shirt. The air was cold, and Raymond took warm clothing and held the garments out to the four men.

The keeper, other warrior protectors, and lions had returned to Ashaise simultaneously with the arrival of the remaining expedition members on Mt. Kilimanjaro, leaving behind with Sahure three camouflaged warriors and two lions.

Sahure motioned to Raymond and the four expedition members to go into the cave. Allan paused for a moment and turned to face Sahure for a second time. The two men simply looked at each other again. Allan wanted to say something but could not. There was a twinkle in Sahure's eyes. Was it pity, or was it cockiness Allan saw? It did not matter.

Sahure and a lion followed Allan, Chris, Robert, Springer, and Raymond in the cave. It was a trek that had taken several hours, and at no time Sahure had spoken other than to urge the group to move quickly.

The warrior soldier focused his attention on the job his chiefs had sent him to do, and also on Allan. There was a creepy silence, except for the rhythm of men's footsteps moving through the cave. At times, the situation was tense. Allan had felt uneasy with Sahure right behind him, and he had looked around frequently. He sensed other Ashais soldiers were following them.

They had finally reached the place where they had entered the cave months ago, and all exited it except for Sahure. The group then turned and looked at him. He waved them to move on their way. As he did so, he looked directly at Allan. The warrior watched until they were out of his sight, then returned to the bowels of the cave.

Not long thereafter, the explorers and Raymond heard a roar. They stared up the mountain and heard another roar followed by an explosion. The mountain rumbled under an avalanche of rocks that cascaded and crashed over the slopes. Their eyes did not leave the scene for a long time. They felt no one would ever find the cave again, or Ashaise. Their hopes were shattered. The only images of the treasures it hid were on Ashaise.

Sahure, on his beast, bolted through the path before most of the cave eroded. He reached the chamber with the reliefs of his ancient forefathers. There he and his fellow warriors would wait until the next crossing of the sun. He thought of Jiena and said to himself that he would wait for many moons.

CHAPTER 36

When Charmaine awoke, Brother Caftie was sitting at her bedside.

"Now, tell me, how I would have found you without my God?" he asked.

She smiled and said, "Maybe it's no coincidence that we're here. Maybe we would have experienced a terrible fate on the mountain. Who knows whether there's a strange land with wise people, black lions, and crystal birds?"

"So you don't believe James, do you, Charmaine?"

She liked how he said her name. "Oh, yes, I believe he's genuine about what he saw, but whatever it was, it could not be on Kili."

"He didn't say it was. He said the mountain was the path to get to a place called Ashaise. Considering that we walked through a cave that spans two countries, anything is possible. The caves could hold a city. We just don't know. What does it matter now anyway?"

She looked at him from the side of her eyes and thought he was not bad looking. He was a good man, and he enjoyed nature in her original outfit.

Caftie could not persuade Charmaine to attend church on Sundays and read to his students from the Bible. She said it was a history book written several hundred years after Jesus died, and Armageddon would happen when some idiot dropped a nuclear bomb. He could not convince her Jesus would come again. She told him that planet Earth was the last place in the universe he would want to visit. A Maasai elder married them under a banyan tree.

※

The biologist, the geologist, and the soldiers told their stories of the strange beasts and men who chased them on the glacial mountain. Their description of the lion was consistent with James's story. People believed the tall people dressed in red were Maasai.

It was Caftie's and Charmaine's accounts of the caves that convinced many people the mysterious land was in a cave. There was a continuation of myths, tales, and babble about the mountain. The facts did not matter.

James's body was never found. Many months later, when Chris and Allan were documenting the events, they speculated whether Sahure had instructions from Meleke to kill James.

Major Raymond Johnson knew what he had seen and heard on the mountain. He had seen when the arrow hit James, and he reported that. The keeper's gentle and patient manner had affected him. He'd accomplished his mission, and that was all that had mattered. His term of office had ended, and he decided to stay in Kenya. Raymond became friendly with Springer. At times they felt as though they were being watched.

※

When they returned to camp, Robert, Springer, Chris, and Allan spent time in the embrace of their relatives, who listened with delight as they related their experiences on the mountain. They made no mention of Ashaise. Their desire to open the silver urn was overwhelming. They would wait until they were alone.

They met with the dean, and in the privacy of his bungalow they carefully opened the gift. Leaves layered the top, and inside was another container stuffed with damp moss, dark soil, gravel, and feathers. Carefully Allan removed each layer. He stopped, held the silver vessel close to his chest, looked up, and said softly, "Meleke."

They all tried to look inside, and Springer exclaimed, "It's an egg. My God, it's an egg!"

"Quick," said Chris. "Let's cover it back and get it to a safe place. We have to get it home safely. I wonder if it will hatch."

"But where will we keep it? They've done this in a way to simulate its natural environment. We have to find an environment similar to Ashaise. It has to be an area where there is no pollution."

"Where on earth could that be?" asked Robert. "This is our evidence. They've given us evidence of Ashaise. We must see this as a sign. Perhaps they want to be found."

"No way. If that's the case, Sahure would not have blown up the cave, which was already difficult to find," Chris responded.

"OK, OK," Allan said quietly. "Calm down. Let's think, because if this egg hatches, the future implications will be enormous. We have to commit to keep this to ourselves, at least for the time being. I trust we all commit to that."

They responded together, "Yes." Members of the team felt they could rely on each other.

"The best conditions will be on the mountain," Hackshaw said, "but there's too much traffic, and it will be difficult for us to monitor progress and restrain the bird. On our return home we'll put the egg in the laboratory, where we can isolate an area and make a nesting place. It will be easy to check on it there. How long is the incubation period?"

"I'm not sure. It's probably about six months. We can't be certain because there is a difference in time zones. But based on what Aatum told us, the Ashais's year is sometimes shorter than ours by a month. We have to assume this is a new egg, so it may hatch as early as September," said Allan.

They were not sure, but figured Meleke would have given them a newly laid egg.

They decided how members should respond to questions about their project. The archaeologists, the anthropologist, and the geographic writer reaffirmed their decision not to discuss their experiences. They agreed Robert could write about their discoveries in the Magamba rain forest and Mt. Kilimanjaro caves, and about a solitary group of Maasai who visited the mountain from time to time. They refused to respond to media requests, except to describe what they had discovered in a cave on the mountain. They had to be skillful and candid in their words as they related the discoveries. They spoke in detail about the cave on Mt. Kilimanjaro and left it to the audience to conclude what had happened on that mountain.

In response to a direct media question about whether there was a place called Ashaise, Springer said yes. "It's a name given by ancient tribes to the Valley of Life." The reporters asked about Timothy, Joe, and Cazeau. The response was that Timothy and James had left the other expedition members, and a lion had chased Timothy into a gorilla's habitat. Springer said Joe and Cazeau also left the team, and they didn't know what had happened to them.

The group felt a strong obligation to the Ashais because Meleke had spared their lives and responded to their need for the medicine.

※

Springer continued to hunt, haunted by the memory of the crystal birds. He drew beautiful scenes, sometimes of the birds nesting in the forests of Kenya. Often he visited the domain of the silverback gorillas, searching for signs of another species. Together with Raymond he went to the snow-capped mountain for several days and looked to the sky, hoping another opportunity would come to visit the mystical land of genteel people. If he ever got another chance, there would be no return.

He sometimes saw the faces of the keeper and Aatum in rivers, as well as the odd shadow. Whenever he went hunting, he stopped to listen for a low whistle. Springer became a different hunter—one who, since his stay in Ashaise, never killed another animal.

﹡﹡﹡

Robert was profoundly affected by his experiences in Ashaise. He now saw the world through a different lens. He often walked at midnight in his garden in Surrey and reflected on current affairs, history, and science. His wife, Sylvia, would look at him from the window and feel depressed because he seemed to have little interest in the things that once had given him pleasure. Kiserian's gray eyes danced in his mind. He realized how much he had grown to love her. He hoped to see her again.

The theme and tone of his writings changed from descriptive accounts of his journeys to soulful, inspiring portrayals of the power of nature's forces. More than ever his sojourn had reinforced his belief that man had so far only scratched the surface of his potential.

He kept in touch weekly with Allan and Chris on the bird's progress. They agreed to meet in August to await the hatching.

The following year Robert visited Kenya. He bought a house in Kakamega, where he and Sylvia vacationed. He had frequent contact with Springer.

﹡﹡﹡

Allan and Chris did not pursue the expedition to Ethiopia as planned because they were busy documenting the details of their discoveries in the caves. They went back to the Magamba rain forest with a heavy contingent of soldiers. They obtained evidence to prove their proposition that Kushites were the first builders of grand pyramids and sphinxes. Video and print materials of the unprecedented artifacts, illustrations, sculptures, and images in the cave established the identity of the ancient civilization that had inhabited the regions stretching across Northern Africa.

They wanted to find out more about the lost Saharan civilizations of the Garamantes and the Kingdom of Yam, which had existed long before recorded history. Research indicated the Garamantes had been among the early architects of underground tunnels, and inhabited a region close to or within the region known as Libya. Chris and Allan wondered whether there was a connection between these civilizations and some of the earliest people who had inhabited the caves. They decided to explore that later.

The impressive evidence of literate civilizations contained in their new book did not quell some skeptical voices. The publication fascinated archaeological communities across the world as well as historians and anthropologists, among others.

They kept a document on the profile of Ashaise using a code name: the Valley of Life.

Allan spent his free time alone or with his parents. Because of his father, Meleke was often in his mind. After the explosion on the mountain, Allan understood what Meleke had meant when he'd alluded that Allan may not have been able to return. He loved the compassionate king.

His face broke into a smile and he chuckled. He would never want to play a game of poker with Meleke.

Allan drafted documents on the prehistoric lifestyles, religion, and traditions of Africa. He drew Jiena's face on notebook pages and wrote poems. He was often depressed, and he longed to see and hold the woman who lived in the land beyond the sun.

Frequently he went to the local lakeside, where he would sit for hours thinking of the Ashais. He thought about his loving, fun-filled, last night together with Jiena. He loved her coquettish innocence and playfulness. She had run outside with his shirt; he had chased her and bumped into Meleke, who had stood before him with his arms crossed on his chest.

"How will you protect Ashaise if you cannot hold a woman?" Meleke had said with a dimpled, mischievous smile. Allan had not been able to stop laughing, and ran past the king. The king had shaken his head from side to side and gone on his business.

Sometimes Chris would not hear from Allan for several weeks. Chris would go over to his apartment and find him in a depressed mood. They would talk about Ashaise for a while, and Chris would persuade Allan to go to a football game, or do things that lifted his mood.

Allan circled the first week of September on his calendar—the earliest date he predicted the bird could be due.

Every morning the dean visited the high-security area of the laboratory at the university to monitor the bird's progress. On the seventeenth day of October, he peeped in, his face flushed and his hands trembling. As he lifted the swaddling feathers and leaves, he saw the cream-colored egg dancing. The bird was getting ready to peck her way out. The dean raced to the phone and called Allan and Chris, both of whom must have risked speeding tickets to get to the university as fast as they did. Allan figured that he had miscalculated the week of hatching because of the time zone difference between Ashaise and Earth.

They immediately called Robert and Springer to inform them of the remarkable development. The dean, Allan, and Chris were like mother hens around the incubator. They paced the floor; looking out the window and drinking cups of coffee as they awaited the birth of Kriziantu. Finally, at six o'clock, the bird pushed her head through the hole she'd pecked. Gradually she worked her way out of the shell, stood on wobbly legs, and collapsed on her belly. The three men gasped. The bird stood up again and shook her wings before opening them. She rested again.

"What do we do now? How do we feed her?" Dean Hackshaw asked.

"Baby chicks feed from their mothers," said Chris.

"I know that," the dean said with anxiety in his voice. "I mean where do we get a mother?"

"You, my dear Professor Hackshaw," Allan said.

The dean stared at them over his glasses.

"You need to drip water into her beak. Within a couple of days, we can get fresh water and baby fish, and blend them."

"Hmm... Well, get on with it then," responded the grumpy dean.

It was well after midnight when they left the bird. They returned early the following morning.

In the hours before dawn, the chick nestled between the feathers of her mother and some leaves. At the crack of dawn she stood up and greeted the dean. He smiled and took photos of the special creature, which was about thrice the size of a domestic chick. Her down was silky; her webbed feet had well-formed, long claws; and her still-misty eyes were pink.

The dean gently placed one gloved hand into the tube that extended inside the incubator, and he left a small petri dish full of water. He put a little in his gloved hand and offered the bird a drink. She gave a low squeak and stayed in her warm bed. He tried on several occasions and got the same response. The chick repeated the performance over the next day, and by the third day her caretakers were very concerned. They pureed food for her, but she would not eat.

"She must feed, so the only option is to try doing so intravenously," said Chris. Allan chuckled at the suggestion.

"We cannot do that," said the dean. "That may kill her. Let's leave the food and water for another few hours and see what happens."

They returned after three hours and found the bird quite active and happy in the large incubator. She squeaked and walked around. The dish was empty. They were delighted and left her for the evening. They named her Asha, which Springer said was a Kenyan name meaning "life."

By the end of the first week, she was twice her size and showed signs of becoming a very glamorous lady. They noticed an iridescent, cerulean patch between her eyes and beak. Their next task was to increase the incubator's size to perhaps half the room, but the rate at which the bird pro-gressed posed a problem. The wingspan of an adult crystal bird was nearly thirty feet, so it was not possible to keep her in a laboratory room, but the polluted external environment was an immediate threat to her life. They could not create the conditions in Ashaise, where human life expectancy was fifty years more than the average in their world.

They considered whether there was anywhere in North America that would be conducive to the bird's survival. In every case there were issues. Nature trails in pristine forests were frequently traversed by hikers, hunters, and research-ers. Rivers were likely to have traces of chemicals, and even the natural flora and fauna posed a problem.

Even if a place for this bird existed, the chances of keep-ing her hidden for any length of time were poor. The three men pondered the seriousness of the situation. They sur-mised that if Asha could be protected at least until she laid eggs, the chances of her chicks surviving in their place of birth were pretty good.

Chris suggested they call Springer to determine whether prospects were good for her survival in Kenya. They wanted to keep her away from prying eyes. The suggestion excited Springer. The next challenge was to get the bird to the African continent without questions about her genus. They devised a plan for Asha to travel within a week.

It was four in the morning a week later—exactly three weeks after the bird's birth—when the dean, Allan, and Chris entered the laboratory to make the final preparations. They panicked. Something was wrong. She was not in the incuba-tor. She had struggled during the last few hours and clawed her way out. Asha was no lightweight chick; her body was sturdy and she had quadrupled her size since birth.

The three men looked around the room, which had a high, cathedral ceiling. They heard a low whistle and looked up at the bird happily perched on a wooden beam. Time was not in their favor. She had grown accustomed to the dean, so he made an effort to coax her down, but to no avail. The stubborn chick had her own exciting plan.

They hatched another scheme. They would go out of the room for a few minutes and see whether she would come down from her lofty position during that time. They did, and she complied, except as they were reentering she squeaked. Her body stunned the dean as it collided with his head. Before the other two conspirators knew what was happening, Asha squeezed through the door and between the bodies of her caregivers, striking with her talons, and was out of the room. She made her way like a mad victim until she found an entrance to the wide world of snow-capped trees. She did not stop flying and continued an uncharted course in the freezing, early morning air until she reached mountains. It would not be easy to spot her, as her white down blended perfectly with the snow-capped Sierra Nevada Mountains.

The chick stunned her mothers. They did not know what to do next. There was nothing that could have been done, since they did not know where she was. It would have been extremely difficult to catch her. Seeking help was out of the question, since that meant revealing the origins of the bird. The rejected mothers left the laboratory and made frequent checks in the event the ungrateful child returned to her artificial nest.

Asha had no intention of returning. She stayed hidden high in the mountains and learned to feed herself, an activity she carried out at night. She rested during the daytime. By the end of six weeks, the lady was awesome. Months passed, and spring brought a renewal of life. Asha felt a pull. She had to go where genetic predisposition directed her.

One evening, just after sunset, she left her secluded place in the mountain and made her way toward the Atlantic. She traveled above the clouds without rest for many days until one night she reached the pinnacle of the Pyrenees between Spain and France. There, high in the mountains, she was safely camouflaged. She rested throughout the night and during the following day. On the second night, she fished in the mountain's creek, and on the third night she took off and made her way to the African continent. It was not long before her migratory instincts took her to the glacial summit of Kilimanjaro.

Her grieving caregivers read the occasional reports of sightings by skiers and hunters of a huge, white bird, much bigger than an eagle that flew across the mountains and disappeared in the clouds. Some said they heard a strange, low whistle, but there was never any concrete evidence of the existence of such a creature. An excited cruise-ship tourist told the captain she had seen a large, white bird during the night on deck, but she was the same person they had escorted to her room drunk out of her senses the previous night.

The caregivers knew it was Asha. Her disloyalty devastated them. As consolation, the dean said it was encouraging to learn that the crystal bird could survive in their environment.

CHAPTER 37

In March 2000 Allan Cline left for the Rift Valley, where he built a cottage. He researched and prepared extensive reports that he sent to the dean and Chris. Over the next two years, he coauthored with Chris two books on civilizations from 5,000 BCE in Central and East Africa.

When Allan was not delivering lectures at universities or archaeological conferences, he was at his cottage. Often he would go up the mountain, where he spent nights watching the stars. During the day he continued to conduct research and became familiar with the forest and virtually every ridge, crevasse, plant, and animal species in it.

Another year passed. A patch of gray at the temples distinguished Allan's handsome, coffee-brown face. He would hold the chain Jiena had given him and touch the pendant, longing and hoping for an opportunity to live in Ashaise.

Whenever he explored the mountain, he took the path that had led his expedition to the cave, but there was no evidence it existed. He thought of Sahure then and believed that returning to Ashaise would be impossible.

He spent longer and longer periods at the camp closest to Uruhu Peak. It was the nearest he could get to Jiena. One night, just over three years after the fateful day he had arrived in Ashaise, he strolled a little distance from the camp. He thought he had seen a shadow. He stood on one spot, waiting and watching. He shook his head, reflected on his mental health, and then laughed at himself.

Two months later he got permission from the authorities to establish a cabin near the camp where he had spent at least eight months every year. Climbers and returning tourists knew him well and began to refer to him as the keeper of the mountain. They knew not the meaning of this to him.

There were times when Springer, Chris, and Robert visited. They would sit around a fire and reflect on their experiences in Ashaise. The Ashais had changed their lives. The explorers wanted more of them. They wanted to feel the rays of the sun god. It was their secret that bonded them as brothers.

The last time Chris visited, he and Allan discussed revisiting the Ethiopian project. It was a cold night, and they sat in front of the fire in the cabin. They explored the prospects. Chris leaned back. He swirled the wine in his glass. He lifted it to the fire and watched the reflection of light play on the glass and the ruby red wine.

"You're pensive. What's wrong?" Allan asked.

"My mother always told me to go by my hunches. I don't think I will see you again after this time."

They were silent.

"Who knows, Chris? I don't know how long I will stay here."

"It's more than a premonition. They're calling you. You hear their call."

The following morning they said farewell to each other.

"Give the dean and Jennifer my love," Allan said.

"I will. Keep this for me." Chris gave him a pocket book of psalms.

"Keep this for me." Allan gave him his father's silver chain.

They embraced. He watched as Chris disappeared from sight.

The following night Allan sat by the campfire under the shelter of a clear-blue, starry sky. He read the psalms until his lids drooped. Later he suddenly awoke because he thought he had heard a familiar sound, like a low whistle. He looked up. The night was cold, and a gentle breeze blew. He felt soothing warmth and relaxed as he looked at the stars. Allan smiled at himself because there was no bird. He felt close to Jiena and imagined her head on his shoulder, as she'd done when they'd sat by the lake. This night he felt at peace when he went to his lodge and to bed.

At least once a moon week, Jiena would sit with Matai on the Seat of God, looking at the mount on which Allan once had stood. The mountain on Ashaise and the ridge on Mt. Kilimanjaro were in the path where there were breaks in Ashaise's gravitational field. The breaks happened during periods of eclipse. The event propelled matter from either side. Ashaise was undetectable because of its magnetic field. Reflective rays created as a result of the interplay between energy matter from the sun and moon absorbed Ashaise's light. With the eclipse of the sun, an unusual gravitational phenomenon occurred that thrust materials into the stratosphere. The atmosphere on Ashaise was also neutralized by the same phenomenon of energy, allowing people to breathe normally.

The visitors had returned home. Sahure had skillfully executed the mandate from King Meleke. He had ensured the path from Mt. Kilimanjaro was no longer aligned with Ashaise when the shield broke. He wanted to eliminate the potential for future accidental or planned arrivals. The scientists had shown Sahure how to make a significant explosion and collapse the opening of the cave as well as the exit where crossover occurred.

The explosion had caused changes in the physical profile of the mountain. Sahure had been precise in his timing and crossed back at the same time the second explosion occurred. He had done his job well, and there was no longer a gravitational path to Ashaise. Any person or thing on either side when the phenomenon occurred would sail the skies around Ashaise.

※

Allan was always in Jiena's thoughts. He was the remarkable visitor who had travelled to the land of the crystal bird, where she knew not his power to seduce her vulnerable mind, to turn her head to elusive stars, and to shatter her dreams. Had it been the twinkle in his earthy eyes or maybe his mischievous smile? Had it been the shell he'd placed in her hands or the magic of his touch? Had it been the hearty sound of his laughter by the cool, deep, languid lake?

She thought love knew not the path to freedom. Her heart was bound to his. It was a dream, a void to bridge, with the memories of a time that was so real and true, but they were not free. Unfulfilled love blossomed in the secret of time. It was a mystery, like the moonbeam's flight; it was the pleasure of forbidden fruit plucked from friendship. There was warmth and sincerity, a bond shared. It was real and not a dream, but something that would be forever more in the tide of a time when they were younger. Their passion was like the rush of water on shifting sands or bamboo breaking in the wild wind over the mountain of the sun. Their emotions flowed like many rivers running to the wide, deep lake.

Her parents saw her pain, and they knew she had fortitude. Her infectious laughter was not heard again. She spent most of her time with children and with the elderly in the garden. She loved Fathiya, whose name meant "triumph." She was the 155-year-old mother of the keeper. She was the wise one—wiser than her son.

Fathiya loved to tell Jiena stories about the keeper when he was a child, and tales of ancient tribes that came to the Valley of Life. Her life was a fascinating story—a story that exposed the fullness of her remarkable world. She had accepted with dignity the unpredictability of daily challenges. The fine, dry rivulets on her brow did not speak of age but accentuated an exquisite profile. Fathiya's eyes were dark-brown crystal balls which twinkled precociously. They were windows that opened to the trees and saw not just the dense forest but every single leaf, bud, petal, and twig. In her distinguished face, Jiena saw enduring love.

When Jiena was not with the elderly, she was working or on the Seat of God with Matai. The keeper brought her fruit and nuts. He loved her; she was the only woman he'd ever cared for, and he suspected she was aware of his affection for her. He understood the reality of Jiena's bond with Allan. He was content to be her confidante and protector and knew she would fully realize her potential if the man from the other side came back, or if she found him.

The keeper often thought about the probability of Allan returning to Ashaise. The chances of a safe crossover were even more remote than before the explosion on the mountain because Ashaise had experienced strong vibrations. The quakes shifted it slightly in relation to her host. The Ashais knew about these small shifts and the impact on their land.

One morning, after a restless night, the keeper went to speak with Meleke, who, during a lengthy discourse, asked him to get advice from the chief scientist, Kiente.

Meleke was eager for new ideas and skills. He had grand plans for Ashaise and often reflected on his conversations with the arrogant man from across the sun. Allan had touched them all in some way. He had stimulated Meleke's thinking. The king felt his daughter's pain.

"Chinua, why is it he seemed so close to us?" Meleke asked.

"I have thought much about that from the day he first came. His chi reached us. The sun god sent him. I spoke with the storytellers who know the past. They believe he is our blood."

"How could that be?"

"Many moons ago, in the time of our father, Mbtani, storytellers related that men took Mbtani's brother. Ancestors who came after Mbtani wrote in the chronicles that slavers continued to take away their brothers and sisters. Maybe they took the boy on the ship to where Allan lives. We cannot be certain, but he may be a great son of our lost ancestor. He looks like us. He looks like you."

The king considered what he had just heard. He went to the temple and looked at the image of Mbtani. He thought of his grandchildren and Meke. He remembered what Teye had said about Allan's voice and eyes. He called the keeper.

"Find him." The king's voice was strangely forceful. His eyes glistened. "Whatever it takes, bring our son back to us."

The keeper had wasted little time in arranging a meeting with Kiente—chief of the council of scientists and philosophers. The council discussed prospects for a safe crossover. "There is a remote chance. Let us go to the temple." said Kiente.

They went to the Temple of the Sun, into a chamber where scientists and philosophers explored the universe and the scope of man's powers.

"See here?" said Kiente. "This is the spot where the shield broke, and when we moved an ant's step the core plates moved. We are probably in line with this spot on the mountain. The ancient passage can no longer receive us, but there is another area on the mountain that leads to the great valley of man. There is a chance. We can send Matai. Matai knows him. We have no guarantee he is there, but as you say, Jiena communicates with him through the powers of her mind. He may be there. He said he and his friend, the one called Chris, will be exploring Alkebulan, so there is every reason to believe he is there. If that is so, Matai will find him."

"I will go," the keeper said.

"No," said Meleke. "Not yet. There is a danger, since there may be no alignment. Let us send Matai first. If anything happens to Matai, Jiena will understand."

When they left, Meleke stood in the Temple of the Sun looking at the image of Mbtani. He thought of Allan and remembered the chronicles. He whispered to himself, "Masigonde."

CHAPTER 38

On one unusually warm night, the eccentric American the people of Kenya and Tanzania came to know as Nuru stood outside his cabin and looked, as he always did, to the sky. He had long ago discarded Western clothes for the traditional Maasai wear. On that night in January 2004, he draped the red shuka over winter clothing. His Rasta locks hung to his shoulder blades—the place where, according to the Ashais' folk tales, people once had wings. His face was lean and weather-beaten.

The people said Allan represented light, hence the name Nuru. He had spent nearly four years enlightening visitors about the history of the continent. He, an American, reminded them with passion of a legacy of extraordinary kingdoms and empires including Ta-Seti (Nubia), Punt, Ashanti of Ghana, Songhai, Benin of Nigeria, Mali (Sudan) or Mandingo, Axum of Ethiopia, Kanem-Bornu of Nigeria, and many others that thrived with enterprise many centuries ago.

He traced in vivid color the inspiring deeds of heroes and icons of Africa and its diaspora. He told stories about heroes of other continents, England and the Caribbean Archipelago, who had been distanced from Africa by hundreds of generations and knew little about the continent. Allan concluded his story with the deeds of Martin Luther King Jr., the heroic children of Soweto, and a noble, peaceful man named Nelson Mandela.

His audiences huddled with enthusiasm. Their eyes danced with excitement as they saw the travails and splendor of the dauntless heroes. They grabbed memorable moments in a cabin of hope. They wanted water to wet their minds. He satisfied their thirst. They wanted food to feed their esteem, and he satisfied their hunger.

A stream flowed through time, carrying the leaders of tribes, kingdoms, empires, and modern communities. They were the rocks around which the water splashed. They were great men and women, as ruthless or benevolent as the leaders who flowed through many other streams. They were courageous people who fought tirelessly for freedom, who had repelled foreigners for thousands of years before Satan had entered Alkebulan with the power of the gun. They were people who fought for civil rights and are today walking with dignity and contributing to shaping the destiny of the world.

Tourists took photos of the American meditating in his red shuka. They whispered about his increasing reclusiveness as he spoke to the mountain. He was often in the company of Maasai people, and on chilly nights they would sit around a fire outside the cabin and share stories. He learned more about their customs and taught them about the world. They heard about the lion of the sun god, the crystal bird called Kriziantu, and Apti the gorilla. Some thought him a strange person; some said he was crazy. The Maasai said he was an ancient light flashing through the Valley of Life to shine on them.

One evening students from a foreign university on a research expedition engaged him in a conversation about his life and the continent. He spoke with them in the warmth of his cabin. He said, "The continent of Africa is like a crystal bird. She is a magnificent and vulnerable bird that can soar beyond boundaries. Her children must know about her and discover who they are. They must love themselves as no other can love them. She is a crystal bird that can fly high above the clouds and whistle to the universe."

He said to them, "My foreparents were people who came from here and arrived in the new world in 1619. I am an American with an ancestry of strong and resilient people who walked this valley. You must know slavery for what it was and what it is now."

He continued, "The word had not yet been written eons ago, when strangers invaded tribal villages and later kingdoms. Throughout history, kingdoms have invaded other kingdoms, and tribes have invaded other tribes. They invaded each other's territory to get manpower to build cities and strengthen armies. The conquerors took men, women, and children—the spoils of war. They became slaves of every race, color, and creed who worked in kitchens, in factories, and on river banks, and built the temples, citadels, and palaces of the world. They were more valuable than gold.

They were, and still are, economic tools that each group—the Arabians, Africans, Indians, Chinese, English, Romans, Greeks, Russians, Scandinavians, Americans, and others—sold. They all sold their own people to the highest bidders."

He told the students that slavery thrived. Throughout six continents, wicked people trafficked more slaves today than during the peak period of trans-Atlantic slavery. Every minute Satan bought and sold children and women under the noses of the most modern armies and police in the developed world. Satan plied his trade for exactly the same perverse reasons he had in the past. He forced people into armies of prostitutes, and factory, plantation, and domestic slaves.

Allan told his visitors that children had to appreciate their unique beauty and value their talents in a world that was a fascinating place. "You must sit around the table of innovators. You must learn from history but have two feet in the future."

Allan learned how to meditate and go deep within himself to feel and hear what he could not feel and hear before. He began to discover the power of his mind. He was ready to be set free, but his spirit was a force so strong he could not release it. It struggled with his mind and battled his heart, trying to escape from the chains of his will. It was part of him, yet it seemed not, for there was no way he could reach the invisible door.

In deep meditation, he heard a call from within. The call resonated throughout his being. He wanted to be set free, to come out of himself and shine like a light that Jiena would see. At other times he was dancing to a tune—the song she sang. It was quintessentially supreme, reminding him of the ocean's mood, which sometimes was calm. He would feel a deep ease. There was no one, no force to ripple his sense of self.

He would hear her voice again like a tidal song, the song of his tribal soul and of an ancient time. He reflected on the power of changing life that responded only to its unique laws. He thought of love, pain, sorrow, and the serenity of natural light, and the strength of tranquil nights. He saw the lake spreading miles and miles to its edges, revealing the beauty of its fullness with hues that reflected passages of the new day. It was the day when he'd lazed with her in the grass between the rocks. His spirit danced to a tune that was gloriously redeeming of all anger, hatred, and envy. He began to appreciate its awesome authority and boundless energy to move him to greater heights. He began to discover Allan, and that Allan and Nuru were one person.

That night he wandered off from the cabin in deep thought. He played with Jiena's chain. He heard a noise and stopped. There was a shadow, and a sense of familiarity overcame him. Jiena danced in front of his eyes. He stood still, watching into the night. He heard his voice calling out to his father: "Papa, tell a story. Tell me a story about the birdie up in the mountains. I want to go with them to the sun, Papa." In the space between mountain and sky, there was a mirror in which he saw an image of himself sitting on his father's lap.

There was something out there. Morning came and found him the same place, and he had an urge to go higher up the mountain. He went back to the cabin and prepared to go to Uruhu Peak. Before he left the cabin, he sent a message to Chris to let him know he was going to do further exploration of the mountain and might return to his lodge within seven days. He told Chris he should not worry.

Allan left Barafu Camp and began to make his way to Uruhu. The biting cold on the mountain and the changing temperatures were now second nature to him. He shod his feet well and protected his body with triple layers of clothing under the shuka. Blizzards and deafening thunderstorms battered him, and the glacial landscape became increasingly threatening. To renew his energy he learned how to tap into his inner refuge. As the day progressed, visibility became increasingly difficult and eventually it was a complete whiteout. A powerful wind picked up speed and rolled and tumbled his body. He finally came to a halt against a rock, where he curled into a ball with the woollen shuka pulled over his balaclava. It provided another layer of protection against the beastly wind.

It was dusk when the severe weather stopped, but he had no notion of time. As happened on the mountain, conditions changed rapidly. Soon the sun burst into a furnace, and the day was beautifully clear and crisp. He thought he heard a whistle, and he looked around, confused. Perhaps it was the wind. He was not familiar with the scenery, although he knew the mountain well.

He wandered over the rough terrain and climbed boulders and ridges. Again the weather began to change, and there was a creeping, thick mist within which he was sure something moved. He saw a shape, and his heart pounded. Allan moved with speed, trying to follow the shadow. He scrambled and crawled his way forward. The evening had an orange-brown hue, and he looked up and saw the orange ball. He stood up and moved quickly, farther and farther up the mountain. There, coming out of the mist, was a black lion. The beast stopped its advance and looked directly at him.

Allan looked up at the sun, then at the beast. "No, it cannot be." There was only one lion like that. He saw the shining blue streak of fur. Only Matai had a streak like that. Softly he said, "Matai."

The beast moved forward. Allan ran toward the lion, shouting, "Matai, Matai!" It licked him down. The sun was disappearing, Matai bowed, and Allan climbed on its back. Matai took off like a bolt of lightning and reached a peak just as the sun vanished. Allan heard a whistle. It was dusk.

CHAPTER 39

Meleke sat regally on his beast at the place where Allan had arrived and barely gave the young man time to catch himself. Allan heard the king's voice.

"Stranger, how many books about Ashaise have you written?"

Allan turned on Matai and looked at Meleke, whose benevolent face now had a white beard down to his chest. Frizzy hair of the same color framed his face. It hung over his shoulders. His eyes twinkled. Allan tried not to laugh. Meleke saw the laughter in his eyes.

"None."

"Why not?"

"I planned to do it in Ashaise."

"You have not lost your arrogance."

"I did not want to disappoint my king."

"Do not try to bring about too many changes, stranger."

"Call me Allan, or Nuru."

361

"Come, my son," said the king. "Let us go home, but take those things off your feet."

The king sped off. Allan looked down at his Nikes and cracked up. He felt for his laptop and Chris's book, then followed the king. On their way they stopped at the Seat of God, where the keeper was. Allan dismounted Matai and embraced the keeper, who hugged him and said, "Welcome home, my brother."

Allan saw a youth sitting on a rock where he and Jiena once had sat. He looked at the boy, who was quite tall. He moved away from the keeper as he saw a face that looked familiar. Then he saw Zete. It was a face that also reminded him of another one he'd seen in the Temple of the Sun—the image of Mbtani. Tears welled in Allan's eyes. "Meke."

Meke responded by jumping off the rock and moving quickly to the untidy person standing near the keeper. He threw long, skinny arms around him.

"Father Allan."

Allan embraced him. "You're very tall, Meke. I missed you, son."

The irascible bull grunted and went to Allan for a pat. Zete glared at him. Meleke sat proudly on his beast and smiled. It was customary for children and youth to call adult relatives father or mother, followed by their first name. It distinguished them from their biological parents.

Meleke allowed Allan and Meke to talk for a short while, then said, "Aatum will take care of you. Jiena is at the usual place." He left them.

※

It was a night of the midnight sun, and Jiena was sitting on the boulder by the lake where they had first met, writing a poem:

Out of the depths of a midnight-blue sky that sheltered the shining lake,
a beautiful sight was mine to behold as the sun suddenly smiled at me.
The warmth of its rays enfolded my heart, longing for a loved one;
it comforted my mind and made me realize it was a gift of life.
The gentle waves made music and serenaded my lover, the sun.
The rolling tide whispered to the shore. I yielded to its call.
I thought I heard a tinkled clang welcoming my lover, the sun.
Was it the Aries, or was it the Splendor anchored on the lake?
Gently, softly, the sun crept over me and whispered words I longed to hear; what joy it brought to me.
Midnight sun, you shine with a special glow on your face;
the radiant smile in eyes that tease;
how I melt under your heat.
I sense the aura of your presence; my sun comes to brighten my night.
Midnight sun, my love sunshine, when morning comes you must rise
and flash your light in nature's way. You must, you know you must.

Will I retreat to a long night, to a life without sunshine? Oh, dawn, please, never come.

She heard a rustling and looked up. She saw Matai.

"Where have you been all these moons? I have been looking for you."

She had missed her companion and went toward him. He sat down, and she patted his body while rebuking him at the same time. The animal conveniently ignored her. Then she saw it. Blood rushed to her face. She stood up transfixed and nonplussed. This could not be. *I gave that to him*, she thought. Tied to Matai's fur was the chain and pendant she had given to Allan. She examined it and looked around.

Far away, under an enormous banyan tree, she saw a man dressed in red. She squinted and began to walk slowly toward him. He did not move. She quickened her pace, then held up her gown and began to run. She stopped, and through blinding tears she looked at the man who had left Ashaise a little more than four moon years ago. Mountain climbing had sculptured his lean body. He was stronger than the archaeologist of four years ago. His unruly Afro locks were a tangled Ras. His shuka billowed in the wind. He grinned, and before she could take another step she was in his arms.

From the far end of the garden, Meleke, with a child in his arms, Teye, and Nehsi with his wife and children watched them. The family members smiled and went about their business. Way up on a ridge stood the keeper. He also smiled, looked at Meke, and they turned to the forest, followed by Zete. A klipspringer bounded in their path, and the cantankerous bull charged it.

The keeper was aware that Sahure watched the couple from where he stood, in the shade, across the river. Within a few moon months after he had returned from his mission, to blow up the path across the other side, the warrior soldier realized that his quest to marry the princess was hopeless. He had become depressed and displayed erratic behaviours.

Allan and Jiena examined each other's faces. He covered her with his shuka, and she absorbed the scents of bark and seawater. They held on to the cord of life as time danced, not letting go for fear of separation by some force.

As he buried his head in her shoulder he heard a child's voice: "Papa, Papa comes from the sun." He thought he was back on the mountain and sobbed. He heard the child's voice again. It came in the wind like a musical chime.

"Papa." This time it was closer. It came from behind him. He lifted his head. "Papa comes from the sun."

He looked at Jiena confused. He pressed her body to his as if to make sure he was there in Ashaise. The voice was closer. He turned around. About thirty meters away he saw a child standing near Matai—a lion and a speck. Allan squinted. The child's voice chimed, "Papa comes from the sun."

He turned and looked at Jiena. She beamed. Her eyes twinkled. He moved away from her and slowly walked toward the child. In the distant background, Meleke retreated.

The child began to walk toward Allan. The little feet picked up their pace. Allan moved quickly until they were a meter from each other. He knelt to be at a closer level with the child. He held out his arms, and the child ran to him. He felt the warmth of the tiny body against his. The boy hugged his father and snuggled in his embrace. Allan felt light. The emotional weight of the past four years had gone. He understood then, the forces that had tugged at his core. Allan looked at the child's beautiful face.

"Papa came from the sun." The child pointed to the sky.

"Yes," Allan whispered. "Papa came from the sun."

Jiena approached them and caressed Allan's head. He stood up with the child in one arm and embraced her with the other, and they walked to her home where Aatum greeted Allan. He said, "Welcome my chief," and embraced the new Ashais member.

Later that evening, Allan and Jiena went to the lakeside where the mercurial mass shimmered and licked itself lavishly. On the sandy slope creatures scurried, and the giant trees that lined the path romanced the wind, bowing, bending their tall trunks to a hum, like musicians strumming soul music for the couple lost in the essence of each other. The young trees arched over the path as if teasing them. Love ambushed their one-track minds. Their bodies floated on invisible beams of a sun-moon, which gloated in its fullness over the stupendous beauty of the lake. It disappeared as the full moon rose and a star pitched across the velvet space. Night fused with dawn. A calm breeze blew, trees yawned, and leaves swished gently. Allan and Jiena heard the sounds of the lake calling, courting, crooning, lusting, loving, and laughing.

EPILOGUE

Ten days had gone by, and Chris had not heard from Allan. He called the embassy in Kenya, and they said they would investigate and send a report. The tour guides and inspectors who regularly checked on climbers had reported earlier that Nuru had left his cabin and gone higher up the mountain. There was nothing unusual about that. He had gone for longer periods before. They said he would return when he was ready.

Another five days passed. Chris heard nothing and informed Springer, Robert, and the dean that Allan had gone to Uruhu. Fifteen days passed, and there was no information. Chris and Robert met Springer at the cabin. There they found a manuscript on which Allan had been working. There was no reason to believe that he had left in a hurry, or that anything was wrong. They checked for his computer; his laptop was not there. They decided they would go to the summit.

At about three hundred meters, they found Allan's camera and diary, which must have fallen from his bag. Chris opened the diary and read entries for the period January 1 to 10. On January 10 there was a record:

It is a lovely day, and having meditated all night I feel exhilarated.

I wish Chris was here so we could go to the summit together.

The intense feeling that they're calling me has returned. I feel a sense of calm and expectation.

I'm sure I saw a shadow in the mist.

I heard a low whistle but saw no bird.

I hear the keeper calling me.

I sense Jiena's presence, but I know she is not here.

I must pursue what I see and hear.

Chris, Robert, and Springer looked at each other and smiled. Tears ran down Chris's face. He got up, and the others followed him. They still went to the summit, and continued to search. They stayed for a long time, looking around the mountain of myths and tales. They returned to Allan's cabin, and Robert and Springer left a couple of days later. Chris stayed for another three days. He went through Allan's books and albums. He took a shuka he had given to Allan.

Although Chris had strong feelings that Allan would return to Ashaise, he still could not believe they would never see each other again. He came out of the cabin and looked at the mountain. He took some of Allan's belongings. He left books and clothes to give the impression that Allan had not gone away permanently. He went down the mountain.

Chris returned to the cabin often. Ashaise was always in his mind. At least twice a year, Robert and Springer joined him. They told Allan's friends he had returned home and probably would be back in the future. His parents knew where he was.

※

Allan and Jiena were on the Seat of God. He was sitting with his back against a smooth rock. Jiena's head rested on his shoulder.

"Are you thinking about when you were a child and the place you visited in the summertime?" He did not look at her. He grinned and said, "Are you trying to bait me?"

"What do you mean by that word—bait?"

"You want to know whether I am thinking about my other family. I am thinking about the future my darling—about our lives, and the other children to come, hopefully." As he said this, he looked at her. Jiena's eyes had the familiar twinkle. "I was thinking about tomorrow's work with the students, and the many things I want to do in all of the tomorrows." He turned and admired the landscape, and began to recite, softly, a poem. "To burrow deep in tomorrow's expectations and whiff the earthy essence that seeps through the pores of promise. The germinating seed is pressing toward the surface of yesterday's womb. It protects the embryo that will explode into millions of particles of light upon the pristine mass of darkness. See there infinity's capaciousness, and how it humors the assaults of now, whose ripeness erupts to memories." Jiena sat up and began to smooth the Rasta locks from his face. She ran her fingers around his face, and touched his lips. He continued reciting,

"And into the bowels of the future, today's song sinks, and yesterday's unique wine ferments, bubbling, burbling, and babbling. Enough of yesterday and today does not need itself any more. Accept with gratitude inevitability of tomorrow's reality."

Allan drew Jiena close to him. He kissed her neck and shoulders, then removed her shawl and explored her body with kisses. She slowly took off his shuka and returned his love with a generous measure, which deepened his pleasure. She sensed his urgency and manoeuvred her body to indulge his passion. He whispered her name. Their bodies were undulating waves. Deep within her, the seed of tomorrow's life quietly parachuted to its welcoming host.

They heard low whistles and got up from their secluded spot between the boulders and looked for the birds. The crystal birds came out of the clouds and flew in unison. The last one swooped low across the seat, whistling raucously. She circled twice, then landed near Allan. She inched her way closer to him. He observed the cerulean patch between the eyes. He patted and stroked her. He said softly, "Asha."

She looked at him, whistled, and flew off to join the chorus of crystal birds.

The End—Part I

SOME FACTS

D uring the 1980s archaeologists excavated a seventy-five thousand to nine thousand year old site in Katanda, on the Upper Semliki River in the Western Rift Valley of Zaire. Research at the site revealed that early Africans had manufactured specialized tools about thirty-five thousand years before European, Central Asian, Siberian, and Near Eastern people made such tools. The evidence suggested the need to update views on human and cultural evolution. It pointed to the fact that Africa was not only where anatomically modern humans originated, but also where modern human behavior originated. There was evidence of sophisticated, cultural practices as well as diverse commercial and agricultural activities.

Seventy thousand years ago, Southern African communities had social networks. They used personal adornment, and they sustained control of plant output.

Long before the Pharaohs and the Egypt of antiquity, Nubians established the earliest known centralized food production system along the Nile. Disastrous changes in the flow pattern of the river destroyed traces of ancient civilizations.

Source: John Reader. Africa—A Biography of the Continent, published by Hamish Hamilton, 1997, and Penguin Books, 1998; chapters 15 and 16, pages135-145.

⠶⠶⠶

According to Reader, the oldest surviving languages originated in Africa, among the San Bushmen, whose dialect is Khoisan; the people of the Niger-Congo, who speak Bantu languages; the Maasai; and other pastoralists who speak Nilo Saharan languages, and the Ethiopian and North African peoples who speak Afro-Asiatic languages. *Source: Reader, chapter 12, page 107.*

⠶⠶⠶

The Walls of Benin consisted of an immense earthen bank and ditch with a vertical height from the base to top of the bank of 17.4 meters and a circumference of 11.6 kilometers. There was a network of interlocking enclosures consisting of more than 145 kilometers of earthworks. This suggested that walls had surrounded several interconnected towns and villages to create a city. The estimated total length of the wall was sixteen thousand kilometers. It was longer than the Great Wall of China. Based on historical information and oral tradition, there was no evidence to suggest there was external influence.

Source: Graham Connah. African Civilizations—An Archaeological Perspective, Second Edition, published by The Press Syndicate of the University of Cambridge, Cambridge University Press; chapter 3, pages 160-163.

※

In Southern Africa the earliest humans drew on walls of shallow caves or boulders and rock protrusions. These artworks did not survive because of exposure to the elements, unlike European Paleolithic paintings found in deep caves. African rock art done in the late prehistoric period reflected early ancient traditions. There are sufficient archaeological, paleontological, and genetic studies to support the hypothesis that Africa made a significant contribution in the cultural and physical development of the world's recent human populations. The emergence of cultural practices that represented significant advances in human development began about two hundred and fifty thousand years ago and continued up to about thirty thousand years ago. Africa was mainstream in modern, cultural innovations. "Both humanity itself and cultural/anatomical modernity were African developments. No longer can Africa be seen as peripheral to, or laggard in, the cultural innovations which distinguish modern people from their predecessors."

Source: David W. Phillipson. African Archaeology, Third Edition 2005, University of Cambridge, Cambridge University Press; chapter 4, page 95, pages 111-116, and chapter 5, page 146.

Made in the USA
Charleston, SC
28 March 2013